NAKED SOUL

GWYNNE FORSTER

Genesis Press, Inc.

Indigo Love Stories

An imprint of Genesis Press, Inc.
Publishing Company

Genesis Press, Inc.
P.O. Box 101
Columbus, MS 39703

ISBN: 1-58571-212-4
Manufactured in the United States of America

First Edition 1998
Second Edition 2006

Visit us at www.genesis-press.com or call at 1-888-Indigo-1

CHAPTER 1

From her gray-walled office window on the sixteenth floor of the United Nations Secretariat Building, Della Murray gazed at the bleak February scene and sighed. Why was it that most of the men she saw in her building who had any appeal also had a low level job, low income and poor prospects for a better life? Take the one repairing the keyboard of her computer. Any reaction to his handsome face, self-assurance and good manners took a back seat when she looked at the couple of dozen tools, two flashlights and a hundred keys hanging around his hips. Every time she sent for a repairman, regardless of the machine, this one answered the call. He was good at what he did, so she didn't consider him a washout, but she couldn't help wondering why, with his seeming intelligence and charismatic personality, he didn't reach higher.

"Ms. Murray," Erin's voice came through the intercom. "Call on line two."

Della walked over to her desk, taking care to avoid touching the workman. It was enough that she could barely keep her gaze off him; she wouldn't risk his thinking that she invited his attention. "Ms. Murray speaking." She listened only haphazardly.

"Granny's sick, Mama? Did she ask for me?" More attentive now, alternative plans formed in her head, in case she'd have to put her work aside and go to North Carolina. "She didn't?" Well, thank goodness, because I can't come home right now. This is the worst possible time for me to leave the office. I'm just finishing organizing an important conference, and I know it's going to be one of the best the UN has ever had. If it goes well, the Secretary-General will have to take notice of me. Everyone will know who I am. You understand, Mama?"

"Ludell, honey, you know how proud we all are of you, and I know you'll come when you can. I thought you ought to know she thinks the doctor's concerned about her."

Tentacles of fear shot through her. "Good Lord, Mama, you know how Granny exaggerates sometime. Ask Doctor Jim if he really thinks that. I'm up for head of the Standing Committee on Adolescent Girls. I'd be an Assistant Secretary-General (AS-G), and if I don't attend the conference and see it through to the last sentence of the report, the man who's trying to get the same job will go in my place. I'll try to get home soon as I get back. But please keep me posted, Mama, if she seems any worse."

"I sure will, and I know you'll do the best you can, child; you always do. When is that conference, Ludell?"

She glanced down at the workman, whose pair of pliers seemed to hand in the air, took a deep breath and plunged on. "The conference is just tow weeks away, and I'll be going to Nairobi for the first time. Mama, you tell Granny I'm sorry and give her my love. I'll see her as soon as I can."

The phone company hadn't bothered to string a line in her grandmother's poor rural neighborhood, and she couldn't call her. It was another reason why she hated the backwardness of that village.

"Alright, Ludell. I'll tell her tonight."

"Mama, I wish you'd try to remember my name is Della now. I've had it changed legally. You give Granny a hug for me, and a kiss to Papa and the rest. Goodbye." Della looked at the receiver, as though she expected it to criticize her, and slowly returned it to its cradle. Against her will, her gaze locked with the repairman's censoring stare. To her surprise and annoyance, his gaze didn't waver. Chills crept down her arms, and her trembling fingers shoved her hair away from her dark brown face.

"I'd appreciate it if you'd please hurry up and finish that," she told him, her voice hollow and dry. But he took his time, and she couldn't complain about that. For over two years, he had repaired all of her department's office machines, and she could attest to the fact that when he finished a job, it was properly done.

He shrugged. "I'll be out of here as fast as I can."

She couldn't believe it took that long to tighten a couple of screws. And his rapt concentration on his job, seemingly oblivious to her existence, when she stood just two feet from him, made her want to throw something. She resisted the urge to loosen the bow at her shirt collar. "Get a hold of yourself, girl," she silently admonished herself.

"Would you please hurry?"

"Yes ma'am." He took a longer time putting away his tools than she though necessary. Then, he raised himself to his full height of over six feet, took his red woolen cap from where he'd rested it on the corner of her desk, looked directly into her eyes for a second and then headed for the door.

"Yes ma'am, indeed," she mimicked to herself. The man had to be older than she. Her gaze locked on him as he sauntered out of the office with his ridiculous keys and things on that low slung belt emphasizing his sleek, slim hips. Why couldn't such a man have gone to school, prepared himself for a good position and made a really good life for himself? Still, something set him apart. Unlike other workers who came into her office, for instance, McKnight pulled off his hat at the door and acknowledged her presence with at least a nod. *And the looks of him.* She'd give anything to find for herself a man like him whom she could admire. His eyes. Almost chocolate brown and always twinkling. She could hardly stand to gaze into them. And he wasn't one bit shy either. Not that man. If she glanced at him, he never wavered his gaze, and she always had to be the one to look away. He was as brazen as he was clever.

She whirled around at the unfamiliar knock on her door, certain that it wasn't Erin, her secretary, who always tapped softly. She couldn't imagine who would come to her office unannounced.

He stuck his head in the door and offered her a smile worthy of Eddie Murphy. "Ms Murray, did I leave my pliers in here?"

Her heart did a waltz in her chest. "Pliers? How would I…?" She caught herself. "I'm sorry. I haven't seen them."

His grin was as much notice as she needed that he had his pliers on his belt. "Thanks." Was it possible that he wanted her to notice him? Well, if he did, he could forget about that.

She got up and went to the window, fanning her face as she walked. Maybe if she gave in to her feelings and jus…She rushed back to her desk and go to work. Her road up had been turbulent, rocky and perilous, and she had no intention of caving in to her periodic lust for a man who'd lead her straight back to poverty. And McKnight would do exactly that. She picked up the gold plated pen her boss gave her when she received the coveted promotion to director and twirled it monotonously. Who was that man that he had the temerity to mock her? Oh, he never said much, but he didn't need to; his eyes spoke volumes. And what a pair of eyes!

At her desk in her new-age kitchen that evening, Della ate a turkey on whole wheat sandwich and drank a glass of skim milk. She tackled the last preparations for the conference-the choice of delegates who would serve as conference officers, made notes for her memorandum to the Under-Secretary for her department and closed her briefcase just as the phone rang.

"Luddell, you coming home soon?" Tate Murray asked his eldest child. "Your Granny's poorly right now."

She supposed it was too much to expect them to call her Della. "Mama called me at the office to tell me Granny's not too good. She's not worse, is she?"

"I can't say for sure, but she's old, and she ain...isn't perky like usual."

"Oh, Lord, Papa. I'm so sorry. I told Mama, I'd get there soon as I could."

She knew he wouldn't speak long, because he never uttered more words than he had to, scared he might mispronounce something. It didn't have to be that way, and it wouldn't be if he'd gone to school.

"I'm sorry you can't make it right now. Here, Mark wants to speak with you."

She shuddered at the prospect of talking with Mark, who was sixteen months her junior. Her brother said whatever he thought and didn't whitewash it.

"Ludell, why don't you come home at least overnight? Anybody'd think that building would sink into the East River if you didn't spend your every waking minute in it. I know you're busy, but don't forget you have a family down here. And don't think that if you the that job you're after, you won't be killing yourself for the next one within a week. Thank God you didn't decide to get rich by stealing, 'cause girl, you *love* money."

She sighed. If only they'd try to understand. "Nobody stands still in this place, Mark; you're either going up, down or out. Besides, if you'd seen what I saw, you'd love money too."

"I've seen plenty."

She shook her head as the ghastly pictures flashed before her. "I'll get there as soon as I can, Mark." She told him goodbye and hung up. The tiredness began with her toes, withered muscle by muscle as it seeped up her body, depleted her nerves and crippled her every sinew. Twenty-three years hadn't dulled that horrible scene. The picture jumped out at her, shouted at her until she was seven years old again and pulverized with fright, as she clutched at her mother's sweater in the waiting room of Payne General Hospital in Wilmington, North Carolina. She dropped on the bed and cradled her head with both hands.

…She huddled close to her mother in the chilly room, terrified as Rachel moaned in pain and prayed aloud that someone would help her.

"We don't have any beds available on the ward for black children," the receptionist said, "but we may be able to manage something private. Do you have insurance or a credit card?"

"I don't have anything. And he's so sick, so hot," Rachel wailed.

"I'm sorry, but we don't have any beds," the woman insisted, before turning to the next person.

Ludell stared down into her little brother's dark, ashen and almost colorless face, then into the tortured visage of her mother. The hunger pangs receded as hours passed, and Rachel's clothes soaked up in her tears. Ludell ran to a nurse who passed nearby and grabbed her hand.

"Please help us, lady. My little brother's sick and my mother is crying."

The nurse stopped, looked down at her and smiled in a patronizing way. "Everybody here is sick, dear. Just wait your turn."

"But we've been here so long, and I'm hungry," Ludell insisted. She began puling on the woman's arm. "Please just talk to my mother. *Please, lady. Please.*" Seeing that the child refused to let go, the nurse went with Ludell to Rachel.

"What's the matter?" she asked, then glanced down at the baby in Rachel's arm and gasped.

"Oh my God, he's dead." She took the baby from Rachel, put her arms around the sobbing mother and ushered them into a little room. Coffee and chocolate-covered cookies arrived along with a solemn-faced social worker but for little Morris it was too late. Rachel and Tate hadn't taken Morris to their local doctor because he was to ill. The neighbor who had driven Rachel and Ludell to the hospital found them and drove them back home in his pick-up truck.

From that moment, she had saved every penny she could get, even picking up bottles and cans to sell. Her schoolmates had ridiculed her because she wrote on both sides of her notebook paper, wore no make-up or nail polish and brought her lunch from home. She didn't buy candy, soft drinks or chewing gun and, on many occasions, they taunted her for her miserliness. She withstood it stoically, not caring what they thought, but saved and doggedly hoarded her money. At age eleven, she opened her first bank account. Poverty wasn't for her, and that meant getting to the top by any honorable means and staying there. Let Mark judge her; he hadn't been in that hospital on that awful day. Black and poor in the rural South. Shudders raced through her as she thought of what the people suffered and tolerated. Well, she was black and comfortable with her race, but she would never again be poor.

Della dragged herself to the bathroom and washed her tearstreaked faced. Her mother had given birth to six children and had lost two. The eldest had been a victim of pneumonia and of her parents' lack of money for a decent doctor and the penicillin the child had needed. She tried to imagine what it did to a woman to have six children and lose two before their second birthday. And for what? For lack of money. Nothing and nobody was going to prevent her saving at least one-third of every dollar she made. She got ready for bed, crawled in and began a last check of the conference delegates.

Tate and Rachel Murray sat with several neighbors around their fire place, the four room house's main source of heat. Rachel lifted the hot kettle from the coals and poured boiling water over the sassafras bark in the discolored tea pot and inhaled deeply as the sweet, invigorating scent filled the room. She gathered the plant in summer and dried it, guaranteeing that she'd have company all winter. The woman claimed that sassafras soothed the nerves, eased rheumatic aches, cleaned out the digestive system and assured a good night's sleep. Rachel wouldn't think of throwing away a nickel on store bought tea or coffee; put a few of those coins together, and she could buy a pound of rice. She poured the tea for Mariah, Lizzie and Ada, who huddled there mainly to save on their own wood.

"Boney coming to take you over to see Old Miss Ludell?" Ada asked, though she knew he would. Granny had gotten that appellation when he insisted Della be named Ludell after her.

Mariah blew her hot sassafras tea and took a long, loud sigh. "How come little Ludell don't get y'all a car? Plenty second-hand ones that run right good. She's making all the money up there and ain't got a few hundred dollars for an old car? Children different these days from when I was a girl. We did all we could for our parents."

Rachel hastened to her daughter's defense. "Ludell's a good child. She works hard, and she sends money to our girls that have gone as far as my Ludell."

Lizzie picked up Tate's iron poker and stirred the coals. "I bet Little Ludell's got seven cents for every dime she ever made."

Mark walked in with Boney and stood before the open fire. "Yeah," he said, "and one of those other three cents went on her back."

"Lord, and don't forget her feet," Ada put in, rocking back and forth on the chair's hind legs. "That girl loves her shoes."

"Now, y'all leave Ludell alone," Rachel said. "She has to look good up there with all those important foreign folks. Besides, Ada, you've worn more than one of my sweaters Ludell sent down here."

Ada shifted uncomfortably in the chair. "Well, shut my mouth."

Boney packed them all in his pick-up and drove to Tate's mother's house.

Rachel huddled near her husband, when he pulled up a chair and sat beside his mother's bed. "Mama, It would be best all round if you'd just come stay with us. We don't have much, but we'll make you comfortable. I worry myself to death about you off here by yourself."

The old woman's piercing eyes told him he wasted his breath, and her words reinforced it. "Tate, you're a good son, and I know you mean well, but I lived here for going on sixty years. Your father built this place for me before we got married, and all my children were born right here.

Judah Murray lived and died here, and I'm going to die here, too. Right here in this bed. I wouldn't be happy any place else, Son."

Tate patted her hand. "I don't aim to force you to do nothing...anything you don't want to, Mama. We'll take care of you; don't you worry none."

Rachel wondered how he'd get the wood to keep Granny warm; he could scarcely afford enough for them. The wind whistled around the old house and seeped beneath the loose window sash, through the cracks between the old floor planks and under the doors. She tucked some of Granny's quilts in the cracks. If she hadn't just gotten that job making a wedding dress, thank God, she'd come over and stay with her mother-in-law. She couldn't, because they needed the money. Boney announced that he had to leave, and one by one they kissed Granny good-bye, as the darkness settled around them.

"Maybe little Ludell can pay somebody to stay with Old Miss Ludell," Ada said. "Course, I don't know how much she makes, but I'd sure stay over here for a few dollars."

Rachel loved her friends, but Ada could be tiresome, and Granny wouldn't want her within a mile of her house. "Ludell always does what she can, and since she's not here to defend herself, I think we all ought to leave her good name alone."

Della stood by Erin's desk waiting for her to pause in her word processing. "I'll be at the bank." She couldn't imagine how she'd manage without Erin. She'd hired her against the wish of her staff, all of whom later admitted that Erin had killed the bias against Irish redheads. Decorous, even tempered and professional, the eighteen-year-old ran the office with the efficiency of a seasoned hand.

Della took a low-rise elevator to the fourth floor and rushed to beat the line that would form in the bank just before morning coffee hour. As she passed the *Times Herald* newsroom, she looked into the face of Ambassador Craig Radcliff, the tall, handsome African American delegate to the Economic and Social Council. The smile he threw her way sparkled against his brown skin, and she noticed that, while he smiled at her, his left arm went around the shoulder of the tall Nordic woman who walked with him. He seemed to know everybody of importance, and maybe he fit the description of a lightweight, but he knew how to run a conference. She intended to maneuver if so that he chaired her meeting in Nairobi. If anybody could put it over, he would.

Good Lord, just her luck that Raf Besa should be in line right in front of her. Some women might find the constant attention of the little delegate from tiny Chagallen flattering but, to her mind, the man bore watching. Corridor gossip had it that Besa acted as a courier, seeking and getting status by staying in the good graces of certain power blocs. Right then, he was seen most often with the Russians and Middle Easterners. He'd started courting her as soon as her responsibility for the Nairobi conference had been announced in *Delegate World* newspaper. He wanted something from her that was bound to be unsavory, and she'd give anything to know what it was, though she wasn't foolish enough to find out.

Besa finished his business with the bank teller, turned around, saw her and beamed. "Ah, Miss Murray. My eyes are happy to see you. We could have a coffee together for a few minutes. Yes?"

One of these days, she'd run out of excuses and have to give it to him cold. "I'm sorry, sir, but I have a staff meeting, and I'll barely make it if I hurry. Some other time."

His smile barely touched his face, and that meager effort faild to camouflage his anger. He bowed. "Of course. Some other time." She nodded and took her turn at the teller's window. Something about the little man reminded her of slime, and she wanted nothing to do with him.

"Ms. Murray, Mr. Pillay wants to see you," Erin told her when she got back to her office. She didn't waste much time disliking people; that ate up too much energy. But Praker Pillay gave her the willies; a little snake coiled and ready to strike.

"Tell him to come in." Might as well get over with it.

"Any news about SCAG, Della? I hear the General Assembly's Committee on Adolescent Girls, but if we're going to have one, I'm the best person to head it up."

She made herself laugh. "No doubt about it. Anything else? I'm busy, Prakar."

He narrowed his eyes and strutted from one side of her office to the other. "You're not going to make me believe you're not interested in that job. Everybody knows you're betting this conference will make you the front runner, but it'll never happen. How many women do you see around here at that level?"

Della pushed back her chair, crossed her legs and let her gaze roam over him. "I know there's been a policy of promoting some of you men for spending your afternoons in the North Delegate's Lounge sipping Scotch and worming yourselves into the good graces of the delegates. But even those guys worked *sometime*. Work. Get acquainted with it, Prakar." She lifted the receiver.

"Erin, Mr. Pillay is leaving, and I don't want to be disturbed anymore this morning." She watched him saunter out the door. She'd treated it lightly, but she knew he spelled trouble. He wanted that job, and he'd stoop as low as he had to in order to get it. She worked through her lunch hour, fortifying herself with a banana and an apple, and on into the afternoon.

"Anything before I leave?" Erin asked. She shook her head and wished Erin a safe and pleasant journey home to New Jersey. Where had the day gone? Her shoulders ached, and the pangs of hunger sliced through her. On the way home, she stopped at Zabar's famous delicatessen and bought an assortment of gourmet items for her dinner, paid nineteen dollars and walked the six blocks to her apartment on Riverside Drive at Seventy-Fourth Street. She pushed aside the thought of how much food her mother would buy with that amount of money. Collards cost twenty-nine cents a pound in Pine Whispers, North Carolina. Zabar's didn't sell it, but you could find them at a supermarket near her for a dollar sixty-nine a pound.

She slammed her front door shut, dropped her parcels beside it and raced to the telephone.

"We went to see your Granny this afternoon," Tate, her father, told her, "and she talked to us. She seemed a little better, but all that talk about dying did shake me up. Just thought you wanted to know she asked about you."

She thanked him for calling, and the conversation ended, because Tate never engaged in small talk. She ate her dinner, rinsed the dishes and stored them in the chrome and glass dishwasher. If she could get in three hours of solid work, she'd have that report ready on time.

Instead of making progress, though, Della flitted away time. Jolted by her father's calm acceptance of his mother's talk about impending death, she couldn't keep her mind on the work. Her computer's cursor locked, probably because she'd hit a wrong key, and she couldn't sign off without losing her data. She had to finish that report before nine o'clock in the morning, so she found the card in her briefcase and called the repair service that the United Nations used.

An hour later, she opened her door to Luke McKnight. It hadn't occurred to her that he would answer the call. She wanted to kick herself after she patted her hair in place and ran her hands down her sides to smooth her wrinkled slacks, annoyed that his opinion as to how she looked mattered.

"You're the last person I expected to see. Don't you have regular working hours?"

"May I come in?" he chided.

She tried not to see the man before her, but to picture the fellow who worked around the UN in jeans, brogans and either a baseball hat or a wool knitted cap and whose tools announced his arrival. This man wore a gray business suit, gray shirt, yellow and gray paisley tie and polished black shoes.

She nodded. "Of course. Unless you can fix my computer standing out there. When *do* you knock off?"

He strolled leisurely into her study, removed his jacked and looked at her top-of-the-line computer. "Four-thirty this afternoon. Did you save the data?"

"Uh…No." She tried not to see his sleek waist and the fit of his trousers over his slim hips. "No, I hadn't saved it."

"Not to worry; we'll have it going in no time," he assured her. She'd swear her own eyes played tricks on her when she noticed that the shape of his head and his broad countenance fitted her image of an intelligent man. He smiled, and she knew he'd caught her tallying his assets. Well, so what? She hadn't seen him dressed, and Heaven knows he looked good. Real good.

"Find something to do," he admonished. "This may take a while. I won't steal a thing. Cross my heart."

She told herself not to let him rattle her. "You know, I think I'd get a bang out of sticking pins in you. You're trying to aggravate me."

He stopped working and cast a benevolent smile in her direction. "If I'd had any idea that you practiced witchcraft…or is it voodoo, you bet I'd have treated you with more deference. Please accept my apologies, and I'll be out of here as soon as I can finish this."

So he was a smartass, was he? He wouldn't have dared needle her if they'd been in her office. Well, she wouldn't dignify it with an answer. His left eyelid flicked, while his other eye suggested merriment. A wink that left her feeling exposed, though she suspected it sent plowing through her, it had the power of a live wire.

He rebooted the computer. "Darn thing's still stuck. Any idea which key you struck?"

If he hadn't grinned in that sex-charged way of his, she might not have gotten annoyed. Mad was more like it. "Don't answer him, Della," she silently cautioned herself. "He knows he gets to you." But her silence evidently served to embolden him.

"Whatever happened to that crisp tongue of yours? Don't tell me you've suddenly taken a vow of silence. Or wouldn't you deign to carry on a conversation with the help?"

Della stopped herself just as the paperweight she'd grasped was about to leave her hand. Shocked at what she'd nearly done, she wanted him out of there; she didn't trust herself with him.

Luke eyed first the paperweight in Della's left hand and then shifted his glance to her face. "I'm glad to see you've got your wits, Honey. You'd like to brain me, but not because of anything I did or said."

She had to get out of there. She was still a senior UN official and he, a UN repairman. He'd already been there at least an hour and half, and there was no telling how much longer it would take. She went into her bedroom and closed the door. If he'd only hurry. She had to work, and a few more hours of him wouldn't leave her in any shape to do that.

An hour later, he called out to her "It's all yours, Ms. Murray. Keep your mind on your work when you're word processing. This computer'll do any stupid thing you tell it to do."

Della barely heard him. She'd been musing over his comment that she'd like to brain him. She looked up at him standing there with his jacket open and his hands in his trousers pockets and swallowed hard. His half smile and slightly narrowed eyes brough her back to her senses.

"Oh, by the way, I hope your grandmother's better."

"Are you clairvoyant?"

"Hardly. I was working in your office when someone called and told you she was sick. Remember?" When she hesitated in answering, he asked, "She isn't …didn't…"

"No." She hastened to tell him. "Not that. I…I…"

He looked closely at her. "Don't you know how she is? You have to watch it, Ms. Murray. When old people make up their minds to go, they leave here."

She started for the door, making no attempt to conceal her displeasure. "Thanks for your concern."

He stared at her. "You haven't been to see her?"

Della slanted her head to one side and shot him a commanding look. "Mr. McKnight, you're"

He spread his hands in a gesture of surrender that his words belied. "I don't mean to meddle. I know you're busy, but any place in this country can be reached in six hours. She isn't in Alaska or Hawaii, is she? Anywhere else, and you could go and come back the same day."

Her hands went to her hips, but she quickly dropped them to her sides. Eben if he was right, it was none of his business. "Let's drop this topic. Okay?"

"Sure, but if she was my grandmother, and I could crawl, I'd have seen her by now." He shrugged. "But I suppose you know what you're doing." His gaze shifted to the karaoke on the corner table. "Is that karaoke? Don't tell me you sing?"

She didn't want him to know anything about her personal life. It was tough his having the smallest bit of information about her would make her more vulnerable to him. "I uh…I record poems and short stories." She picked up her checkbook. "How much do I…"

He cut her off, seemingly eager to probe. "You do that as a side line?" His manner had changed and he projected a demeanor of camaraderie.

"No. I… Well, I… volunteer at The Lighthouse."

A look of incredulity covered his face. "You record for the blind?"

She nodded, uncomfortable beneath his suddenly intense scrutiny.

"Doggoned if you're not a bunch of surprise, Lady."

The warmth of this gaze seemed to draw her to him, threatened to envelope her, to lasso her willing body. She clutched her checkbook. "Thanks for your help, Mr. McKnight. How much do I owe you?"

She resisted clutching her chest when a shadow of a smile drifted across Luke's face, as he lifted his small leather satchel and reached for the door knob. "We only take corporate accounts, so this one's on me. Have a good evening, Miss Murray."

Cold as it was, he hadn't worn an overcoat, she realized, as she watched him leave in his perfectly tailored suit. What an enigma! And she'd stupidly gotten herself into his debt. She went back to the computer, but she couldn't work. What sort of a person was Luke McKnight? He'd known it was she who called. He couldn't change her, and he hadn't had an ulterior motive fore coming because he hadn't mad a pass, not even an innocent one. She wondered if she'd regret making that call. She'd just as soon she'd never seen the dressed-up Luke McKnight.

Luke walked two blocks to his minivan, drove to his apartment at Eighty-seventh and Central Park West, put the van in the garage and walked back outside. He had intended to visit the youth center, but he had to deal with his encounter with Della; it had practically unraveled him. If she'd get off her high horse, he'd try to get to know her. But the woman was such a snob; she wouldn't admit her attraction to him, thinking him a mere repairman. And she could go right on believing that. He wanted her to know him, to desire him for himself, not for his wealth and status.

He hadn't been on duty when her request came in, and he didn't ordinarily take night calls, because his workers jumped at the opportunity to earn the time-and-a-half pay. But he hadn't been able to resist the chance to se how she lived, to see her at home. Softer. More feminine. And she hadn't disappointed him. She'd gotten her back up when he'd teased her and when he'd asked about her grandmother, but that business about her grandmother was pure guilt. He bunched his shoulders against the brisk wind and turned back toward his apartment building. More important than getting a glimpse of the woman behind the professional shield, he'd wanted her to see him as he saw himself-as a successful, desirable man whom she couldn't ignore as she did when he worked in her department and, sometimes, in her office.

A tough one, that Della. She heated up when she saw him, all right, but she hated her rejection to him. He grinned. "I'm not going anywhere; baby," he said aloud, "so you may as well make up your mind to deal with me."

CHAPTER 2

Luke made his regular Saturday morning call to his family in Polk Town, North Carolina and, as usual, his parents, sisters and brother took turns speaking with him.

"What's this about your leaving school to get married, Dolores?" Luke asked the oldest of his three sisters. "Mom seems to think he's a nice guy, but what about our degree? If you don't finish your studies now, you never will."

"I want to marry him, Luke. I know you think I ought to wait but I'm already twenty-five, and I want to start my family."

"Listen, Sis, you may love him, but when you realize you fluffed your opportunity while he goes on for his dream, you'll resent him. Get your PH.D and then get married. If you want to quit work and study full time, I'll pick up the tab. Our people are never going to get ahead if the ones with sharp minds like yours take the easy way out. I have to tell you, this news disappoints me. Terribly."

"Luke, you've made up your mind what my life's going to be and I'm sorry. I appreciate your sending me through school, and I know I sound like an ingrate, but Dan and I want to get married and that's what I'm going to do."

His oldest sister had always taken his advice, but this time well, he supposed Dan whatever-his-name had replaced him as Dolore's confidant. He didn't like the feeling that he'd become an outsider to his family. A look at his watch told him he could get an eleven o'clock flight and be in Polk Town by three-thirty.

"How's school?" Luke asked his second sister, Wanda, at dinner that evening.

She had a special place in his heart; not only did she look enough like him to be his twin, but they'd long known that their minds worked like a pair of matched bullets. "Just great," Wanda replied, but he had a sense of alarm when she didn't look at him. "I'm thinking of taking ROTC."

"What on earth for?" he asked. "You're not the military type."

He saw that she glanced around the table at their parents and siblings and wondered about the covered looks. Had he missed something?

"I don't know what type I am," she hedged, "but the course'll get me six credits toward my degree. What more can I ask?" He let it slide, but he figured he hadn't heard the last of Wanda and the military.

"Luke, what do I have to study to be an engineer?" his brother Nelson wanted to know. Luke hoped his perfunctory answer satisfied his brother, because right then he couldn't think past the directions in which Dolores and Wanda seemed headed.

"I got all A's this semester," Irene told Luke. His youngest sister possessed an endearing humility along with a wit and style that prevented the less cautious from attempting to take advantage of her and hugged her.

His "you're the tops, Baby Sis," earned him her shy giggle.

After dinner, Rudolph McKnight went out back to get a bucket of coal from the old shed that seemed to lean forward in the eerie, shadowed night, and Luke followed his father. "I'll take that, Dad," he said. Stars blinked in the clear moonlit night, and the frigid air let him see the vapor of his breath. His glance fell on what looked like a thatched tepee sitting on the hard bare ground, and he could imagine the energy it had cost his mother to build it as a winter storage place for her sweet potatoes. In the distance, he could see smoke furling upward form their neighbor's brick chimney that stood fixed to the side of the shingled house as though it had been an afterthought. He wanted more than that for his sisters. His father picked up the bucket of cal, ignoring Luke's offer, enough of a gesture to let Luke know of his displeasure.

"You didn't say word during dinner, Dad. What's the matter?"

Rudolph McKnight, who supported his family with the proceeds from his small general store, set the bucket on the porch, braced his sides with his roughened hands and looked his son in the eye. "If Dolores wants to get married, that's her right. Nobody here is entitled to interfere. I don't think I have the right to meddle in something so important as her marrying the man she loves. It's her life." He picked up the bucket and went in the house.

Luke leaned against the doorjamb, oblivious to the cold. Being able to send first Dolores and then Wanda to the university has given him a sense of accomplishment and satisfaction in knowing that he could give his siblings every opportunity for a good life. They'd come up poor, but that would change; he'd see to it.

He looked toward the kitchen door when he heard the knob turn. Patsy McKnight cracked it open and peeked at him. "Son, you come in here before you catch our death of cold. It's freezing outside."

Luke walked in, stopped before her and tweaked her nose. "Mom, who do you think checks on me in New York?"

"That's what worries me, Luke. You ought to be thinking about getting married. Have you found a nice girl?"

He'd walked right into that one. "When I do, you'll be the second person to know." He hoped his grin softened the words.

She wasn't put off. "And who'll be the first?"

He wanted to make it light, to have it appear unimportant, but his tone shocked him. "When I find her, she'll be the one who knows it first." He hadn't meant to sound so solemn.

From his mother's worried perusal of his face, he knew she had detected his deep desire. "You just trust God, Son. You'll find her."

He loved his family, but at that moment, he needed to be alone. But where? Up to bedtime, a McKnight could always be found in the kitchen or living room. That left his parents' room, the girls' dormitory and the room he'd share with Nelson. If he went there, his younger brother would follow immediately. Somehow, he had to reason with Dolores. But the question of his motive tormented him, and he fought his nagging conscience. Was he bothered that Dolores would waste all the money he'd spent on her? He wanted her happiness, didn't he? He went into the bathroom, closed the door and leaned against it. He didn't want to be unfair, but didn't owe it to him to follow through? He kicked the side of the tub. She no longer needed him, and she'd proved it by making her plans without consulting him. He opened the door and closed it again when an inner voice accused him of a fear of losing his status as his sister's sainted brother.

He found his mother in the kitchen putting up bread for the family's breakfast. "Mom, is Dolores pregnant?"

She straightened up and wiped a hand across her forehead, streaking it with sourdough. "Of course not. How could you think such a thing?"

He let out the breath he'd been holding and held both hands up, palms out. "Alright. Alright. If she isn't, how can she blow her only chance of getting her Ph.D? I told her I'd pay for it and support her 'til she finishes."

Patsy cleaned the dough from her hands and leaned against the kitchen table. "Luke, Dolores loves Dan, and he loves her. Nobody's life goes the way they plan it, and Lord knows if you try to run somebody else's, you'll regret it. Let it be, son."

He turned away and bumped into his father. "Dad, I'm gonna have to talk with that guy. Can't he wait another year and a half?"

After all these years, the touch of his father's hand gentle on his shoulder still comforted him; not even Rudolph McKnight's strongest reprimand had ever been accompanied by a heavy touch. "Luke, it's not your place to cross-examine Dolores's boyfriend. I have spoken with him and welcomed him to the family. I'm satisfied with her choice."

Luke restrained his left foot just as it would have kicked the frayed carpet. "Alright, sir. I'm not happy about it, but

I'll back off." Were they telling him they didn't need him? He smothered his sense of dislocation in the place that had always been his rock, and kept his feelings to himself. Later, leaving his family to return to New York, he had a sense of rootlessness. His place, his role in their lives, seemed less secure, and he hated the feeling of vulnerability that it gave him.

The next morning, back at work, Luke rushed along the corridor of the first basement to answer an emergency call from the Secretary-General's office. Whoever purchased those substandard copy machines had made a mint for themselves, not that he had a complaint; the more often they broke down, the more money he made. He turned to go through the glass doors, saw Della coming from the other side and stopped. At times, like now, just looking at the woman could send heat hurtling through him with stunning force.

"Good morning, Ms. Murray." Keep it cool, he told himself. "I hope your grandmother has improved. How is she?" She hesitated long enough for him to guess that she didn't know. "I wish I had a grandmother," he said, his tone wistful. "One of mine was gone before I was born, and the other died about ten years ago."

"Why have you decided to judge me, and what gives you the right? You know one thing about me."

"Oh, I know something about you, Ms. Murray. Quite a lot, in fact. And have I judged you, or have you passed sentence on yourself?" He flicked the bill of his baseball cap with his right thumb and index finger and let a grin light up his face. "Have a good day."

Della stared at Luke as he sauntered over to the high rise elevator bank, the keys, tools and flashlights that hung from his hip slung belt clinking as he went. Nothing and nobody aggravated her the way that man did. She sucked in her breath and steadied herself. What a time for an image of herself wild beneath him to flash through her mind. She hurried on to Conference Room Three where the planning committee was to meet. She'd done all she could to assure her success with the Nairobi conference, and all she needed now was for the Committee to elect Craig Radcliff as Secretary-General of that meeting. She took her place on the dais and, within minutes, the delegates with whom she'd spoken in advance nominated Craig. Representatives from Africa and the Middle East made his election a certainty. The Japanese delegate who presided over the proceedings banged the gavel and declared in a loud, profound voice, "Mr. Ladcriff is *erected*."

Along with everybody else in the room, Della smothered her amusement at the classical mispronunciations that were the trial of many of Asian descent and watched newly elected Craig Radcliff approach the dais, unfazed by the errors that would have embarrassed many men. His ease of maneuvering might annoy some people, but she knew that translated into polish, charm and suave manners. Besides, any man with his looks, height and build could be expected to use them to an advantage. As far as she was concerned, his demeanor was merely the deportment of a smooth diplomat. He had her respect and, she suspected, that of his peers in UN circles. And nobody could contest the fact that he was one good-looking, sexy brother. Della dropped her glance to the notes in front of her when she realized he'd caught her glance to the notes in front of her when she realized he'd caught her looking at him, but it didn't pain her one bit when he sent her a purely masculine smile. At the meeting's end, she walked out of the conference room triumphant. Radcliff was her conference S-G.

"It went well, don't you think?" She hard Craig's voice at about the time she felt his hand on her arm. "I'd like a word with you, if you don't mind."

"Want to sit over there and talk?" She pointed to a leather sofa along the corridor. That didn't suit him, he said, ushering her toward the North Delegate's Lounge, a place in which she didn't allow herself to be seen during working hours. He acceded to her wish and sat with her in the corridor, but she realized at once that he had no plans to talk business, and that he didn't intend to thank her for getting him elected.

"You and I make a great pair," he began, leaving her no doubt that he referred to their physical attributes. "I've seen you around, Ms. Murray, and wanted to get to know you, but you don't give a guy an inch. I was getting frustrated enough to eat nails, and then you walked into that conference room this morning and sat on the dais. I don't mind telling you that gave me a bigger charge that getting elected S-G of the Nairobi Conference. I figured it was time something like that came my way, but getting a chance to know you…Now, that's what I call a real coup."

Della pressed her lips together so that her mouth wouldn't hang open. He leaned toward her and took her hand. "We *are* going to be friends, aren't we?" His breathless baritone and brilliant smile allowed her the full force of his charisma, a blatant come-on that, in less skilled man, would still hold her. Anybody who thought her job wasn't dangerous hadn't met the men who prowled the halls and corridors of the United Nations.

She walked away from Craig Radcliff, but when she turned the corner, she almost knocked Raf Besa off his feet.

"Just my luck," the little man beamed. "Could you spare a few minutes? My country wishes to make a contribution to the Nairobi conference, and I need your expert guidance."

You're out of luck again this time, buster, she thought, but smiled and told him, "All contributions go directly to the Under Secretary's office. I'm sure Miss Kian, his secretary, will be glad to make an appointment for you." Before he could tell her that he hadn't meant a contribution of money, as she knew he'd planned, she escaped into the elevator. She didn't want to report him to the US Government, but if he persisted in trying to get her into his web of political intrigue, she wouldn't have a choice. One thing was certain: she wasn't letting anybody or anything jeopardize her job or her chances of getting ahead. Nothing.

She remembered that she'd left some papers in the conference room and went back for the, hoping she wouldn't see either Besa or Craig. But Craig hadn't moved from where she'd left him and stood talking with a woman who seemed to soak up his company the way a mushroom drinks wine. He glimpsed Della and, at once, bade his companion good-bye. Della couldn't help pitying the woman for her stricken look.

"Ah, Ms. Murray-may I call you Della? I wanted to tell you how happy I am to be working with you." To her amazement, his fingers grasped her elbow, and she didn't care for that. Still, he ranked high in the US Mission to the UN, and she'd do well to remember that.

"We *will* be working together," she stated in a tone that discouraged the intimacy of first name usage, and gently removed her elbow from his grasp.

"There's no need for formality between us, Della. We're going to be friends. Very good friends."

"If you say so," she answered, suddenly nervous at the prospect of having to deal constantly with his blatant suggestiveness and proprietary manner. They reached the conference room, and she ducked away from him. But too late. From the doorway of the film production room, Luke McKnight gazed at them, his face a cloud of disapproval. Her heart tumbled to the pit of her stomach, as she withered before his knowing look. For a second, she hated him. He had no claim on her, so why was he looking at her as though she'd committed a crime? His mocking grin jarred her poise, and she turned quickly into the conference room and sat there in the silence, wondering at her reaction to him and why he had made her feel as though she'd been caught stealing. "Oh, the devil with him," she muttered, got up and left.

"Miss Murray, there's a Mr. Besa on line one," Erin told Della when she got back to her office. She had to deal with him.

"I see you were able to postpone your staff meeting after all. We could have lunch today, perhaps?"

So he meant to harass her into doing what he wanted, did he? Well, she could be as obstinate as he was tenacious. "Mr. Besa, I don't consort with delegates unless I have a project that involves them directly. You know the staff rules."

"Of course," came the soft reply, "and you'll pardon me if I suggest that not every man among us commands the attention that Mr. Radcliff exacts."

She bristled, and she wanted him to know it. "No, I don't pardon you, Mr. Besa, Mr. Radcliff is a Secretary-General of the Nairobi conference for which I am responsible."

"Yes, of course. My apologies. Good day."

She knew she hadn't heard the last of the little man; she'd bet her mink that he had a mission to carry out, and it involved her. The next time he called, she'd have Erin monitor the conversation. Not that that would do much good; if he inflicted any damage, it would happen somewhere along the corridors.

Unable to get on with his work, Luke simmered just below boiling point. He wanted Della Murray out of his head. Only minutes before he'd seen her walking with Radcliff, he'd watched the man turn up the heat with a young tour guide. Couldn't a savvy woman like her tell the difference between a man and a six-foot peacock? He hoped he was wrong in thinking she looked down on anybody who got his fingernails dirty when he worked, and he hadn't pegged her as a climber. He didn't want to think that of her. But what in Heaven's name was her problem? He headed for the cafeteria, got a cup of black coffee, sat in a back corner and thought about the pain he got in his chest when he saw Della with Craig Radcliff. Anybody who frequented the General Assembly and Conference buildings recognized in the ambassador a womanizer and shallow cad. He stared down at his cold coffee, realizing for the first time that he had more of a felling for Della Murray than was healthy, but he was damned if he'd let her get next to him. He threw the paper cup with its cold coffee into the refuse bin, put his cap on his head and went back to work.

Craig Radcliff looked over the women and men who crowded the North Delegates Lounge eavesdropping on private chats, chasing rumors and hunting secrets. Some looked for company-for the moment or, as luck would have it, the evening-but most wanted to satisfy their thirst for alcohol in the company of notables. He knew that some of the women and men who habituated the place worked it as

lounge lizards, cataloging for their governments the habits
and political associates of other delegates. Craig knew all of
the, why they hung out in the Lounge and what they did
there. He ordered a glass of club soda with ice and mint
leaves, knowing that all who saw the drink would assume it
to be a Tom Collins. He wasn't foolish enough to drink
anything alcoholic in that scene; many a diplomat had
dropped out of sight after liquor and unhinged his tongue.

Craig leaned against the bar. He needed to digest his
good fortune of earlier in the day and to figure out Della
Murray's motive for engineering his election to Secretary-
General of the Nairobi Conference. He'd wanted it badly,
but his career hadn't advanced to that level and, in his
wildest dreams, he wouldn't have given himself a shot at it.
But he had it now, and acting the part wouldn't be much of
a sweat. Della and her staff would do the work. He sipped
the bland drink and winked at the reporter who joined
him.

"That stunt you pulled this morning really shook up a
few people," the reporter began in what Craig recognized as
a backhanded compliment. "You really snowed 'em, man.
Nobody knew you were in the running for the honor.
How'd it happen?'

Craig sipped his club soda, showed his perfect white
teeth and shrugged. "Beats me, Frank. Biggest surprise I
ever got."

The reporter took out his tape recorder and hooked it
to his lapel where Craig could see it. "Okay?" When Craig
nodded, he went on. "The news around here is that the
Conference will propel you into the world prominence and

that your government called in some favors to get you in. What do say to your being the first American Secretary-General of the United Nations?"

Craig feigned disinterest. "Not a chance, man. No Russian or US citizen will ever get that job, you know that." He watched Frank for signs that he knew something, saw none and took another sip of soda.

The reporter put away his recorder. "See you 'round, Mr. Radcliff." He moved on, looking for news.

Craig told himself he'd just fluffed the best opportunity he'd ever had to start a rumor that would have had every delegate kowtowing to him in the belief that he was in for something big.

As it was, that reporter would consider him a dry pond and wouldn't look to him again for news. Gunning for UN Secretary-General had never occurred to him, but black was in right then and, if he put that conference over big, he might have a good chance.

Craig stopped his musing and bowed to the Indian ambassador, a tall man, whit haired and distinguished. "Thank you for your confidence, sir. I value the trust you showed me in voting for me this morning. I'll do everything I can to put that conference over the top, and any suggestions you'd care to make will be most welcome."

"You'll run an excellent meeting," the ambassador told him, barely pausing before he moved on.

Craig bristled at the obvious slight. Considering the importance of the role he'd just been given, he expected that even the much-heralded gentleman from India would show him some deference. Well, to hell with him. To hell with every damned one of them. He went over to the bank of phones and called Della's office.

"Craig here," he said, adopting the European way of announcing himself. "We have to get together and work out a strategy for running the conference." He thought he detected hesitancy on her part. Well, too bad. He meant to have his hand in every single operation of that meeting.

"Hello, Craig. I'd planed to be in touch with you. I'm calling a planning session for next Tuesday."

So she intended to use him, did she" Well, she'd better not hold her breath. Neither Della Murray nor anyone else was going to use him for a stepping stone; that was his specialty. He'd been looking for a way to get maximum visibility, and she gave it to him when she maneuvered to get him as conference S-G, not that he'd ever let her know he knew it. He'd see that her conference made a splash around the world, but the credit would go to him, not to Della Murray.

"Della, love," he began, giving his voice the sound of patience about to expire, "I think tomorrow would be better *and in my office*. Plenty of space for a meeting. Have one of your people bring the documents over to me sometime today."

He couldn't believe his ears when she said, "Craig, I'll send you the papers when they're ready, and that won't be before Monday. The meeting will be in the Under-Secretary's office, and he's already scheduled it. And Craig, there's no *love* attached to my name. Okay?"

He'd blown it again. The Under-Secretary outranked him, and he'd have to cool his heels and go to the man's office. "Just see that I get those papers before the meeting," he said, salvaging as much as he could. "That'll suit me fine." He hung up. Two setbacks in less than fifteen minutes. He'd have to watch it. And he especially couldn't afford mistakes with Della; she figured big in his plans.

Della hung up, walked over to the window and looked down at the East River. She'd roughed him up, and she hoped she wouldn't regret it, but that conference was her baby, her ticket to the coveted position of AS-G for the Standing Committee on Adolescent Girls. She'd worked her behind off for it, and the credit was going to *her*. The clanking of metal drew her attention to her office door, and she walked to it just as Luke took off his tool belt and crawled beneath Erin's desk. She beckoned to the pretty young redhead.

"Erin, what's he doing out there?"

The girl's eyebrows shot up, and her eyes widened. "It's Thursday. Don't you remember it's the day he services the copy machines?"

A bit ashamed, Della muttered. "Since when did you have a copier on your desk? Why is he under there?"

"Miss Murray, did you forget my disk sits over the plate that has all the electric outlets? Why don't you like Mr. McKnight?"

"Who said I don't like him?" Della sked her, pretending annoyance. "He's a nuisance. Every time I look up, I'm staring in his face."

Erin laughed. "I'll bet your eyes don't complain. He's a terrific guy. Don't you think he's handsome?"

Della didn't like being backed into a corner, and her young secretary had done it without trying. "Handsome is as handsome does," Della replied, parroting her mother and regretting it. "I mean, he isn't my type."

She supposed that her words and attitude perplexed Erin, whose thoughtful word lashed at her conscience. "He's not handsome because he repairs office machines? He's a heck of a lot better looking and more of a gentleman that most of these diplomats swaggering around here."

"Not to me," Della replied. "Anyway, that isn't what I meant."

Erin walked around to stand directly in front of her boss. "Are you sure you're alright? Luke's a dream of a man."

Della let herself smile. She adored Erin, but she wouldn't let the girl have the better of the conversation, especially since she wasn't sure how much of it Luke could hear.

"Well, I suppose he is, if you want to spend your life in a two-family home, waiting for the next pay day. That's not for me."

Erin pushed her glasses higher on the bridge of her nose and took a deep breath. "But if you love a man, you don't calculate it that closely, do you?"

Della walked toward her desk, signaling a return to work. "As far as I'm concerned, Erin, it ought to be easy to love a man with money as one without it."

"Did you see the note I put on your calendar?" Erin asked as she left the room.

"Thanks." Della looked at her message calendar. Besa had been to her office. Thank God she'd been in the ladies room. One day, she'd have to deal with that little weasel, and she didn't look forward to it.

"Mr. Besa on line one."

Della groaned. "Thanks, Erin. Yes, Mr. Besa."

"Ms. Murray, I've spoken with Mr. Radcliff, and he's sure there's room for my small country to make a contribution to the conference. We have solid contacts in Nairobi and can help with transportation and hotel arrangements."

In his dreams. "I'm sure the Under-Secretary will appreciate your offer, sir, but the Scandinavian governments are taking care of all that. If there's nothing else…" She let it hang.

"We wish to make a contribution, and we'll find a way. Thank you so much" He hung up.

Damn Craig Radcliff. So he made up the rules as he went along, did he? She walked out to Erin's desk. "Erin, please send Mr. Radcliff a copy of conference rules and procedures and underline the section on contributions and participation. Thanks." That should take care of *him*.

"Headed for lunch?" Luke's voice taunted, as she stepped out of her office an hour later and closed the door.

She stopped short, unprepared for the encounter. "Yes, I'm going to lunch. Why?"

"Just though you might like to know that Craig Radcliff is renowned in these halls as a womanizer, and a not very discriminating one at that. You wanna watch him."

"Why, of all the—"

"Tish, tish. That's what I thought when I saw you two this morning."

She wanted to erase the mocking grin form his mouth, "Is what I don any business of yours?"

He hooked a bunch of keys to his belt, as if to annoy her with that sound that always announced his presence, and raised his hand in a mock salute. "Well, 'scuse me."

Della gazed at his manly strut, as he walked off with the litheness a prowling tiger, his hips swinging in a strange, exotic rhythm. She swallowed hard and turned her back. Was it abnormal to hate a man, when what you really wanted was to... She forced herself to stop thinking about him. If she's slowed down for one second, he'd charm her stupid, and she'd never get back on track.

CHAPTER 3

She couldn't postpone it any longer, every other day her mother, her father or Mark called to tell her about Granny. It amused her in a way, because everyone who knew Granny was aware that she tried to control anybody who'd give her the time of day. Bigger, the dog she'd had for years, faithful though he was, had learned not to run to Granny every time she called him. Though tired from weeks of working fifteen to sixteen hour days, Della worked late into the night for most of that week, s that she could spend the weekend with her family in Pine Whispers.

She walked out of the Wilmington, North Carolina airport into the bleakest morning in her memory, though the occasion might have added to the desultory appearance of all that she saw. Shivering in the harsh ocean-borne wind, she glanced up at the gunmetal gray threatening clouds and prayed she wouldn't get snowbound in Pine Whispers.

Thank Heavens she had remembered to order a rental car before leaving New York. After a bleak forty-minute drive, she parked the Cougar in front of her parents' weather beaten house. Her spirits drooped at the sight of its grimness. Wealth versus poverty. Beside the Mercury Cougar's sleek beauty, the old house seemed three times its age and more dilapidated than it was.

She did her best to smile and tugged her tweed coat tighter. She hadn't dared wear her mink; as it was, she'd be a conversation piece for their neighbors. Rachel Murray rushed out of the house to greet her oldest child.

"Honey, I'm glad to see you," she said, and Della reveled in the warmth of her mother's arms. She kissed her mother, stepped back and looked at her. "Hard as you work, you look younger than New York women your age."

Rachel beamed. "That's because I don't worry. No matter how tough it gets, I don't worry. I just have faith, and whatever it is usually takes care of itself."

Della bit her tongue and told herself not to react. As far as she was concerned, that kind of fatalism put limits on what a person could achieve. "How's Granny?"

"She's holding on. She eats right good, and her voice is strong. We're all thankful for that. Come on in the front room and meet some of the neighbors. They just couldn't wait to see you."

"Child, you sure is a sight for sore eyes." Della knew Mariah Jenkins well enough to wait for her next remark before answering. "I'd a though you'd a been here soon as Old Miss Ludell got sick. You all she ever talks about." Della fixed a smile on her face and greeted the three women as warmly as she could.

"I got here as soon as possible," she replied and let it go at that.

"Now would you look at that coat," Ada whatever-her-last-name-was exclaimed.

"That's the way they're wearing their hair up in New York?" Mariah asked, refereeing to Della's hair hanging straight down around her shoulders.

"It's the way I wear mine," Della said. "If y'all will excuse me, I'll go change." She put her things on her sister's bed and took a deep breath. Two long days, and she didn't look forward to another minute of it. She changed into a dark skirt and woolen sweater, went back to the front room and stopped at the door.

"The only way the church can raise money is with those Sunday dinners, and it costs more to eat them than it does to eat at home," someone said.

Lizzie pulled what sounded like several centimeters of air through her teeth and shook her head. "Seems to me the Pastor could do with a little less money. He oughta know times is hard."

"Yeah," Ada said, "and prices getting higher and higher. I wish I had whoever it is up there in Washington saying there ain't no inflation. I'd let them eat on my budget for a couple a months."

Rachel and the three women laughed. "Wouldn't help a bit," Lizzie said, adjusting the little stool so that her considerable weight wouldn't land her on the floor. "Rachel, you gotta do something about this old broken-down stool. Talking 'bout politicians, you know they never was human."

"You sure got that right," Mariah put in, stirring the coals in the fireplace with the iron poker. "If they had any feelings, they'd do better by us poor fools that put 'em in office."

"You tell it girl," Rachel said.

Ada nodded and folded her arms. "Speak for yourself. I don't plan to go back to the polls 'til they do something about these doctor bills. Sometimes, I can see why people steal."

"*Ada!*" they all said in unison. "Shame."

Della looked at the women. How could they chat about their impoverished lives as though speaking of someone they'd never met? Thinly clothed in cotton dresses and threadbare sweaters in the dead winter, when her woolen skirt and cashmere top barely kept her warm. Thank goodness she'd gotten out of there or she'd just like them, chatting about their problems as though they didn't contribute to them, didn't have any control over their lives.

"When can we go over to Granny's house?" she asked her mother.

Rachel sighed. "Maybe late this afternoon. Boney's gone to Wilmington. Said he'd be back around one or so. He's good as his word, so I know he'll take us. Your father and mark ought to be home around one, so I 'spect we'll leave right after dinner. You just make yourself comfortable." *Dinner*" She relaxed when she remembered that people there referred to the noon meal as dinner and the night meal as supper. Still, if they waited for Boney, her parents' faithful neighbor, it could be almost dark before they got to see Granny.

"Mama, I drove, so why don't we go in my car. We don't have to wait for Mr. Boney."

"Honey, I wouldn't a thought all of us could get in the car you drove here. Everybody wants to go, so you take some and let Bone take the rest."

Della nodded. "Fine with me."

"Lay your clothes out on my bed, Ludell," Rachel told her. "Let me see what I can copy. I made a pattern form that pretty little pink dress you wore down here last year, remember? Well, I changed it up lots of ways, 'cause so many of the young girls asked me to make it for them after they saw it on the pastor's daughter. We don't get those designer patterns in Woolworth's and, even if we did, they cost too much."

She made a mental note not to wear that dress to Pine Whispers again. "I already put my suit there, Mama. I didn't bring a dress."

"Alright, honey." Rachel turned back to her friends. "Ludell's so thoughtful. The end of every season, she gets yards and yards of that designer fabric and sends it down here to me. Everybody thinks old Miss Farrell shops at those big stores in Wilmington, but she buys that cloth my Ludell sends here, and I sew it myself. Ludell's a fine girl."

Mariah rocked back in her chair. "Hmmm. Yes, Lord."

Della crossed the hall, opened the back door ad stepped out on the porch when she heard her father scraping the dirt form his shoes. She had welcomed that sound as a child, for he would always open the door with a smile, pick her up and twirl her around. She winced, recalling it, and though of the wide gap that separated them now.

"How are you, Papa?" she asked him.

The big man gripped her in a warm welcoming hug. "Well, Ludell, I've seen better days, but I've got my health and strength and, right now, I've got my elder daughter. I'm just fine. Just fine."

Della took her usual place t the table beside her father. Just as she'd guessed they would, the three neighbors joined them for dinner. If times were so hard, how could anybody afford guests for a meal? Nobody seemed to notice the chipped plates and cracked teacups, and she supposed that a frayed linen cloth on the table didn't matter to anybody but her. Rachel had starched and ironed it and the matching napkins and had hidden the fading print of a hot iron with some artificial flowers. Every time she sent her mother money for another tablecloth, Rachel found something more important on which to spend it. As far as she was concerned, such things were for show, and they had other, more pressing needs.

"Everything sure does look nice, Rachel," one of the women observed.

Ada added. "Not use mentioning it. You know Rachel is fancy with things like serving a meal. For somebody that never worked in service, she's up on everything. Rachel, these have got to be the best candied yams that ever slid down my throat."

Della turned toward her father when he laughed and said, "There's not much my wife can't do; putting some syrup and butter on a few sweet potatoes doesn't take much out of her. She's smart."

He looked at Rachel and smiled. Good Lord! How had she missed that? Hot rays of passion ricocheted between them until her mother lowered her gaze. Della shuddered. An acute sense of loneliness seized her, for she had never felt that close to a man. She had often wondered why her mother, an intelligent, hardworking woman, stayed with her father whom Della regarded as a failed human being. She shook her head and wondered what her mother would say to a relationship between her daughter and Luke McKnight.

"Ludell, honey, you better eat some of these pork chops," Mariah advised. "You need something to stick to your ribs and keep the cold out. Nibbling on them collards and letting these good old biscuits and chops go by don't make a bit of sense to me. It's a wonder the wind don't blow 'way those women up north. Nothing but skin and bone."

Della had to laugh. Mariah weighed two hundred if she weighed a pound, and she was surely shorter than five feet three. "I haven't had any collards since the last time I came home, and I'm catching up. Nobody has to urge me to eat Mama's biscuits," she added and reached for one.

"How long you staying, Ludell?" her father wanted to know.

She cleared her throat. "Well, I'd hoped to leave in the morning."

"In the morning?" the five voices parroted.

"I have to be at work Monday," she told them in a tone that she hoped left no room for argument.

Rachel cleared the table and put the remainder of the food in the oven to keep warm for Mark, Bitsy and Matthew.

"I'd hoped you'd stay for a while," Tate grumbled. "It's not like we get to see you often, Ludell."

"Now, Tate, you know Ludel has a real important job up there at the United Nations. She can't do her work and stay down here same time," Rachel said, trying to pacify her husband.

Her father's gaze appeared to shrivel her. "I seem to remember that when Abraham Lincoln got shot, the North went right on and finished up things just like he'd started 'em. And when Roosevelt died, Harry Truman took p right where he left off. This world never done…did stop turning for anybody, because nobody is indi…indispensable, Ludell. Nobody on this earth."

Della groaned inwardly. If she'd had a knife, she could have sliced the hush that descended over the room. She could think of a dozen retorts, things she'd wanted for years to get off her chest, but she pressed her lips together ad said nothing.

Probably because of the anger that simmered in her, she didn't hear Mark when he entered the house followed by Bitsy and Matthew wrapped themselves around her, but Mark kept his distance.

"Granny asks for you with every other breath," he accused. "Maybe now that you're finally here, we'll be spared some of that. There's no consoling her."

Della jerked forward. Stunned. "Nobody told me that Granny was asking for me."

"Now, Son," Rachel began. "Ludell does the best she can. There aren't many women – black or white – with her responsibilities. So we have to be understanding. You all come on in the kitchen here and eat your dinner. Mr. Boney will be here any time now, and we'll all go to see Granny."

"How are you, Mark?" Della asked him.

His grin reminded her of Luke McKnight. "Just dandy." She had no idea what that meant, and his facial expression didn't help, but she didn't' understand Luke's grins either.

"Ludell," her father called from another room. "Could you come in here, please? I want to show you this statue I'm working on."

Statue? Since when had he picked up that hobby? She went into her parents' bedroom and gazed at a nearly finished sculpture: a man with a hoe, slightly bowed as though carrying the weight of the world. Her eyes widened, and she knew her mouth hung open.

"Papa, this is beautiful. Exquisite. How long have you been doing this?"

He stood taller, pride illumined hi face, and his ashy, roughened hands caressed the life-like form. "A couple of months. I always loved to whittle. The principal of our school retired and I helped him move. He gave me a lot of stuff, and I found some real ebony wood that he got in Haiti years ago and never got around to carving. So I tried my hand at it. You think it looks good?"

She fought back the tears. "Papa, I've seen pieces in museums that didn't look this professional."

"Well, I don't hope to get into any museums, Ludell, so don't go getting fancy. I just wanted something nice to give to your mother for our anniversary next year. We'll be married thirty-three years."

She knew it was no use pressing him. He didn't envisage himself as talented, so nothing would prompt him to use his talent to better his life. "Papa," she said, her tone more harsh than she intended, "why do and Mama keep calling me Ludell?" You know I had my name officially changed to Della."

She stepped back as his gaze scorched her. "Ludell, I'm having a hard time getting used to that. After a while, you'll call here and say Murray is too old-fashioned or too something and that you've changed it to Clinton or Bush or maybe Roosevelt. I named you Ludell, and that's what I'll call you." He put a black rag over the statue, rolled it up and placed it in a trunk. He then walked out and left her standing there wondering why she was so different form the rest of them.

Boney arrived with his pickup truck. The neighbors and Matthew piled into the truck, and everyone else rode with Della for the four-mile trip to Granny's house. Della wasn't sure what she'd expected, but certainly not a chipper Granny sitting by the fireplace stroking Bigger, her beloved German Shepherd. She tried no to show her excitement for fear Granny would conclude that everyone thought her end was eminent.

"Ludie, child," she exclaimed, "you came to see your old grandma. Come here and give me a hug."

Della hugged the old woman, fighting tears as she caressed the bony shoulders.

Granny's shrewd old eyes perused her favorite grandchild. "It's time you gave me some great grandchildren," the old woman said, waving an accusing finger at Della. "But you young girls run around in your pants and men's jackets, cussing and swearing like lumberjacks. You can't expect men to treat you sweet, marry you and be faithful like my Jonah was 'til the day he died and like your father here. But you go on. You know everything."

Della sat down on the cold floor beside her grandmother's rocker. "It's not easy, Granny. And I don't own a single pair of jeans and no leather jackets."

"Humh," the old woman said. "Pant are pants. But never mind. I think you're a little disappointed that I'm not on my death-bed, Ludie, like you made the trip down here for nothing. Oh, I saw the look on your face when you walked in here. But I can't say I'm sorry for the inconvenience." She laughed and Della looked down at the wrinkled fingers that covered her hand. "I want you to remember, Ludie, you aren't the first woman to amount to something. I went clear through normal school and got my teaching certificate, and that was rare down here in my day. A little humility wouldn't hurt you one bit, child." As if in afterthought, she added, "You're my heart, though. My own heart."

The old eyes perused Della as though doing research and making notes. "I'm trying to figure what you've done to yourself, and I see you've gotten rid of your glasses."

"I'm wearing contacts," Della told her and steeled herself for the tart reply she knew would come.

"You youngsters pick up every new gadget that comes along. Now, you're sticking things in your eyes. Don't be so vain. You looked better with those glasses; at least they won't blind you."

"But I don't lose them the way I used to lose my glasses," Della replied. Granny didn't mind a little sass, Della knew. What the old woman couldn't stand in people was milquetoast.

Granny's laugh and the squeeze of her fingers buoyed Della, but when the old woman said, "You always had a little of me in you. You've to my spunk," it was as though she'd been rewarded for the hated trip to Pine Whispers.

Later that night, the family sat in Rachel's kitchen around a super of cold fried chicken, potato salad and collards. "Soon as I get out of high school this June, I'm going to New York, get a fancy job and make a lot of money," Matthew announced.

Bitsy stopped eating and looked at Della. "Me, too and I can stay with Ludell. Can't I Ludell? If I make enough money, maybe I can go to college."

Cold shivers furled up Della's spine. She had no answer. What would she do with her younger sister? The girl was years behind New York girls her age, without a sense of style, unpolished. She'd never been to a museum, a concert or any of the things that were a commonplace with big-city girls her age. She'd feel like a misfit, and she'd be one. Della hated to admit it, but Bitsy would be a fish out of water and easy pickings for those New York boys. And wayward as she was, she could be uncooperative and ruin the image of herself that she'd so carefully established among her New York friends. When Rachel began fidgeting with her napkin, Della knew her mother was looking for a way to change the tenor of the conversation.

But her father mired them in it more deeply. "Does the United Nations have any good positions for an experienced janitor?" Tate Murray asked his daughter.

"What?" Della sprang up from the table, knocking her chair over. "For goodness sake, Papa. I'd be humiliated if my own father cleaned the toilets at the place where I work. The idea's ridiculous."

Tate leaned back in his chair and strummed his fingers on the table long enough for Della and everyone else present to know that he was having an unusually difficult time controlling his temper. "I didn't know you were ashamed of me, Ludell." His accusing stare disconcerted her, and she'd have given anything to be able to get away from it.

"I hope you never give me occasion to be ashamed of you, Daughter."

"I'm sorry, Papa, it's just that I-"

"Let it rest." He ordered. "I've had enough." He got up, started toward the kitchen, turned and looked at her. "I wasn't a bit serious. I don't like what New York does to people."

Della helped her mother take the dishes to the sink, clean them off and stack them for washing. She couldn't help thinking that her mother's kitchen and Granny's were the only ones she knew of that didn't have a dishwasher. Rachel thought the appliance ate up money that could be better spent on something else. Della didn't mention her father's annoyance with her, because she knew her mother wouldn't tolerate criticism of him.

"I'm glad you stayed here with me, Ludell, because I wanted a chance to discuss Bitsy with you."

"Mama, I'm not home much and I travel a lot, so I don't…"

"Please hear me out, Ludell. I just don't know what I'm going to do about her. Bitsy doesn't keep her head stuck in a book the way you always did, and there's nothing 'round here for her to do 'cept work in service, and I want more for her than that. Cooking and cleaning for "Miss Ann" is honest work, but that's all it is. Besides, Bitsy wouldn't pick up a broom if dirt piled up to the ceiling, "less I made her. That girl doesn't like work. I don't know what I'm going to do with her when she gets out of high school."

"Mama, you can't live Bitsy's life for her."

"I know that, but I'm her mother and I care about her. She idolizes you, Ludell. Wants to be just like you. Trouble is you too far apart. You know I had a miscarriage and two children in between Mark and Bitsy, and I lost both of my babies. I still cry sometime when I think about Morris. Died because of people's meanness. You think about what we can do for Bitsy. That's all I ask."

"Alright, Mama, I'll think about it." Long after Rachel left the kitchen, Della remained, pondering all that had transpired that evening. She looked out of the kitchen window at the night, pitch black but for a few scattered stars. And quiet. Not even a dog howled. How did they tolerate the isolation? She removed the apron that her mother tied around her and started toward the room she would share with Bitsy, but she didn't want to deal with her sister's pie-eyed dreams right then, so she headed back to the front room.

Half way there, she paused at the sound of her father's voice. "I'm proud of what Ludell has done, Rachel, but I think she's ashamed of us," she overheard. "She says she's got a nice big apartment. Well, if that's so, why can't Bitsy visit her for a couple of weeks and see how other people live. Bitsy needs to as…aspire to something, but she don't – I mean doesn't know what to look to."

"Now don't you mind, Love. It'll work out. It always does," Rachel soothed.

Shaken by her father's words to her mother, Della rushed back to Bitsy's room. Mark and Matthew had wolfed down their supper and gone to their room where Mark planned to help Matthew apply for a scholarship to summer camp. Mark hadn't said a word during supper, and she was glad. She hadn't needed the added discomfort of his biting remarks. She looked at Bitsy huddled under the cover except for their head and hands, reading a true confession magazine, crawled in and tried to sleep. If she could get through the night, tomorrow morning she could leave.

After Della assured her father that he wouldn't join the family for church service, Tate called the family together for prayer, and they then gathered on the front porch to bed Della goodbye. She forced a smile and controlled the tears that threatened to spill out of her as she drove off. She reached the bend in the frozen road and, driven by a sudden impulse, swung away from the direction of the highway and headed for her Granny's house. She might be late for her flight, but the old woman's joy made up for the inconvenience of the detour. Fortunately, the sparse traffic let her speed to Wilmington in record time, and she had an hour's wait before her flight to New York. She thought of calling her mother to say she'd arrived safely, but remembered that they'd gone to church.

Della greeted her doorman as he opened the door of the yellow taxi, held out his arm to assist her and took her bag. "Afternoon, Mike. How are things?"

"Just as you left them, ma'am."

He walked with her to the elevator, placed her suitcase inside and went back to his station. She pressed the button for her floor, and not before Pinski, a giant of a man, stepped in. She hadn't seen him in the lobby. He looked at her steadily, neither glaring, snarling nor lusting. Just looking. She'd gotten used to his inane behavior. And though she wouldn't say she liked his constant attention, she didn't fear him nor did she speak to him. Still, she had a sense of relief when he stayed on the elevator after she got off.

She saw from the note sticking on her font door that Kate Hamilton, her next door neighbor, was having a "few friends over for drinks, snacks and good conversation." Could she join them? Della put down her bag and telephoned her.

"Kate, I'll be over as soon as I slip into something, but listen for the bell. Pinski's hovering around again. I know he's harmless, but his kind of adoration gives me the willies."

"Not to worry, honey. I'll even leave the door unlocked," Kate told her.

Della put on a red velveteen jump suit and went next door, where Kate greeted her with a hug and clapped her hands for her guests attention. "Everybody, this is my buddy, Della Murray, mover and shaker of people and things over at the UN."

After greeting them, Della sized all five of Kate's friends up as yuppies, everyone of whom wore something that bore the logo of a famous designer. Bradford Carter's silk shit probably cost more than her father made in two or three weeks. Manhattan hair styles in the latest shades of blonde and jet black; sepia, peaches and cream complexions; and four different scents of expensive French perfume. Della looked at the people assembled there. Not one of them cared whether the Tustsi and Hutu fought to the death of the last one had an interest in the civil war that raged in Zaire or the festering hatred in Bosnia Hertznagovina. Local homelessness wouldn't bother them either. She took a seat in one of the low slung, three thousand dollar leather *Roche Bobois* chairs and looked around at the complementing furnishings, luxuriating in the comfort. The ceiling-high, hand-carved totem pole, modern art and hand knotted Iranian carpets had a something effect, but she wouldn't have minded seeing of the work of at least one African American artist in all that splendor. Quickly, she banished from her mind pictures of what she'd left in Pine Whispers and settled back to enjoy the urbane, sophisticated strangers with whom she, unfortunately, had more in common than with her family.

"I'm tired of vapid plays," one of the women said. "I long for something engrossing, good entertainment, food for the soul."

Just what she needed after her weekend, Della thought, a morose mood settling over her. It occurred to her that Craig Radcliff would fit right in with the group, though she was perhaps accusing him unfairly of superficiality.

"I thought Mercer's opening was a bust." Bradford said of their friend's new Broadway play.

"The whole thing stank. And where'd he get that girl who played the lead. What a curse!" Della turned to see the speaker, a tiny drugstore blond with big green eyes.

"You named it, baby," Bradford confirmed. "All boobs and no brain. Somebody ought to tell hem if he's looking for another Dolly Parton, Dolly can act."

"Yeaaah, man," an African American fellow sitting behind the green-eyed blond chimed in.

"I've taught play-writing for years," the Clairol brunette – a woman – stated, "and I can tell you the trouble with that fiasco was the plot. Every time you saw the hero, he was parked on his ass on the floor. What's funny about a man who always falls down? Didn't Mercer see any of those boring Jerry Lewis movies?"

Drama should be uplifting," big green eyes interjected. As far as Della was concerned, the elfin girl was her favorite among them. She hadn't seen *End Of The Line*, but she knew the critics had panned it.

"We'd better cool this," Kate told them. "Carla will be here any minute."

"Carla's an airhead," Bradford stated. "Any poet ought to know better than to read behind David Brinkley and Walter Mosley. Plain stupid."

"You mean they were on the same program?" Green eyes, whom Della had discovered, was named Marilyn, asked.

"Oh for goodness sake, Marilyn," Bradford groaned, giving her a withering look. "Stand up and let your mind get some air. I'm talking about two different occasions, for Pete's sake." He took a deep, impatient breath and rolled his eyes skyward. "Women!"

Kate laughed. "Carla's real problem isn't Brinkley or Mosley. The girl can't write poetry or anything else. If her uncle wasn't in the publishing business, we'd never had heard of her."

"Tell me about it," the man who sat behind Marilyn said.

The doorbell rang. "Shhh, everybody," Kate said, as she darted to the door. "I'm sure that's Carla." She opened the door. "Carla, darling, how *are* you? We've been holding our breaths waiting for you to get here. Imagine being on the same show as Walter Mosely and the great Brinkley. You were marvelous. Darling, come on in."

Della nearly slid from her chair as Bradford rushed to Carla and enveloped her in a warm, tight hug. "Carla, love, you were absolutely magnificent night before last. You put Mosely to shame, darling. And you look great, positively stunning. He hugged her again.

Della tried to shrug off her discomfort. She despised duplicity in anybody, and this group, through interesting, reeked of it. Still, she rationalized, though they were opinionated and critical, at least *they had opinions*. And they did things. She told herself she had no rights to judge them. *But you judged everybody in Pine Whispers*, her conscience screamed.

They munched on the smoked salmon, caviar sandwiches, sable roll-ups, shrimp, tiny empanadas, cherry tomatoes and other finger foods and washed it down with whatever liquor they chose.

Kate gave each of them a brochure and invited them to her design show. "I'm exhibiting photographs of my interior designs at the Bethany AME Church next Sunday," she told them. "It's a benefit for homeless children, so don't be stingy with your contributions."

Della hadn't been in Bethany church nor its modern recreation annex, where Kate had set up her show. She marveled at the church's accommodations for various sports, classes and community activities.

"You haven't been with us before," a man who was obviously a church elder said, joining her. "Let me show you around." He took her through the impressive plant that offered recreational activities for people of all ages.

"It's wonderful," she told him, as they reached the gallery where Kate's photographs hung.

"Yes," the old gentleman agreed. "There are many ways to nourish the soul. Perhaps you'll join us for morning services some Sunday."

Della nodded, having no intention of being penned down to a promise she doubted she'd keep. "Everything here surprises me," she told him, "but I guess I'm most amazed at how racially integrate this place is."

"Like our church." His gaze found something or someone that gave him pleasure. She followed it and looked into the eyes of Luke McKnight.

CHAPTER 4

"Have you met Luke McKnight, Miss…?"

Della had a sudden feeling of suffocation, and her words came out in a subdued gasp. "I'm Della Murray, and I've met Mr. McKnight." She would never have expected to see him in an art gallery at a show for homeless children. "We have the same employer," she quickly added, embarrassed at Luke's mocking bow and his unspoken, *fancy seeing you here*.

"I see," the old gentleman said, his face creased with pleasure. "So you're in the machine engineering business, too, Miss Murray. How nice."

"I'm not sure Miss Murray would deign to look inside a FAX machine, Dr. Gray. She's a senior UN official, a regular ramrod."

"Come now, Luke said, and Della had to look away form his brazen stare. He'd as much as said that she thought herself better than he. Well, if he considered himself inferior, it was no skin off her teeth.

"Our future would be in good hands," Dr. Gray told her, "if all our young men could stand shoulder to shoulder with this one. He's a role model for old as well as young. Our church is proud of him."

"If you don't stop this, I'll have to get a new baseball cap, Luke said, and a grin spread over his face.

"I'm not worried about you getting a big head," Dr. Gray told Luke. "You've had plenty opportunities for that. I still don't know how you've survived as a bachelor in this pool of eligible women. Perhaps you'll finish the tour with Miss Murray, and I'll see to some other guests."

Della tried hard to keep her face blank, because she knew that if she let it mirror her thoughts, she'd give Luke McKnight a good laugh at her expense.

But Luke didn't appear amused. Or, at least he wasn't laughing at her. Instead, to her amazement, he starting walking with her into the next room, explaining what she saw and the Church's original plan for this space.

"You may relax, Ms. Murray," he said when, tense and ill at ease, she released a deep sigh. He looked down at her fingers, held tightly entwined before her, and stopped walking. "Let's both admit, Ms. Murray, that we don't know anything about each other. Then, we'll each get over our surprise."

Della threw him an unfriendly glance. "Why would you be surprised to see me in an art gallery?"

"Same reason why you didn't believe your eyes when you saw me here, only you thought I'd more likely be seen in a bar guzzling beer or some place shooting pool."

"I never…"

"Maybe not the bar or the pool room, but something comparable. You can't judge a man by his shoes; the best dressed men in this country used to be mobsters. Still may be for all I know."

"You're not being fair," Della huffed. Dressed up, the man was even more arrogant than when he was crawling on his knees behind cabinets and under desks and benches repairing machines. More arrogant, smoother, sexier. A knockout. She tried not to squirm. "Besides, I haven't spent enough time thinking about you to place you anywhere. I'm too busy for that."

His easy laugh added to her discomfort. "And don't try putting me in my place, either. You have an advantage when we're in the UN building, but out here, lady, it's even Steven. If you don't want to catch it, don't throw it."

Della stopped, whirled around and faced him. "Do you want to continue walking through here with me? If you do, please try to be pleasant."

He winked at her. "I'm pleasant, but I have to swallow your uppity behavior every time I go near your office. It's great to be able to tell you off with impunity."

Too late, she tried to hold back her audible gasp. She'd heard overbearing female executives referred to as dragon ladies and barracudas, and she'd thought she deported herself in such a way as to avoid being placed in that class. She'd have to watch it with Luke McKnight.

As if to appease her for his bluntness, Luke adopted a different demeanor. "Tell you what," he said, interrupting her thoughts, "why don't you stay and attend serviced with me this evening?"

"No" lay easily at the tip of her tongue, but a light seemed to capture his face, transforming it until her heart raced with the warmth of his smile's brilliant glow, and she couldn't say a word. Immediately, the smile vanished and the hot rays of his sexual heat plowed through her. Fool. She had let him see her attraction to him and, within the second, the man in him had shot out to her.

"Yes, why don't you stay for evening service?" She hadn't known that Dr. Gray had rejoined them, because her thoughts and all her senses had been centered on Luke.

"I wanted to get home and do some work," she laughed.

The old man's snow-white eyebrows slowly elevated. "On the Sabbath?"

Caught out, Della agreed to stay and found herself sitting thigh to thigh with Luke while the minister repeatedly admonished those present not to judge other people unless they wanted to be judged. Rather than elevate her, the sermon depressed her so much that she welcomed the warmth of Luke's hand as it covered hers. But when she glanced at him, her spirits crumbled; he wasn't' looking her way, but seemed totally absorbed in the sermon.

They walked out of the Church half an hour later, and Luke couldn't help noticing Della's subdued air, a marked difference from her usual energy-charged self. "How about stopping for some coffee?" he asked her, as they walked up Broadway, not speaking or touching. Maybe a fiery Della was easier to take than this quiet, seemingly chastened woman.

"Coffee? Alright." The words were spoken as if she hardly knew they'd left her mouth. He decided not to press for an explanation of the change in her, because he though she knew. Della hadn't wanted to hear what she'd heard in that sermon. Truth didn't sit well with some people. She was strong, and he admired that, but it took toughness to face reality in oneself, and he preferred to think Della capable of hanging tough.

They stopped in a little coffee bar, took seats beside the window and ordered coffee. When she persisted in being quiet, Luke figured it was due to her mood rather than her snobbishness and decided to satisfy his curiosity.

"That sermon upset you, didn't it?"

Immediately, she bristled. "Why would you think that?"

Never one to back away from a position he thought secure, he told her, "Because it depressed you, and because you know you need to hear it."

He watched, fascinated, as the woman with whom he was more familiar reemerged. Her shoulders went back, her chin moved upward and she slanted her head to one side as tough to look down her nose at him. He grinned and had the pure joy of seeing her react to his masculinity at the very moment she'd planned to put him in his place. Thinking about it, he laughed out right.

Della drained her coffee, the best she'd tasted in a long time. "I'm ready to go."

His half smile didn't lighten her frame of mind, nor did his words. "If I'm wrong about the effect that the sermon had on you, say so. I've been wrong."

"I find that hard to believe," was her facetious retort. "I'm ready to go."

He stood and grabbed her wrist just as she opened her pocket book. She'd been sworn at and reviled in numerous languages, but she doubted she'd ever receive a look that equaled that one in unspoken furor.

"If paying for the stupid coffee is that important to you," she muttered, "go ahead and do it."

"My, but you do give in graciously, don't you?" he needled.

"You don't give me an incentive to be gracious; if I told you what was on my mind, you might like it even less."

Rain drops spattered them, and Luke whistled for a passing taxi. He got them into the cab just prior to the onset of a blinding shower and gave the driver Della's address.

A shiver of panic raced through her as Luke turned to her, and she was conscious of acute disappointment when, without taking his gaze from hers, he moved as far away from her as possible, leaning against the car door.

"I suppose I can thank the rain for saving me the embarrassment of having you dismiss me. I had intended to see you home, Ms. Murray, and for no reason other than the fact that I always see a woman safely to her door when I'm in her company at night. Call me old-fashioned."

She shifted form one ip to the other and, to her disgust, crossed her knee. The man had the ability to disconcert her at will. "Luke, I appreciate your seeing me home, but we needn't make a great deal out of it. You may keep the taxi and go on home, or wherever."

Did she imagine that he snarled? "I said I'd see you to your door and, to the best of my knowledge, you don't live in this cab."

"It isn't necessary. Really."

Luke got out, walked around to her side of the cab and opened the door. Then he paid the driver. "I'll see you to the door, or are you afraid the doorman wouldn't approve of me?"

Sheltered by the navy blue and gold canopy that extended form the building to the curb, Della walked rapidly to the front door of her apartment building, conscious of Luke at her side.

"Good evening, Mike."

"Good evening, Ms. Murray," the doorman replied. "I'm glad to see you've managed to stay dry."

Della didn't pause, but proceeded to the elevator. When she reached it, she turned to Luke. "I'm as safe as a person can be Luke. Good night."

Pinski walked to the elevator, gazed at Della then looked at Luke and frowned. Luke took Della's arm, stepped into the elevator and pushed the button that closed the door.

"Who was that, and why was he staring at you?" Luke asked her.

"Oh, that was Pinski," she said, waving her hand to show that the topic was of no importance. "He's a few blocks behind everybody else, but he's harmless."

Luke seemed less certain. "I sure hope so. Anybody that big and stealthy can do a lot of damage. Going to invite me in?" he asked in front of her door.

She shook her head. "The evening is over, Luke. It's been interesting."

She watched as he assumed a casual stance and leaned against the doorjamb, as though making him self comfortable. "Lady, you're a snob. You call me by my first name but you haven't given me permission to call you by yours." He extended both hands, palms out. "Oh, I know it's because you'd die if anybody at the UN heard me use your first name. But that being the case, why do you call me Luke?" He reached out and held her hand and, without warning, heat spiraled through her. She wanted to tell him to leave her alone, to let her be. She didn't want to be attracted to him, didn't want to feel anything for him. Yet, never before had the touch of a man's hand and the fire in his eyes sent excitement and eagerness for more roaring through her and settling in her loins.

His voice came to her icy and confident. "You think you want to be rid of me, don't you? Well, let me tell you that's far from the facts. You don't have the guts to face what you want. Good night, Ms. Murray. This *has* been interesting, indeed."

She opened the door of her apartment, closed it and clicked on the light. Angry with Luke, herself and her existence, she flung her handbag onto a chair, looked down at her eight-hundred dollar bar cart with its unopened bottles of high priced liquor and kicked it. If there had been anybody to hear her scream, she would have opened her mount and let it pour out. Of all the men in the world, why did she have to want an arrogant repair man? She slumped into a chair. He'd said she didn't have the guts she needed *not* to take what she wanted; he wasn't the man for the life she planned.

Luke walked the fifteen blocks from Seventy-fourth and Riverside Drive to his apartment at Eighty-seventh and Central Park West. The rain had slackened to a drizzle, but he was hardly aware of the dampness that clung to his clothing. Something about the woman just plain got next to him. For months, he'd watched her, elegant, cool, running her office with the finesse of a grand master at bridge. He'd admired her dignity, to say nothing of her long, shapely legs. Lord, but that woman had a pair of pins. Compared to a lot of African American women around New York, he wouldn't say Della was a raving beauty, but she had the kind of face you could look at forever. Arresting. And she had the presence and carriage of royalty. He might have ignored her, if he hadn't glimpsed isolated rays of gentleness in her, her kindness to her secretary, and even temper with her staff. It had stunned him to learn that she'd sent flowers for the funeral of the maintenance worker's wife and that she'd written him a not of condolence.

From what he knew of her character, she was full of incongruities, personality conflicts and heightened her intrigue, intensified his curiosity about her and ultimately, triggered his desire. What man wouldn't want to explore such a woman? Fully. To the hilt. But Della Murray wasn't for him. Oh, he wanted her; no point in denying that, but he didn't intend to go for her. He needed a steady, loving woman like his mother, a relationship such as he saw in his parents.

He got home without realizing the distance he'd covered and shed his coat and jacket. He'd achieved success; that much was undeniable. He looked at the evidence around him. His gaze swept the stucco walls of his foyer, the soft sand color of which soothed his eyes; the brown and beige marble tiled floor, the gilt-framed glass table over which hung a lithograph of Ulysses Marshall's *Sunday In Savannah,* and on which sat a leather bound copy of *The Norton Anthology of African American Literature.* He hadn't acquired things that would make an impression on his friends, but had bought what felt good and comfortable to have around: books he wanted to read, paintings he wouldn't ever tire of seeing, comfortable furniture and *objects d'arts* that felt good to the touch and were easy on the eyes.

He'd surrounded himself with things that made him feel at home, and when he settled on the woman who would be his life's mate, he wanted one who made him comfortable, at ease, like a well worn shoe. Della wasn't that woman. He doubted she'd share his dreams, because what he wanted wouldn't take him to diplomatic functions and a steady round of cocktail parties. As soon as he got his siblings educated, he intended to open a design studio and concentrate on inventions. He didn't plan to go through life repairing what other men created. For half and hour, he prowled from one room to another, opened closet doors and pulled out a few drawers. What the devil was he looking for? He thought of calling Gene, his buddy from col-

lege days, but Gene wasn't on his mind. He wanted Della.
He found her number and dialed it.

Della couldn't imagine who'd be calling her; she rarely
received calls at home, except from her family, and she'd just
spoken with her mother. It couldn't be Kate, she thought as
she wrapped a towel around her and hurried to the phone,
because Kate had left the gallery with Bradford, which
meant she was, by then, flat on her back. She welcomed the
interruption of her thoughts, which had lingered on Luke
McKnight.

"How did you get my number?" she asked Luke, recog-
nizing his voice at once.

"You gave it to me the night I repaired your computer.
Remember?"

She felt the chilling hand of fate tighten around her. She
knew she could get rid of him if she wanted to, because he
was, if anything, proud, and such a man didn't go where he
wasn't wanted. But if she were honest, she'd admit she did-
n't want to be rid of him; she wanted him more with every
passing second, but she wasn't going that way, not even if
she had to go on a diet of salt peter. She pulled the towel
closer, as though drawing strength from it.

"How may I help you, Luke?"

His low laugh held a growl-like tremor that skittered
through her nervous system. "You can start by not being so
ridiculously supercilious."

"What?"

"You heard me. If you ever found your way down to earth, you'd be good company. Look. I just wanted to say good night, make sure you found everything alright in your apartment, since you wouldn't let me go in and check it."

She didn't believe a word of it. "What are you after, Luke? If you expect every woman to start trembling with passion the minute she sees you, you must be in shock."

His answer came so fast that she wondered if he'd read her thoughts. "You've just let me in on the way your mind works, and if you've given me a shock, that was it." His voice was suddenly tinged with mocking laughter. "So you think women find me irresistible. Wonder what that means."

She wasn't going to let him entrap her with his wily comments. Not that she disliked clever repartee; on the contrary, she enjoyed bantering. A good mental workout always refreshed her, enhanced her confidence and broadcast her intelligence to her adversary. "I have to be in my office by eight o'clock in the morning," she told him, "so I'll have to say good night."

"I thought UN office hours were nine to five, but if you've loaded most of the world's problems on your own shoulders, I expect you need a little extra time there."

"Luke!" She'd come close to screaming at him. "You're going to have to stop saying everything that pops up in your... your mind. Good night." She hung up. Distracted, she let the towel fall away from her body as she went back to the bathroom to finish her nightly ablutions. As she passed the full length mirror, she stopped and gazed at herself. Fascinated. Would Luke like her? Angry at her tell-tale thoughts, she slammed the bathroom door shut and leaned against it. Nothing and nobody would make her settle for less than she wanted. And she wanted the security of knowing that she'd never be poor, never watch her child die because she didn't have the money for a hospital room, and that she'd never have to use a bucket to catch water from the leaking roof of the house in which she lived. Love wouldn't cover that. *Never!*

Her friend, Madge Altwood, had married Mr. Altwood when she was thirty-seven and he'd just reached fifty. He had boasted of an inherited trust, a string of annuities and a big bank account but, not long after her marriage, Madge had learned that her husband's total assets hadn't been worth a drunken shout. He hadn't lied; he just hadn't added it up. Twenty-five years later, the woman still dragged her arthritic limbs to work every day, while he stayed home and cultivated his mind, as he'd done ever since they married. Last heard, he was on his third reading of Prousts's *Remembrance Of Things Past.* She didn't see herself as a Madge Altwood, and neither approaching middle age nor her libido was going to enmesh her in Madge's kind of gentile poverty.

She knew the caller was Luke at the first ring. "Luke, have you lost your—"

"You didn't give me a chance to tell you good night. Sleep well." He hung up.

In the act of throwing the phone, she began to laugh. The man was her match, alright. She sobered up, and the mirth evaporated. Fun was fun, but he'd never see her rolling beneath him.

The next morning, Luke parked his van in the UN garage and struck out across First Avenue to the delicatessen on the corner of Forty-sixth Street where, standing beside the cash register, he swallowed his first coffee of the day. He looked at the long line of office workers waiting to be served and, on impulse, asked the clerk for two more cups of coffee and two bananas. He wondered what kind of reception he'd get after hanging up on her the night before and whether she'd appreciate having him in her office first thing in the morning.

"Come in."

At her tone, which was anything but welcoming, he had an urge to tiptoe away. But what the heck. He pasted a smile on his face, took off his baseball cap and opened the door. "Hi. If you're busy, I'll just ru-"

"Of course, I'm busy. Why do you think I…Luke? What are you doing here?

"You mean none of your machines are out of order?"

"I mean…Luke, you're taking this too far, you're—"

He put the coffee on her desk, amused that she'd opened her mouth and hadn't been able to close it. The elegant Ms. Murray. Nonplussed. Could you beat that?

"I'm what? he asked her, as he took the coffee out of the bag, put the milk in it and placed the banana on a napkin. "What am I, Ms. Murray?"

"Uh…uh…"

"I figured you wouldn't eat a donut or a Danish, so I brought you a banana. Don't you want it?"

"Thanks, but I'm busy."

"I know, but you have to eat, and this'll only take ten minutes. You didn't eat before you left home, did you?"

She eyed the coffee longingly, and he wondered if she'd forgo it out of stubbornness. "How do you know that?"

He removed the lid of his own coffee, sniffed and let the aroma tease his olfactory senses. He sipped it, made a show of his delight as he savored it, looked at her over the top of the cup and asked her, "Sure you don't want some? This is good stuff."

She swallowed hard, and he forced himself not to grin. "Oh, alright. But only for a couple of minutes."

He nodded. "Want me to close the door?" 'Course, I can try to get out of here before your staff shows up, if you'd prefer that."

"Right now, you remind me of a cow, Luke."

He could see that she delighted in having surprised him. "What do you mean by that?" He hadn't meant to growl at her, but it came out that way.

She didn't back down but glared at him eyeball to eyeball. "I mean a cow that gives a full pail milk and then deliberately kicks it over."

He didn't bat an eye lash. "Maybe she's getting even for the bruising some jerk gave her udders. Can't blame her."

"And who bruised your…"

He laughed. "Ms. Murray, I'm a man; I don't have udders. Now, if-"

"Luke, finish your coffee and get out of here. I've got to finish this draft before ten this morning."

He took a napkin and dabbed at the corner of her mouth. "Okay, but not until you eat your banana." She glared at him and began to peel it. "What's the matter? Don't you like them?"

"Luke, I love bananas, and I'm a coffee freak. I appreciate this. I really do, but I've got to finish this draft."

He drained his cup, threw it into her wastebasket and stood. "Okay. Honoring a commitment is a thing I respect. Good luck with it." He took his baseball cap out of his pocket, put it on and waved her goodbye. He winked at her and closed the door as he left.

How in Heaven's name had that man wormed his way into her life? She had needed that coffee almost as badly as she needed air and had been counting the minutes until Erin would walk into her office with her morning caffeine fix. She gulped it down. Luke McKnight could grow on a woman, but he wouldn't have any luck with her. She tried to concentrate on alternative seating arrangements for the dais on opening day of the conference, depending on whether the UN Secretary-General attend the first session. If he did, Craig Radcliff, the ingrate, would get what he deserved. He'd be outranked at his own show. She tried to banish the thought that Luke would have had the grace herself to compare Craig unfavorably to Luke; it was Luke who didn't measure up to Craig. She had always though herself fair, so she admitted that Luke had some virtues, but she pushed to the fore what she saw as his inadequacies. All of her trumped-up reasons why he wasn't the man for her. And like a lion after a gazelle, she set her sights on Craig.

Luke took his first call, a leaking color-copy machine in the Presentation Department. He went into the men's room to clean the ink from his hands and overheard two men talking about Della.

"She runs her shop as tightly as a new soccer ball," one of them said.

"Yes. You have to hand her that, but she's like a bull-dozer, man. Get out of her way. In my country, women give place to the man, but not these American women, and especially not Ms. Murray.

"Why should she?" the other asked. "She's competent. You don't give place, do you? She does her job, and I'd rather work with her than a lot of people I know."

"Well, yes. I agree, she knows her stuff. But why does she have to make everybody else look stupid?"

"You're joking," the other said. "She can't help it if she's more clever than some of these windbags around here. I walked into a guy's office-I won't call his name, -and his incoming basket was crammed. He was working *The New York Times* crossword puzzle. You'd rather have that?"

Luke dried his hands and left. So she was tough; if she wasn't, she wouldn't have that job. He picked u a phone on a desk in the hallway and dialed her number.

"Luke, you're driving me up the wall," she said. "If I pray to you, will you leave me alone?"

"I don't know. I hadn't thought about that. Try it. Where would you like this little ceremony to take place, and how long do you usually make your prayers?"

"Not even if you climb to the top of Mount Everest and put a pennant there that has my name on it. You could land there from a helicopter, and get the same results."

He laughed aloud. "Honey, you're precious. Helicopters won't fly that high."

"Luke, I'm on my way out of my mind. Cut it out. I'm not getting on my knees to pray to you?"

"Good grief; don't take it that hard. Maybe I'll see you later."

He hung up, looked at his order slips and headed for the basement printing offices. He dreaded it. The printer was the best that money could buy, but it didn't stand a chance of surviving ten of its projected fifty years if Boon Einarson, Roosevelt Jackson and Sean McGivern didn't lay off booze during working hours. He understood their need for some relief in that windowless third basement where every footstep carried the sound of a stalking murderer, but his integrity was beating him in the face; either he'd have to report them, or give the job to one of his employees. He made a note to bring Josh along with him when he got another call down there.

When the elevator carrying Luke reached the fourth floor, Craig Radcliff entered, accompanied by the tall, Nordic woman with whom he was frequently seen. Luke returned his unfriendly stare, realizing that the man saw him as a competitor. They headed for the second floor areas frequented by the delegates, but Luke continued to the third basement. He walked down the corridor, listening to his footsteps as he headed for the printing shop.

Why, he wondered, didn't' he leave Della alone when he knew she wasn't for him? He amended that: she couldn't have a permanent place in his life. Honesty forced him to admit that she bruised his ego with her haughtiness and challenged him to conquer her in the most primal way. He shook his head. She pretended not to need him or anybody else, but when he'd held her hand, he'd felt her tremors. A man without scruples would get her just to prove he could. He let out a sharp whistle. It wouldn't do to examine himself too closely.

Several mornings later, Della arrived at the UN building and reached the elevator simultaneously with Luke. Her annoyance at their chance encounter tempted her to take the escalator as far as the fourth floor, but she didn't do it for fear that he'd think her petty. Or worse-afraid of him.

"Hi. Might as well get on," he needled, "we've got it to ourselves. Truth is, everybody else who works here is probably just getting up. How come you're so early?"

"I have a job to do, and besides, I work best when no one's around to disturb me." She wasn't about to ask him why he was on the job at a quarter to eight in the morning. She didn't care what he did.

"I got a call from the S-G's office."

She didn't ask him about it. Had the elevator always moved so slowly? While it crawled, his gaze stayed locked on her, and her flesh quivered in response. She jumped off when the door opened at her floor and, in her eagerness to escape him, tripped and went sprawling into the hallway with her papers scattered around her.

His arms held her, lifted and cradled her and, for one second, she let herself fantasize. Embarrassed, she moved out of his embrace and forced herself to look at him. How was a woman supposed to be cool and detached when the heat of desire boiled all around her? "Thanks. I... thanks, Luke."

He collected her papers and handed them to her. "No problem. That wouldn't have happened if you'd had your breakfast. See you later."

"Later" arrived at eight-thirty when Luke entered her office with two cups of coffee and one banana. "Here. I'll just stay five minutes."

Della couldn't reject what her frazzled nerves demanded, so she took the cup from his hand, got her first swallow and relaxed.

"You can't make this a habit, you know. I'm not going to let anything develop between us, Luke."

"You're right; it wouldn't make sense. You aren't a New Yorker. Where'd you grow up?"

Della told him as little as possible, and when he attempted to lead her into a discussion of her family and background, she balked. "Luke, you said five minutes. It's been ten, and I have to work."

He took their cups and dropped them into her wastebasket. "I work with a group of adolescent boys. Why don't you come along one night and help with the girls; they need someone."

"Look, Luke, I'm—"

"Not too busy. The program is at a junior high school in the Bronx. We'd be there for about an hour. How about it? The girls need a role model, and you'd be perfect. Their teachers are too much like their parents—tired, jaded and cynical. You could help."

"Alright. Alright." She would have agreed to most anything to get him out of her office before Erin arrived. "Now, will you let me work?"

"Okay. Meet you in the lobby at six?"

She groped for words. "Uh… I'd rather… I have to drop something off at FEDEX. You know, the office on Forty-fifth between First and Second. Meet me there." Guilt washed over her when she glanced up into eyes that censored and sorrowed. Well, she couldn't help it; she couldn't afford to be seen leaving the building with him.

"Would it make a difference if I changed out of these brogans and put on a business suit?"

She opened her mouth, but his "No, I guess it wouldn't" saved her an answer.

As Delia was leaving the UN building via the delegates' entrance that afternoon, she saw Craig talking with two men, nodded his way and continued walking. But Craig extended an arm and intercepted her. After introducing her to diplomats from Ivory Coast and Togo and praising her work on the Nairobi conference—more for her benefit than for theirs, she figured—he excused himself and took her aside.

"Della, I need to talk with you about the conference and how you want to run it, but I'm pinched for time. Would you give me your phone numbers? She wrote down her home and office numbers, including her FAX number. He looked at the note and, from his smile, she knew at once that she'd made a tactical error. She should have made him ask for her home number. No use crying over spilled milk. She held her head up, nodded in the direction of the two diplomats and ducked into the Meditation Room. She didn't want to leave with the three of them, because she stood a good chance of bumping into Luke.

She found him leaning against the FEDEX door, his arms folded across his chest and a scowl on his face.

"What's the matter?"

"You said six o'clock and it's fifteen past. I feel like a dunce holding up this door. Come on."

She went inside and mailed an envelope hi order not to be caught lying. Curious as to what she'd find, she looked forward to seeing Luke in the role of counsellor to inner city youths. And what she saw assaulted her prejudiced view of Luke.

"You've undergone a personality transformation," Luke told her after she'd mingled with the girls for a few minutes.

"I've gotten an idea for a project," she told him, "and I can see big things coming out of it." She didn't tell him that by working with those girls, she could legitimate her claim to the UN post of Assistant Secretary-General (AS-G) for the Standing Committee on Adolescent Girls. What a piece of good luck, she thought, barely able to wait until she could begin laying out her plan. So elated was she that she didn't protest when he asked to accompany her home.

She ignored Pinski when she saw him lurking in the lobby, but she could see the hostility in Luke when Pinski joined them in the elevator and fixed his gaze on her companion.

"Invite me in. I didn't get a chance to see how you live."

Flustered because she couldn't think of an excuse, she said, "I …uh…I don't think so."

"What are you afraid of, Ms. Murray. Do you think I'll ravish you?"

"Of course not, I…"

He shrugged. "Don't sweat it. I'll just…"

She put the key in the lock and turned it. He waited, all the while string into her yes. She wanted to tell him to leave, but her hand opened the door. She couldn't look at him, but walked in and waited.

"Am I invited in?"

She looked straight ahead, not daring to see his coal black eyes.

"For a few minutes. I want to turn in early."

In his mind, Luke flirted with the way she'd look as she slowly shed the most feminine of under-garments, bathed her stain skin, let the air day it and crawled into bed naked as though expecting a lover.

Expecting him. His thoughts must have been reflected in his face, because her eyes darkened, she rimmed her lips with her tongue and her left hand grasped her breast. Then, she turned her back, and he knew she realized what her action signified.

"You have mixed feelings about me. You don't want to believe I'm honorable, that I'm worth your time.

She backed away from him. "I never suggested that."

He knew he shouldn't press her, but he disliked being treated as if he was a contagium. "I don't believe you. When is a man honorable and worthy of your consideration? Give me some guidelines." He didn't know why he kept pressing, and maybe he'd stop it if she'd admit he attracted her.

"Thanks for seeing me home." She walked toward the front door, shoulders back and head high. Regal. Dismissing him.

He laughed. It wasn't one bit funny; in fact, it hurt like hell to be attracted to a woman who behaved as though you were of no consequence. He looked hard at her, cataloguing the things about her that made him want her. She clutched at her chest, and a reckless mood overtook him.

"You want more than you're letting on, Ms. Murray." He stepped closer. "What's so bad about kissing me good night? I'll treat you the way I'd want a man to treat my three sisters. You want to kiss me. I know it, and you know it." He moved closer still and brushed her cheek with the pad of his thumb. To his satisfaction, she didn't move. He put an arm around her waist and urged her to him.

"Kiss me?" The hole that was always in him opened wider; God help him if she refused. When she neither spoke nor moved, he tipped up her chin, looked into her compliant face and lowered his head. Violent shudders rocked him when he touched her parted lips.

He might as well have stunned her with a ray gun. His hot mouth singed her, and her arms went around him as though they belonged there. Desired gripped her. She savored his lips. Sweet. So sweet. She clutched him to her and fought with herself until she couldn't help opening her mouth wider in an unspoken quest for his tongue. She took what he gave her. Hungrily. Unable to get enough of him. Warnings thundered in her brain, reminding her

that an involvement with him would drag her back to the life she'd fought so hard to escape. But the men who took her to the one-hundred-dollars-plus-wine dinners didn't kiss like that, didn't make her feel as he did. The hot fire of desire settled in her love nest, a dizziness assailed her body and, when he pulled her so close that air couldn't get between them, her tremors betrayed her.

He stepped back, releasing her, and she couldn't cover her embarrassment, couldn't look at him. He put his arms around her, not speaking, just holding her.

"I'm... I'm okay, Luke."

He shook his head. "We aren't going to gain anything by pretending. This is the way it is with us and, if you don't want it, if you can't accept it, tell me right now."

"And you can drop it...," she snapped her finger, "just like that?"

He shrugged. "I'd lie if I said yes. Let's just say I don't think it'll kill me. I'd better say good night. Watch out for that big fellow who seems to tail you."

"Oh, I told you; he does that all the time. Everybody knows he's harmless."

"Not in my book. By the way, I'm through calling you Miss Murray, so if you don't want me to call you baby in front of anybody who listens, you'd better tell me your name."

"My name's Della, as you probably already know."

He leaned forward and kissed her. "Good night, Delia."

'

Frissons of heat plowed through her and she lowered her gaze.

"Good night, Luke."

She slumped into the nearest chair feeling as though she'd slammed into a loaded freight train. She'd played with fire, and Luke McKnight had singed her, but no matter how much she suffered for it, she would not give in to him. She wanted a family, and she refused to cast her lot with a man unless he offered her financial security and a decent life style. By herself, she could afford whatever she wanted, but she didn't plan to lower her standard of living by taking care of a man and children. She wanted to be at home with her children until her youngest went to kindergarten, and she didn't want to live from hand to mouth—as her Granny put it. Whenever Luke tempted her, she would remember Madge Altwood. And little Morris was never far from her thoughts.

Luke had chided Delia for her attitude toward him, but he wasn't certain that he'd behaved honorably with her in her apartment. He'd felt that kiss as much as she had, but he'd initiated it just to prove to her that he could seduce her. He'd succeeded, but he wasn't too proud of it. He laughed at himself; that kiss hadn't left him unscathed. Oh, no. And he wasn't sure he would have moved into her that way, if he'd anticipated the force of the emotion she wrung out of him. Shivers coursed through him when he thought how easily she could have brought him to his knees. He had to watch himself with Della Murray.

CHAPTER 5

Della pulled herself up and rushed to the phone, thinking that Luke might be the caller. "Hi." With a heavy sigh, she yielded to the letdown.

"Craig Radcliff here. Sorry to call so late, but I just got rid of those ambassadors and dashed home to give you a ring. You know how it is. Those fellows make a living talking, and they never run out of gas. But let's not waste our time on them. Hope you're not in bed."

If she had been, she wouldn't tell him. She looked at her watch, saw that it was ten minutes past eleven and corralled her rising irritation. If she hadn't given him her home phone number without his having asked, he wouldn't have been so presumptuous. She wouldn't make a similar mistake with him again.

"What is it that can't wait 'til tomorrow, Mr. Radcliff?"

"That's what I call mowing a guy down. I wanted to talk with you, and I'm an impatient man; I didn't want to wait until tomorrow. Have dinner with me. We need to talk about some things."

"Yes. I suppose we do, but I'm busy tomorrow evening. What do you say to lunch?"

"I prefer dinner when the day is over, and we're relaxed. Will Tuesday suit you?"

"Uh… yeee… yeah. Okay. Tuesday evening." She saw no point in alienating him; he could make or ruin that conference.

She didn't try to hide her lack of enthusiasm for the middling restaurant he chose. She couldn't remember when last a man had taken her to one where half the men had left their jackets and ties at home. He noticed her reserved manner and confided that it was his favorite eating place, because he loved the curried lamb. She detested lamb, curried or not.

"Tell me about yourself, Della. How'd you get where you are? You're sitting in a high post."

She sipped her martini and then, suddenly alert, put the glass aside when she noticed that Craig had ordered club soda with a twist of lemon. She was familiar with that trick; you stay sober while your adversary makes a fool of himself.

"Would you ask a man that question? I didn't get to the top on my back, Mr. Radcliff; I got there with my brain and hard work."

"Ah, Della, am I so easily misunderstood? Everybody knows you're competent. It usually takes the support of your government for an appointment to your level, but you came up through the ranks."

"Yes." So he'd gotten access to her personnel file. Interesting. "And I fought for every step up that ladder."

She watched him assess her, a big cat circling a prospective kill. "But there's no need to fight *me*, Delia. You and I are going to make great waves together."

She sat up straighter. Don't relax with this man, Della, she admonished herself. "I'm glad to hear you say that, Craig, because the Nairobi Conference should shoot us both to the top. I'm speaking the pinnacle; from then on, we'll be able to call our shots." She wondered at his frown, but went on talking about the conference.

He quirked an eyebrow, and then an expression of surprise lit his eyes. "My dear, we discuss business between nine and five; the evening is for us."

So he'd faked his look of surprise. Alright. She knew how to act, too. She pulled up her lower lip and put a blank expression on her face. "Didn't you say you talked business with two diplomats until late into last evening?"

He leaned back and let a smile crawl slowly over his face. Talking about practiced charm! She didn't want to believe he was mostly shell and little substance, so she shrugged it off as the demeanor of a diplomat.

"Della, whatever I may have intended, my only interest right now is you. I couldn't dredge up a useful thought about that meeting in Nairobi if my life depended on it." He reached across the table and pulled one of her fingers. "You're heady stuff, lady."

"Craig, I don't mix work and... and—"

"Pleasure, Della. And I promise you, it will be a pleasure." He sat forward. "For both of us."

She jerked back her hand. "Not even Hank Aaron hit a home run every time he went to bat, Craig. Thanks for dinner."

What a man! He stood at once, giving the impression that he'd been ready to leave before she suggested it. She'd have to stay on her toes without getting on the wrong side of him, because he mingled freely among the titans of political leverage and, if he chose, could either damage or boost her career.

Pinski seemed to have anticipated their arrival at her apartment building, for he stood near the door and lurked just behind them as far as the elevator. He waited until it arrived, all the while gazing at Delia, then left them. She looked at Craig for his reaction to Pinski, but saw none.

"May I have your key?" he asked her when they reached her door.

She handed it to him and remembered that the first time Luke went home with her, she had refused him that courtesy. A sense of unease, an apprehension of the unknown pervaded her, and she couldn't help recalling that being with Luke had not induced such a feeling in her. No sooner had they stepped into her foyer than Craig closed the distance between them, and his hands, large and foreign, eased around her waist.

"You're a beautiful woman, and I want to see more of you. A lot more." His fingers tipped up her chin and she felt his lips, warm, firm and tasteless moving over hers, asking that his tongue invade her mouth. She couldn't part her lips, couldn't open up to him, but he must have mistaken that for reticence or primness, because he pressed harder.

"I don't want to leave you. I can't leave you. Let me stay with you tonight."

Stunned that he would make such a move while knowing so little about her, she stepped away from him and made herself appear unfazed. "Not tonight, Craig. Thanks for a pleasant evening."

"Next time, then?" He pulled her close, ran his tongue across her lips and let her feel his arousal before stepping away. "I'm sorry. Forgive me, Della; I didn't mean for that to happen, but you... well..." He seemed to search for a word. "I'll let myself out. Good night."

Della walked through her apartment, turning on lights as she went, trying to come to terms with her reactions to Luke and Craig. She told herself that Craig's impervious air prevented her from responding to him. Wouldn't most women be attracted to a tall, dark, handsome, polished and refined man? So why not her?

Craig was all that and more. Oh, Luke was handsome, at least four inches taller than she in her heels, and could hold his own. But could he provide financial security for her and the children they would have so long as he repaired machines at union wages? Wealth was not the only test of a man, but it ironed out a lot of his creases. She didn't want to live as her mother had, and she wanted to remain at home while her children were small. If Providence didn't play a practical joke on her, she'd stop thinking about Luke and fall for Craig.

Sensing the onset of a sleepless night, Delia hooked up her karaoke and began recording poems for the blind, the volunteer activity that gave her the most satisfaction. She read works of Phyllis Wheatly, Robert Frost, Langston Hughes and Carl Sandburg. When her voice wound down, she put the poems and the machine aside and opened her copy of Carson McCullers' *The Heart Is A Lonely Hunter.* If she'd wanted to sink into a blue funk, she couldn't have chosen an easier method. The idea that human beings had been freed of one kind of slavery only to be forced into another—often with their own connivance—sickened her for, as she read, she knew that by virtue of her single-mind-ed determination to avoid poverty, she had saddled herself with a dangerous state of mind, maybe even a kind of slavery. She closed the book, got in bed and fought sleep. But it came and, with it, that awful day in Payne General Hospital.

She got up, sluggish and tired for having spent the night fighting her demons. She knew them well, but this time, they had brought friends. The receptionist at the desk in the hospital waiting room hadn't been a woman from the cast *of Fried Green Tomatoes,* but a man with Craig Radcliff's face who had smiled and told her, "We don't have any rooms here for poor people." The harder she had pleaded with him for her little brother's life, the brighter his smile had shone. The noise of laughter had nearly deafened her, and she'd looked around to see the amused faces of four hundred delegates to the Nairobi Conference. Cold moisture dampened her palms as she relived the nightmare of her dreams.

She paused while dressing, looked upward and begged, "Oh, God, why are you playing this trick on me? All I want is a good life for my children. Please don't shackle me to a poor man; I won't stand for it." She shook her fist, regretted it and clasped her hands in a prayerful attitude. "Why can't I care for Craig? Don't make me choose between Luke and my dreams." She had to pull herself out of that mood and get to work. Along the way, however, her wayward thoughts locked on her dilemma. Why didn't she respond to Craig when she wanted so badly to feel with him what she felt with Luke. Craig was as tall and as smooth looking as Luke, and more debonair. But she couldn't say he was more intelligent, not if she was honest. She nodded a hello to the guard at the front door of the Secretariat Building and hastened to her office.

Minutes after she sat down at her desk, she looked up to see that Luke had poked his head in her door. "Hi. How's your grandmother?"

Too proud to lie, she dropped her gaze. He said nothing, but when at last she looked at him, she didn't have to be told that he'd judged her and found her wanting. She opened her mouth to asked him how he got the audacity to censor her and closed it without speaking. He stepped inside the door, and her gaze swept his solemn face, the red woolen cap in his hand, his green storm jacket, the brogans, and the dozens of tools and keys that always clanked around his hips. In spite of herself, she saw something comfortable in him, and her face must have reflected it, because his lost its somber expression. He smiled, and her heart kicked over.

He walked over to her desk and ran his hand along the edges of the polished wood. "These edges ought to be rounded. Save you a lot of stocking money. Want me to put a couple of hooks under there for your brief case and your hand bag? What you really need are some inside, invisible drawers. It must be centuries since anybody introduced a new concept in desk design for offices. All the differences you see in desks are variations on the same old theme."

"You're inventive."

"I *should* be. But we're off the subject, Delia. Why don't you know how your grandmother is?"

"It's not that I don't know; but you were asking when I'd seen her, and I haven't since… well, you know." When he treated her to a wordless stare that was loaded with meaning, she bristled. "Stop leaning on me. I can't run to North Carolina every weekend."

"I'm not leaning on you; your conscience is doing that. Just wanted to say hello. I'm short of emplo… I've got some things to do over in the Oldenhaus building, so I'd better run."

Saved by the bell, Luke mused, recalling that he'd almost slipped and let Delia know he had *employees*. He dashed across the street to the deli, got two cups of coffee and a banana and sent them to Delia by the repairman he'd assigned to the printing shop. Then he headed for the Oldenhaus Building. Rich McCoy, the man who serviced that building for him, had gotten an acid burn while cleaning a copy machine. Fortunately, the Oldenhaus was walking distance from the UN complex, and he could manage both until he found Rich's temporary replacement.

He wished he could understand his fixation on Delia Murray. God forbid he should be attracted to her because of her aloofness; that would mark him as a sick man. Hell, a man would be sick if he didn't want Delia Murray, he reasoned, but he'd be more comfortable with his interest in her if she wasn't married to that job. That business about being too harried to visit her grandmother every weekend was a screen for something else, and he suspected she didn't enjoy being with her family. He'd be foolish, he rationalized, if he allowed himself to fall for a woman with Delia's outlook.

As soon as Luke closed the door, Delia dialed her mother. "How's Granny doing?"

"Honey, it's so sweet of you to call. The doctor says she probably won't make it, because those seizures are getting closer and closer, and one of them may take her out." Her mother explained that the church ladies who lived nearby took turns staying with her grandmother. "She's never by herself, and Boney takes us over to see her every other day. So don't you worry none. Still, I'll be glad when you get back from Africa, so you can get to see her."

"I will, Mama. I'll get back home as soon as I can." Guilt pricked her when the words left her mouth and, in her mind's eye, Luke's accusing stare floated back to her. But the whole scene down in Pine Whispers depressed her for days after she left there.

"We know you'll try, Ludell. We know you're important, and a lot that goes on up there depends on you. So you just do the best you can. Granny loves you, and I know she'll understand; I feel she will."

Della didn't correct her mother's estimation of her worth to the United Nations, because Rachel wanted to believe that her child had reached the top. She knew her mother regaled the neighbors with tales of Delia's travels around the world and her accomplishments at the UN, and she didn't want to detract from her mother the status with her neighbors that having such a daughter conferred.

"Come in." She glanced up and saw a man wearing a jacket with the words, RPM Repair Company, written on it. He walked to her desk and placed a white bag on it.

"Mr. McKnight asked me to bring this to you." He turned to leave.

Della looked closely at the bag and tried but failed to control the smile that the sight of coffee brought to her face.

"Thanks. Thanks a lot."

"You're welcome, ma'am. No problem."

She had swallowed half of one cup before she wondered at the man's deference and his reference to Luke as "Mr. McKnight." A colleague would have refereed to him as Luke. She shrugged. Who knew about protocol in the RPM company? Maybe Luke was foreman for the UN building. She peeled the banana and sat back to enjoy it, but when she tried to imagine Craig bringing or sending her coffee, she lost some of her joy at receiving the precious gift.

Eight-thirty. She had thirty minutes in which to get some work done before the interruptions began. At that moment, Pillay Prakar knocked and entered.

"I hear you got Radcliff to chair your conference. I hope you don't live to regret it." She saw that the smirk on his face belied his statement; the man was praying that she'd fall flat on her face.

"You can't find a better chairman; Craig Radcliff's first class." If she had misgivings, Prakar would never know about it.

"He's a user. I'll be waiting for you to land on your face when he tells the S-G he made a success of that conference all by himself and in spite of your incompetence."

She did her best to appear unperturbed. "Don't make the mistake, Prakar, of assuming I'm a patsy."

He showed his brown teeth in a feral grin. "Patsy? Barracuda is more like it. But you've met your match, doll. You laid an egg. Thought you'd get the better of me and beat me out for that AS-G post, didn't you?" He laughed. "You just increased my chances of heading the Standing Committee on Adolescent Girls."

She scoffed. "They would never give it to a man."

"Don't be so sure. Logic isn't what turns the wheels in this organization. You know that. Count yourself out."

"Would you let me work? And that's something you might try, unless you'd like to see your department eliminated in the S-G's reorganization." She didn't wait for him to leave, but got down to work. She and Prakar each headed a department, and she suspected he counted on his being a man and non-American to get him the promotion to head of SCAG. She detested his low regard for women, but she didn't blame him; you could get a pig out of the country, but you couldn't get the country out of the pig. He'd try to root if he found himself in Buckingham Palace.

She wanted that promotion, and she'd... She remembered Luke's youth program. That's the ticket, she told herself. She phoned the New York City school superintendent's office and got permission to develop a program for adolescent girls. The man was overjoyed to have her suggestion and her support. Encouraged, she telephoned half a dozen foundations, anticipating strong support, which she received, because her idea was both timely and relevant. What leader in New York City wouldn't support a program designed to prevent pregnancy among adolescent African American girls? Two foundations asked for proposals, and she put her work—including that relating to the Nairobi Conference—aside, wrote the proposal and mailed it on her way home that evening.

When she got home, she found Pinski hovering near the building's front door, as usual. She wished he would at least smile. Since she didn't know what his reaction would be if she spoke, she continued to pretend she didn't see him. She got into her apartment too tired to eat, kicked off her shoes and started for the shower just as the phone rang.

"Your grandmother's had another seizure," her father announced without preliminaries. "I don't see how I can go home right now, Papa, but I'll call every day to see how she is."

"Yesterday, she said you wasn't… weren't coming, but your mother assured her you'd make it. If you call, I'll tell her you asked about her." He hung up.

She eased down to the bed and sat, too tired to think. She told herself that she couldn't do anything to help Granny, and that her grandmother would want her to be successful. If she left her office for any length of time, Prakar would move to take over the conference. Dejected, she wiped the lone tear that settled on her cheek.

"Hello." She almost yelled it, jumpy with the fear that another call from her family was bringing dreaded news.

"What's the matter? Any problems there? You don't sound like yourself."

An unexpected solace flowed through her when she heard Luke's voice. "I… I'm alright." She covered the mouth piece to prevent his hearing her sniffle. "You sure?"

"I… I…Ye…yes. I'm okay."

"You're not okay. Now tell me what's the matter." She told him about her father's call. "You have to go home, even if you stay there only an hour. I'll come get you and take you to the airport."

"No, Luke. I'm alright. Honest." But she wasn't, and suddenly she wanted to see him, needed his strength. She was alone in every crisis she faced, whether at work or in regard to her family. One lousy choice after another. Man your turf, or go see your sick grandmother. Crawl out of bed at five-thirty to get to work by seven-thirty, or turn in a rotten job. Work your tail off because more was expected of women than of men, or watch your bootlicking male colleagues sail right past you up the ladder of success. She got up and began to undress. Frustrated, she tossed a pillow across the room, and anger rioted through her. She didn't want to need Luke or anybody else; once you let yourself lean on a person, you opened yourself to being victimized. She'd seen enough of that to last her forever.

Alternately, she paced the floor and sat on the edge of the bed. Dejected. If only she could know what her life would be a year hence with the conference behind her, the promotion settled and Craig's role in her life clarified. The ringing doorbell brought her out of her reverie. She wondered why the doorman hadn't buzzed her and hoped the caller wasn't Craig. She put on a tailored robe and opened the door.

"I knew it," Luke said. "Come here."

She dived into his arms and relished the warmth she found there. "You idiot."

He hugged her to him for a second and stepped away. "Yeah. I'm that alright. We can make the nine-forty to Wilmington. Want me to help you pack a few things?" When she only stared at him, he said, "Come on. Let's go. If she dies, you'll never forgive yourself."

"I hadn't planned to go."

"Let me have that again. What do you mean, you hadn't planned to go? It can't be the job, and if it's a man you can't leave for a couple of days, he's not worth your time. You want me to pack for you?"

"I can do it. Thanks."

She crammed a few things into her overnight bag while he called the airline and made reservations. She didn't question his staying with her until boarding time, because she'd begun to understand that Luke was a thorough man, that whatever he began, he saw it through to the end.

"You take care and call me when you get back." He handed her the small bag, winked and walked off.

Della watched him go, bemused that he'd neither offered a kiss nor asked for one. A person could make a fortune instructing women in the ways of men and, in her current mind set, she'd be among the first to register. Luke McKnight was a complicated man, an enigma.

She got her parents' home around midnight. Only her brother, Mark, was there. She unpacked her overnight bag in Bitsy's room, changed into a robe and went to the front room where she found Mark gazing at the open fire.

"I hear Granny's leaving you the old cabin along with her forty-three cents. You don't want it and you don't need it, but if I had the place, I'd fix it up so I can get out of here and be on my own."

"Nothing's stopping you from staying there when she's gone. You could stay there now." "It will surprise you to know that I stay here so I can help Mama and Papa. You come down here parading your three-hundred dollar dresses and hundred dollar shoes, and mama could make herself four or five dresses with what you spend on one pair of shoes."

She didn't have the energy to fight with Mark. She'd been tired hours before she left New York. "I didn't realize you resented me. I work hard for what I have, and I have to look right. I could work my tail off, but if I wore cheap clothes and had runs in my stockings, that's what everybody would see, and I'd be a source of shame to my superiors and a joke to my peers. I send Mama bolts of the best fabric money can buy, but she doesn't make anything for herself from it. She clothes her customers in elegant suits and dresses. What do you want from me?"

"More than you give. I can't figure out why everybody thinks you're so great. Mama's always making excuses for you, and I wish the hell I knew why. I make three-hundred dollars a week, and after I give Granny and Papa fifty each, pay my taxes and give Papa a little extra if he's in trouble, I have practically nothing left for myself."

"I make a high salary, Mark, but the cost of living in New York is excessive. I send Mama and Papa money every two weeks and some extra if they're having it tough."

"Sure, and what's a few hundred bucks to you?"

"More than you think. I can't eat lunch in the UN dining room for less than eighteen dollars, and I'd be ashamed to tell you what my apartment cost me every month. I spend one-third of what I earn on it; one third goes for savings; and I live on the rest. I'm careful with money, Mark, because I don't want to be without it. I have nightmares about needing money and not having any. In New York, your neighbors—if you've got any—don't help you out when you're in need. You don't even ask."

"Then you're no better off than Papa; maybe he's ahead of you. If he needed anything, he could go to anybody in town. They'd give him something, if it was nothing but a bag of corn meal."

"I know. Everybody likes Papa. He could have been somebody, Mark. Why didn't he go to school so he could get a better job? School janitor for ten months a year and cleaning the streets the other two."

"Ludell, Papa *is* somebody. You'd rather he was like the principal of Matthew's school? A married man chasing every skirt he sees. Or making house calls with his breath stinking of liquor like Dr. Maynard? You wouldn't mind having for a father that judge who freed a man of a rape indictment, claiming the girl invited it because she was wearing a mini skirt? And what about if he was an educated town drunk like Ben Hooper? You've got some peculiar values, Ludell. Can't see the forest for the trees. Papa cleans up as well as anybody when he gets off from work, and you'd better be glad he has that summer job. Otherwise, you might have to send more money down here.".

"He settled for less than he could have had, and you're doing the same thing. Why don't you learn computers and improve yourself?"

"And what'll happen to your family here if I quit my job to go back to school?" She didn't answer, only looked into the distance wondering at the cruel turns that life could take. Mark possessed an exceptional mind, but if he were to cultivate it to full advantage, she'd have to make more sacrifices, lower her living standard and cut her savings. She had to save; she needed that security. "You're so scared of poverty," he went on, "you're its prisoner anyway, Ludell. Worse things can happen to you."

His demeanor softened, "All I want you to do is increase what you send every time you get a raise. That's what I've done."

"I've done that too, Mark, but I'll send more." She'd planned to increase her payroll savings by three-hundred dollars a month, but she supposed she'd better postpone that. The arrival of their parents and Bitsy ended the conversation.

"Lord, look who's here," Rachel exclaimed and rushed to embrace her daughter. Delia greeted them with hugs and kisses, and she had the surprising thought that she only got such unconditional warmth from her family.

"How's Granny doing, and where's Matthew?"

"She's holding her own," Tate answered, "and Matthew stayed with her."-

"But he'll miss school."

"Ludell, Matthew loves his grandmother, and he wanted to be with her," Tate told her. "When you love someone, Ludell, you'll give up what's important to you if you can make that person's life easier, a little sweeter."

Her father's words stung. She looked into Mark's judgmental gaze and cringed as he turned and walked out of the room.

She shook off the feeling of consternation; who was Mark to judge her? He didn't know her circumstances, hadn't seen what she'd witnessed. If she spread what she earned among all those who thought they had a claim to it, she'd have to move back to Harlem. But she would work two jobs before she'd do that and look poverty in the face everywhere she turned every day of her life. Never. She'd struggled too hard to get away from there. Her clothes seemed tighter, moisture accumulated in her scalp, and she wanted to take off her blouse. If only she wasn't haunted by the fear of becoming the pauper who existed in her nightmares. Dreams so real as to circumscribe her life.

She acquiesced to her father's plea that she join them for church Sunday morning before going to see Granny. Her parents wanted to show her off, and she agreed, mainly to give them that pleasure. The simplest thing she had with her was the gray pants suit in which she travelled, and she hoped the minister wasn't on his "sinners at the angry gates of hell" horse that morning, because if he singled her out for a lecture, her parents would be mortified.

But to her amazement and delight, the minister welcomed her and had only glowing words of praise for the successful hometown girl. Accolades that she would never have expected. And after the service, the church folk crowded around her as though she were a celebrity.

"Why don't you come down and talk about your travels, Ludell?" one of her mother's friends asked. "We need to raise some money to fix up the church, and everybody would come out to hear you. You just about the only person in this town that's ever been anywhere. Well, one of the few."

"That would be just the thing, don't you think, Rachel?" another put in.

"I guess so," Rachel said, "but my Ludell's very busy." '

Della knew her mother feared she might refuse, and she sure didn't want to do it.

"You could talk about anything you want," the woman assured her. "The pastor won't care as long as you don't mention sex and don't take the Lord's name in vain."

Della had to laugh. The world was full of hypocrites, and she stood in the midst of some right then. She hedged. "I'll see about it."

"Oh Lord," Ada, who had just joined them, moaned. "And everybody'll have to listen to old lady Graham's speech about how she brought little Ludell into the world."

"She didn't do any such thing," Rachel told them. "My Ludell and all the rest of my children were born in the hospital. I never had a midwife."

"That won't bother her none," the other woman said. "Mary Graham don't know the difference between the truth and a porcupine."

"You tell it," Ada encouraged. "Shoutingest liar you ever saw."—"How much money do you need to raise?" Delia wanted to know.

"We need five thousand, but that'll take years," her mother said.

"All right, I'll come, but I have to go overseas first. It'll be at least a month from now."

"Oh, Ludell, you're going to be blessed, you hear?" One of the women assured her. She looked at their beaming faces and, though she tried to be sorry she had committed herself, she couldn't hold back her smile.

The visit with Granny proved to be the most pleasant part of her trip, because the old woman's pleasure in seeing her granddaughter was unmistakable. Delia held the frail body close, not knowing whether she'd see her alive again. And joy suffused her when she saw that fading health had not diminished Granny's wickedness.

"Be a good girl and keep your dress down," Granny whispered.

"Most men aren't worth raising it for, and the ones that are will take matters out of your hands." After the previous somber eighteen hours, that humor brought cleansing laughter, and Delia didn't bother to squelch it.

"I'll remember that," Della said, when she could stop laughing.

Events during her visit with her family crowded Luke and Craig out of her mind, as the plane took Delia back to New York. She hadn't realized the meagerness of Mark's salary nor how much of it he gave to the family. When she got home she telephoned him and assured him that, if Granny left anything to her, she would sign it over to him, and that she planned to increase by three-hundred dollars the amount she sent home each month.

"Mama and Papa can sure use that," he told her, but he wasn't grateful for her offer to give him her inheritance from Granny. "I'd be bubbling over with thanks, Ludell, but I know Granny's little place means not a damned thing to you. I bet you wouldn't hand over your Burberry raincoat or your lizard skin brief-case that fast."

"You said you wanted that property, and I'm offering it to you."

"Sure I want it. I need it." She heard the bitterness, understanding that it came from his pain.

"When things are tough, Mark, let me know, and stop thinking of me as some kind of ogre; I'm your sister." Every time she went home, she had to cross another bridge.

CHAPTER 6

Della heard the telephone ringing when she got to her office at seven-thirty Monday morning. Who would be calling her so early, and who knew she'd be hi her office that time of morning? A rush of adrenalin sent her heart into a trot and excitement hurtling through her body. *Luke.* Who else would it be? She greeted him more warmly than was probably wise "How'd you find your grandmother?"

It hadn't occurred to her that Luke would want to know about her Granny. "She's weak, Luke, but she wasn't too sick for a little mischief. I'm glad I took your advice, because she was further down than when I was there last."

"I'm glad you went, too, but you weren't going to call and tell me how she's doing, were you?"

She couldn't lie, but she didn't see how she could tell him he was right. Not after his kindness hi getting her to the airport and waiting with her until her flight was called. "I could have told you when you dropped by today."

"Not good enough, Della. You're not sitting there waiting for me with bated breath. And anyway, I'm not in the UN building today; if I were, you'd be getting your coffee about now. Want to make up for your meanness?"

Here it comes, she thought. "What meanness?"

In her mind's eye, she could see the mischievous lights in his eyes. *And what eyes!* "Your mean little pretense that I don't care what happens to you."

She hadn't remembered how direct Luke McKnight could be. "I never said—"

"You didn't have to. Now you have to make up for it."

"I'm not giving a pint of blood, Luke."

"Then I suppose I'll have to settle for your going to the youth center with me this evening. How 'bout it?"

She'd stumbled right into that one. "Alright. Alright. But I have to go home first. I'll meet you there at seven."

"I'll pick you up at your place at six-thirty. You don't think I'd ask you to walk four blocks in the dark on Webster Avenue, do you?"

She hadn't thought of that. "Oh, alright. You men are so controlling." She wondered why he hadn't commented on that remark and figured she hadn't heard the last of it.

Minutes after they arrived at the youth center, a boy and a girl in their mid-teens began to argue. She noticed that Luke didn't interfere until it heated up. He told them to stop. However, the boy became vituperative and the girl responded first with venomous accusations and then with her fists. Other boys and girls cheered them on, but Luke rushed into the fray, positioning himself between the two.

"One more infraction and you lose all your points," he said, referring to the credits they needed for scholarship recommendations. Delia didn't hide her displeasure at the children's rowdy behavior, and she supposed she earned a low mark from Luke.

"You have to understand where they're coming from," he told her. "In their homes, arguments are more often solved with violence. If you don't have any sympathy for the way these kids live, you can't help them. They need compassion and understanding."

Shaken by the vicious manner in which the boy and girl had assailed each other, she shook her head. "I am sympathetic, Luke, but I don't have any patience with their lack of desire to escape this… this environment, to raise themselves out of the gutter."

He stopped a basketball with his foot and held it in place. "If you look down on them, you can't help them. They're not sitting around waiting for you to save them. Look at yourself. You could be a Martian for all they know or care. But you can change that, if you'll show them what you have in common. Show them that you care about them."

"I do care, Luke, but I don't understand how they can't see what they're doing to themselves."

"That's why you're here, isn't it?"

She supposed so. A beautiful girl of about fifteen, who sat alone filing her nails caught Delia's eye. She was neater than the other girls, better dressed and quiet. Deciding that she might make progress with her, Delia went to the girl and sat beside her.

"Why do you come to this program?" she asked the girl for want of a better way to start a conversation. The girl stopped filing her nails. "What's it to you?"

Taken aback by her sharp tone, Della wasn't certain she'd made the right move. "I'm starting a club for girls at this school, and I need to know more about all of you."

The girl sucked her teeth. "What kind of club?"

"All who join will take an oath to finish the school year without getting pregnant and will agree to counsel girls in the grade below them. You'll also receive school uniforms to identify you as members of the club."

The teeth sucking sounded louder than previously. "Spare me. You do-gooders give me a pain."

Della braced herself. "We're trying to show you a different life."

The girl got up, dusted off the back of her skirt and sneered "No kidding. Will I still need the toilet a couple of times a day? Get lost."

Della sat where the girl had left her. She had thought of poverty as the inability to purchase life's necessities, but had never associated it with impoverished minds. She found herself thinking that lack of money and property didn't make a person low class. Values and behavior did that. Unsettled by the encounter, she welcomed Luke's presence when he joined her.

"Marine looks Park Avenue, as though she doesn't belong here," Luke said, "but she's a hard core delinquent. You stand a better chance with Jennifer over there."

She looked at Jennifer's dreadlocks, cheap and unfashionable clothing and lack of make-up. Not wanting another slap in the face, she hesitated.

Luke's gentle hand on her shoulder encouraged her. "Go on. In your own way, you're as tough as they are, and Lord knows you're smarter."

She walked over to Jennifer, who had seen her approaching and spoke first. "Why do you want to talk to me? 'Cause you struck out with Marine? Everybody thinks she's different, that she's better than the rest of us—'til she opens her mouth. That girl does things I wouldn't even write about."

Della took a deep breath and outlined her plan for the NIA club.

"If you try to save every girl you see around here, you're gonna be a wreck, and you won't succeed."

At least this one would hold a conversation. "Why?" Delia asked her.

Jennifer shrugged. "Mainly 'cause you don't really care. You have to feel like Luke does. He nearly loses his mind if one of us gets into trouble. And you can't favor the ones who dress well; some of these girls would steal your glasses off your nose. Marine might have stolen that dress she's wearing."

Chastened, Delia spoke in quiet tones. "And you, Jennifer. What about you?"

"I'm getting outta this rut. One way to be stuck here is to break the law. I don't steal; don't do drugs; don't sniff nothing; and I stay away from these pimply faced boys. Half of them have a brown egg somewhere. Ain't nothing wrong with the schools; it's these old boys. You want to straighten these girls out? Well, I wish you luck."

Delia figured she'd need it, but she loved a challenge, and this promised to be her greatest—unless you counted the job of walking away from Luke McKnight She hated to expose her ignorance, but she had to ask Jennifer, "A brown egg?"

The girl's grin surprised Delia. "See what I mean? Everybody in these neighborhoods knows what that is. A brown egg is a child born to an unmarried black girl."

Della couldn't help wondering if she'd bitten off more than she could chew. The difference between Jennifer and

Marine was such that she didn't see how a single program could accommodate both of them. She gazed steadily at Jennifer. "What do you want from life?"

"It isn't what I want; it's what I'll get. I'm going to school and be somebody, so I can get me a fine man like Luke. And I'm gonna start a school for girls with brown eggs, so they'll know how to raise kids that won't get into trouble."

Luke didn't have to be told that Jennifer had given Delia another shock. He knew both girls well and guessed that Jennifer had spoken as candidly to Delia as Marine had. And he knew that each, in her way, had promised Delia a difficult task. She related to him her conversations with Jennifer.

"I'd be certain that I wanted to do this, if I were you," he cautioned. "If you're serious about helping them, they can take over your life, but if you're getting in this for personal aggrandizement, you'll rue the day you had the thought. Ready to go?"

She accepted his extended hand, and he held it as they left the building, but he knew she was hardly aware of it. He'd known she approached life as the serious matter that it was, but he hadn't thought her so intense. "What is it, Delia?"

Her voice came to him from what seemed like a great distance. "When I was growing up, I thought city kids owned the world, but these kids could use the grounding effect of green grass and open vistas. I have a feeling that they don't dream of the future, that they have no goals, but just let life happen to them. What a shame."

When he'd asked her about her life growing up, she had practically told him to butt out and, in her present mood, he wasn't going to question her about that or anything else. She was out of her league dealing with those girls, but he'd bet his last penny that she'd come out on top. He squeezed her fingers and ; tucked their hands into the pocket of his overcoat. When she . didn't object, he looked around for a yellow cab. He made it a I policy not to ride unlicensed "gypsy" cabs; too big a chance, but

he wished for one right then. Anything that would give them privacy. He wanted to put his arms around her while her need screamed out to him.

He tugged her close to him and, when her fingers squeezed his own, he pulled her into the doorway of Kayman's Jewels & Things and took her into his arms.

"Luke, this is crazy. We shouldn't do this."

Her weak protest sent butterflies darting through his blood stream, making him giddy, and he tilted up her chin with his right index finger. "I know we shouldn't, but I need to feel you in my arms."

Her eyes reflected the street light that faced the store, and he turned her so that she'd have her back to it. He thought his heart would gallop out of his chest when her heard her halting whisper, "K... Kiss me. Oh, Luke, kiss me."

"Baby... I... Oh my God, don't do this to me," he heard himself say and knew he'd lost his heart forever. Her mouth probed, warm and eager beneath his, but the cold air brought him to his senses, and he released her. Never in his thirty-four years, not even as a hot teenager had he kissed a female in the street. Where on earth were the taxis?

They walked the four blocks to the D train station without speaking. What had come over her. Confusion and a sense of loneliness had suddenly overwhelmed her, and she had needed him. She wouldn't have reacted that way if she'd been with Craig, because he didn't give her the feeling that he was there for her whenever she needed him. Anger at herself began to churn inside of her, anger for having asked for what she didn't plan to give in return. Anger for having trapped herself into getting one more taste of what sweet loving with Luke could be like.

For reasons she wouldn't guess at, she picked a fight. "All I know about you is your name, that you repair office machines and, from time to time, meddle in my affairs."

He stopped walking down the steps into the subway. "It's like that, is it? Well, all I know about you, Delia, is that you're a workaholic, ambitious, tough on the outside and scared as hell of getting involved with me."

She stopped and looked back at him. "Just what do you mean by that?"

"You tell me, lady. Something's driving you in a way you don't want to go, and it's deep-seated. Back there, you wanted me, and now you're trying to put a wall between us, because you wouldn't like this to go any further. Well, put as much distance between us as you like. Even if the Pacific Ocean separates us, it won't help, baby; you've got your work cut out for you. You've got to deal with what you feel for me."

She could do without his bluntness, and she didn't need his truths either. But if she didn't put on the brakes, she'd end up living in genteel poverty and baking cookies for the Sunday church sales. Nothing wrong with that, if it was what you wanted, but she didn't plan to duplicate her mother's life. She searched for a way to calm the tension between them.

"This conversation began with my asking about you, but if you'd rather not talk—" "You want to know who I am? That surprises me, but if you're serious, spend Sunday with me." The train arrived at that moment and she was grateful that, once on it, they couldn't carry on a conversation above the noise without broadcasting what they said.

At Fifty-ninth Street, they left the subway, and he hailed a taxi. Half an hour earlier he'd been able to think of nothing but getting i her into the back seat of a cab and loving her mindlessly. The strangely overpowering urge had slipped inside him, plowing through him like a cyclone, stunning him with its force and giving i him the surprise of his life. She was in him for keeps. He knew that now. Back there, she'd wanted him as much as he'd wanted < her but, in no time, she'd skillfully and deliberately cooled their fire. He didn't need that kind of roller-coaster ride with Delia ;

Murray; she was after something, and he wasn't part of the
I scenario. Maybe if he prayed hard enough, she wouldn't
matter. He wasn't used to lying to himself, so he admitted
that he < couldn't quit. Nothing ventured, nothing gained,
he recalled. He'd give it a shot, but he'd watch his back.

"What would we do Sunday?" she asked after she'd settled into her corner of the taxi. . He pretended not to notice
her tightly folded arms and rigid posture, a woman's body
language for "don't touch me'. "We'd start with eleven
o'clock service at Bethany—"

She interrupted. "That same minister?"

So that sermon about judging people had upset her; just
as he 'd thought. "Same guy, Delia. The worst that can happen is that you'll get a little guidance. Okay?"

She nodded, reluctantly, he thought, but he went on. "I
like the Sunday brunch at Jojo's Caribbean Kitchen. The
jerked chicken is out of sight."

"Stop right there. You're on." She seemed to peruse the
idea.

"But you have to promise me you'll get the recipe from
the chef."

"That's easy. He's my buddy. Don't you want to hear the
rest?"

She unfolded her arms, relaxed her body and smiled. If
the thought of chicken did that to her... He shook his
head; no point hi going overboard. "I'd like to visit that
new age trade show at the Javits Center and, by the time we
work our way through that, we ought to be hungry enough
to appreciate this great Cajun restaurant that I like. I want
your entire Sunday, Delia. How about it?"

"I said alright, didn't I?"

The taxi pulled up to her door, and her doorman let her out before Luke could get around to her side of the cab. In his annoyance, he considered not tipping the man. As they reached the elevator, he looked around for the ubiquitous Pinski, and the man didn't disappoint him. They rode to her floor under Pinski's watchful eye, and Luke couldn't help being relieved when the man didn't get off with them.

"What floor does that guy live on?" Luke asked Delia.

"The third."

"Then what's he doing riding past the eleventh floor?"

She shrugged. "It's probably all the entertainment he gets. Stop worrying about him; nobody pays any attention to Pinski."

At her door, she took out her key and inserted it in the lock. "It's been quite some evening," she told him. "See you Sunday morning at ten."

Damned if he'd press her. He let a half smile drift over his face, touched his forehead with his right index finger and winked.

"As the lady wishes." He stuck his fists in his coat pocket and waited until she'd gone in and closed the door. He walked off whistling as he went. He'd never known a more mercurial woman nor, when she was her natural self, a sweeter one. He wanted her badly, but not getting her wouldn't kill nun, and the sooner she knew it, the better their chance of getting together.

Delia walked through her dark apartment to her bedroom, deep hi thought. Still wearing her coat, she sat on the edge of her bed beset with a sense of foreboding. She shouldn't see him again outside the UN building, but she knew she'd be ready when he got there Sunday morning. She fell back across the bed, rolled over on her belly and swore she wouldn't cry about Luke McKnight. Not then. Not ever. Three hours later, she woke up, washed the tears from her face, undressed and crawled into bed.

Delia told herself to calm down, act nonchalant and keep a cool head, but when Mike buzzed her that Luke was on his way up, every one of her nerves seemed to go on a rampage through her body. She gathered her wits and faced him with a warm but studied smile. She had expected him to greet her with a kiss or, at least, a hug, but he did neither. Instead, he smiled, told her she looked great and asked her for her coat. Stunned, she caught herself as she was about to ask him if he'd changed his mind about them. And that would have been an error of gargantuan proportions; he had never said there was a *them*.

Jojo's restaurant served food for the soul as well as the stomach. Handsome waiters wore Fats Waller derbies, black leather pants, black and white striped shirts with rubber bands just below their biceps, black vests and red bow ties. You identified your waiter by the color of his red, blue, green, purple or orange apron..

"What kind of music would you like?" their waiter asked. Delia thought he'd take the message to the three piece combo and said, *"Ain 't Misbehavin'"*, since he wore a

Fats Waller hat, but he gave them a professional rendition of the classic jazz song.

"Wait 'til the show starts," Luke said. "Half the people in here are frustrated actors and singers. They take turns doing their thing. It's a riot."

However, the young girl who stood on the stage singing "*Cry, Cry, Cry*" while her tears wet the floor didn't make Delia laugh. Not even when Luke told her that the girl had done the same thing every time he'd eaten there. But she couldn't restrain her laughter at the incongruity of an old man reading Longfellow's *The Song Of Hiawatha* to the accompaniment of the combo's jazzy rendition of *Baby, It's Cold Outside.*

When he'd finished, the octogenarian stopped at their table, smiled and told Delia, "I'm so glad you liked it; you made my day."

"It was wonderful," Delia told the happy old man, and watched Luke check his eyebrows before they shot upward in a look of incredulity.

Luke would have given a lot to know whether their waiter hovered over them because he liked looking at Delia or hoped his solicitousness would increase the size of his tip. Finding it tiresome, he told the waiter, "Ask the head chef to come out here, will you? Tell him Luke wants to see him."

"Hey, Buddy, how's it going?" Gene asked, pulling up a chair.

Luke glanced at Delia from beneath lowered lashes to see how she'd take the company of a man in full kitchen attire, chef's hat included. She gazed steadily at the man, but her nose wasn't in the air.

"Delia, this is Gene, my best friend since high school. Gene, this is Delia." He'd have said who she was, if he'd known.

"I see you're feeling no pain, my man," Gene said and extended his hand to Delia. "Glad to meet you, Delia. I don't have to ask what you're doing with this knuckle-head. Turk always scored high with the girls." Luke winced at what he knew would be next.

Her lips parted in obvious surprise. **"Turk?** You call him Turk? I never would have imagined him with a name like that."

Gene ignored Luke's high sign. "Suits him perfectly. Smartest quarterback you ever saw. If he let that pigskin fly, I knew it would be right on target when I got to the five yard line."

She sat back in her chair, folded her arms and smiled at Gene. Damned near coquettish, Luke thought irritably. "Tell me more, Gene. Where did this quarterbacking take place?"

He had to put a stop to it. "On a football field. You're out of line, Eugene," he said, drawing a laugh from his friend.

"Turk always calls me Eugene when he'd like to sock me."

"I sent for you, because Delia wants to know how you jerk this chicken."

Gene wrote the recipe on a paper napkin, gave it to Delia and grinned at Luke. "If you get stuck, give me a call," he told Delia.

Luke laughed. "I hope you remember the rules, Gene."

"Right." Gene replied. "I don't go to bat 'til you strike out."

Luke stood and took Delia's hand. "Thanks for the recipe, man. The food was great." "Yes," Delia added. "And the ambiance is fabulous; I loved every second in this place."

Gene raised an eyebrow. "Coming back?"

Luke wanted to hug her when she looked at him and asked, "Are we?" Gene's booming laughter reminded him of their joyful high school and college days. He took Delia's arm. "See you, Buddy."

New York was bearable on Sundays, Delia thought, provided you didn't go near Rockefeller Center. They took the Fifty-seventh Street cross town bus to the JavitsCenter, and she could sense the energy building in Luke as they neared the booths.He seemed charged with an eagerness that she hadn't witnessed in him.

He held her right hand and read a program that he carried in his left. "Over here. I can't wait to see this new color scanner. It's supposed to work with the efficiency of a super camera." He stopped them at booth number five.

She couldn't believe the conversation. Luke questioned the engineers about their machines, suggested changes in the company's top-of-the-line scanner, all the while speaking with the company's representatives as an equal. One of them excused himself, left and returned a few minutes later with a colleague.

"We're not recruiting today," the man said, "but I'm prepared to offer you a position as senior staff engineer." He handed Luke a card. "We'll pay your expenses to our head office in Arizona, if you want to look us over."

Delia glanced at the card in Luke's hand and saw that the man was CEO of a top Fortune Five Hundred company. A smile seemed to float over Luke's face, and her heartbeat accelerated.

He was going to pull himself up and get into the corporate world.

"Thanks, man," she heard Luke say, "but I'm fixed for now."

"But you could do whatever you liked. Modify. Design. Whatever. This is practically our top engineering level."

She couldn't believe her ears when he said, "Thanks. If I ever get in trouble, I'll get in touch."

The man took Luke's extended hand. "I'll be glad to hear from you."

She wanted to wipe his self-satisfied smile off his face. How could he walk away from such an opportunity. For a minute, she'd seen a chance for them. Anger boiled up in her until she couldn't contain her hostility. "You'd rather punch a clock for the United Nations, taking orders from Tom, Dick and Harry than be an officer in a big corporation. How can you turn down this opportunity when you know you may never get an another offer like it?"

"Wear a pin-striped suit, Gucci loafers and carry a brief-case to work. Right? Well, you've got your values screwed up, lady. You don't want a man who's good at what he does and who does it honestly. You want a dressed-up turkey that you can show off. I'm not the guy. I'll take you home."

The day was shot, but she didn't care. "I know the way."

He dropped the program and grasped both of her shoulders. "I went there and got you and, by damn, I'll take you back."

Conscious of the stares of onlookers, she let him have his way. They didn't say a word to each other during the ten minute taxi ride and, once in her apartment building, Pinski followed them to the elevator.

"Doesn't he ever speak?"

"Never. I guess he gets a charge from looking."

"It's not amusing, Delia. Not one bit."

They reached her apartment and she could see that he didn't intend to ask for her key. She didn't question her acute sense of loss, an opening of her insides as though she'd been pierced. She pasted what she hoped was a blank expression on her face and made herself look at him.

"Sorry it didn't work out as I'd hoped," he said. "If you ever find out who you are and how I fit into your picture, cue me in."

"I… I know who I…" The break between them shrouded her in loneliness, and she turned her back to prevent his seeing her turmoil. With gentle hands, he turned her to face him, and she could see that what he found in her face stunned him.

"What'll it be, Delia? Tell me right now."

Mutely, she shook her head. All she knew was that she needed him, that she longed to reach out to him. She concentrated on controlling the quiver of her lips, but to no avail.

"Sweetheart. Delia. Baby, for Heavens sake, can't you…"

She closed her eyes as if that would shut out her pain, and in a second, she had the glory of his mouth on hers. Her lips parted for his tongue, and she opened to him. He claimed every crevice of her mouth, knocked her senses out of order, possessed her willpower. Her heart danced in her chest and frissons of heat shot like hot arrows to her feminine center. She clutched him to her, begging for more of him as she sucked on his tongue. She wanted him and hadn't the will to hide it. Her hands wound themselves beneath his coat and fumbled at his chest, seeking his bare flesh. He grasped her buttocks, and she clutched at him, pulling him as close as she could and, when he lifted her until his massive arousal nestled at her love portal, violent trembles attacked her body. He pressed her between himself and the wall, letting her feel all of him until his hoarse moans brought her to her senses, and she broke the kiss.

He rested his forehead on her shoulder. "You know I don't want to leave you. Delia, we can't go on like this."

She wrapped him in her arms. "I know. But you have to go, because I'm… I'm too confused right now. I'm not sure I know what I'm doing or saying, and I… I don't want to mislead you."

He straightened up and looked her in the eye. "You do that with your words, Delia, but your body always tells me the truth. I'll be seeing you."

"I'm a masochist," she said to herself as she closed the door. If she'd had any sense, she wouldn't have let him see what she felt; she'd have gone straight into the apartment and locked the door behind her. If he ever took her clothes off her, she'd belong to him forever. No doubt about that. *And what would be so bad about that*? her niggling conscience demanded. Oh, he'd make her happy for a while, and then they'd begin to get all the problems a poor person could have. Love wouldn't withstand that.

What about your parents? her mind nagged. She clapped her hands over her mouth. Startled. And who had said anything about love?

She leaned against the door of the guest bathroom that opened into the foyer. Why had he turned down a job offer that most men in his place would give their eyetooth for? He couldn't possibly be a fool. She mused over possible explanations as she walked to the closet and hung up her coat. There wasn't any answer. And what was that business about his having been a quarterback? Probably in high school. She'd missed her chance to know for sure when she hadn't asked Gene. She told herself to stop thinking about it. If she didn't leave him alone, one day she'd go too far.

Delia was not alone in her concern over the hot scene with Luke at her door. Luke's steps dragged when he left her. He knew he could settle things between them, if he told her about himself instead of allowing her to continue thinking him a union scale repairman. He didn't expect a woman in her position to take up with a man who didn't have her status or financial clout, but he saw nothing wrong with a laborer's work, no matter what it was, so long as the man did the best he could for the wages he got. And why the devil should he set her straight just to get her to admit she wanted him? Scratch that. She'd already admitted it. Trouble was she refused to admit she cared for him, not even to herself.

But sometime, she could be so gentle and so sweet. Like she'd been in Jojo's restaurant with that old man. In the three years the man had been reading *The Song of Hiawatha* from that podium, always to *Baby, It's Cold Outside,* he hadn't seen anyone applaud or smile, except Delia. He stepped out on Riverside Drive and looked across the Hudson River at the low, setting sun. He should give Delia Murray his curriculum vitae and maybe his bank statement, too, just to get her to be honest with him about her feelings? Not in this life. He hailed a taxi and went home.

CHAPTER 7

Della arrived at her office early, as usual, the following morning, Monday, and stopped short at the door. Prakar Pillay examined her book shelves, searched her desk and began to rifle through her Rodolex, checking the names and addresses listed there.

"It never occurred to me that you'd stoop this low." She had the pleasure of seeing his head jerk up and his face reflect his horror at being caught.

But he recovered in moments. "Who can you tell? It's your word against mine, and everybody knows we're after the same AS-G post. Who'd believe you?"

"You ought to know, Prakar, that I'm not so foolish as to leave anything here that I wouldn't want anyone to see. I wouldn't do this again if I were you though. Ever hear of a hidden camera?"

She laughed. The stricken expression on his face was worth her anxiety that he might have found something that could give him the upper hand in their struggle for that post.

"Please leave, and don't let me catch you in here again." Her threat of a hidden camera had been just that, but she wished she'd had the presence of mind to reach into her handbag and flip on her tape recorder. She sat down and leaned back in her desk chair wishing that promotion to the post had been settled, the conference over and she'd sorted out her feelings about Craig and Luke.

The most wonderful thing that could happen to her right then would be Luke's appearance with a cup of coffee.

Or if he'd just bring himself. But she knew he wouldn't come. Not after that gut rending session at her apartment door. She knew him well enough now to understand that he wouldn't expose himself soon again to the pain she'd seen in him just before he walked away from her. God help her. She didn't want that misery either, but she wanted Luke. She sucked on her bottom lip, annoyance surging in her at the injustice of it. He had everything and nothing. But she had better stop thinking about him, because she wasn't going anywhere with Luke McKnight.

The phone rang, and she glanced at her watch. Too early for Erin. She answered it.

"Craig here," came his rough tenor. "Would you join me this evening at six for a reception on the third floor adjacent to the Delegates Dining Room? A senior ambassador for one of our allies is retiring, and I'd like you to accompany me."

"I'd love to." Immediately, she could have throttled herself for appearing so eager. "I'd love to," she amended, "but I remember that I have a dinner engagement." She realized that saying she'd forgotten a dinner engagement only made it worse; a business woman didn't forget engagements without reason, and Craig would consider himself that reason.

"My dear, the reception will be over at seven-thirty. Surely your companion hasn't set dinner for earlier than that." She didn't know what to assume about Craig where his honesty was concerned. He appeared straightforward, a good person. Still, she didn't give a diplomat high marks for issuing an invitation on the day of the event. She agreed to go, reasoning that she couldn't learn to like him unless she got to know him.

"I'd begun to think you weren't coming," he told her, when she met him ten minutes late.

"Since I got a last minute invitation, I figured you'd understand that I might have to shuffle a few things around in order to make it."

She thought it to his credit that he grinned. "Touché." Her mood lightened when he bowed from the waist, clicked his heels and said, "At your service, ma'am." And because her laughter seemed to please him, she was glad she'd come.

But her good humor was short-lived. Craig took her to meet his boss, the United States Ambassador to the United Nations and, though employing a tone and manner that suggested Delia occupied a position of enormous importance, he nonetheless depreciated her status by introducing her as his *right arm* for the duration of the Nairobi Conference.Delia gritted her teeth and explained, "I'm director of the Department of Conference and Meeting Services." She let Craig have a withering look. "I thought Mr. Radcliff knew that." If he didn't acknowledge her status, she refused to give him his title of ambassador. Their needling earned them the more senior ambassador's indulgent smile; to her chagrin, he obviously attributed their crossfire to a lovers' spat. Craig steered her toward the drinks, but she wouldn't let him put his arm around her waist. She stopped walking. "Craig, please remember that I am a senior UN official."

He lifted one shoulder in an air of nonchalance. "You're also beautiful, and it's easier to remember that than your title, so I'd appreciate it if you'd cut me a little slack here, Delia. It's hard to switch roles and styles here in this building. If I don't manage it sometime, that doesn't make me a bad guy. What would you like?"

"Club soda with ice and a sprig of mint," she replied, looking him hi the eye to let him know that his little sermon hadn't made her remorseful.

His eyebrows arched sharply, and his pupils enlarged. She let a smile settle around her lips; from then on, Craig Radcliff would watch his step with her.

"Very interesting," was all he said, and she laughed aloud when he ordered a Sprite for himself, instead of his usual club soda. "Having fun?"

"Absolutely," she said, not trying to hide her amusement. "You don't even like club soda, but you dress it up with a mint leaf and pass it off for a Tom Collins, while you play hound with these unsuspecting foxes around here." She lifted her glass to him in mock salute. "When I see genius, I bow in deference."

He stepped closer, his gaze boring into her, and she sensed his increased respect. "I could go a long way with you. You know that?"

She lifted the glass once more before taking a long sip. "If you can't beat 'em, join 'em. Right?"

His expression bordered on mockery, but she wasn't fooled. He wasn't accustomed to having women take him lightly. "Who do you know capable of rattling your cage?"

She didn't expect him to admit it, but she'd dented his armor and, like the average man whose ego had taken a wallop, his next thought was of conquering. But she wanted more than a few dates with him, and this wasn't a man who chased. If she went after him, she'd never get him. She shrugged. "My cage doesn't rattle, Craig."

His stare, dark and humorless, gave her an unwelcome chill, but almost immediately his perfect teeth sparkled against his smooth brown skin. Laughter transformed him into a prince of a man. "Good. You're your own woman, and all the more desirable, because you are such a rare species."

"Thank you." Maybe he believed that, and maybe he didn't.

She knew her assets as well as her shortcomings; she wasn't beautiful, but she hoped she was a rarity.

At seven twenty-five, she told him she had to leave for her dinner engagement and rushed off, increasingly uncomfortable with her calculated goal of making Craig a permanent fixture in her life. For over an hour, she'd stood within inches of him, flirting, challenging and measuring his attributes. Good looking hardly described him; if a brother's likeness ever belonged on the cover of magazines, his did. Tall. Polished. Flat belly. Clean shaven. Brooks Brothers from his shirt collar to his Gucci shoes. *She hadn't felt one thing.* Neither his Ralph Lauren cologne nor his salon-tapered nails gave him an edge. She'd been thinking that Luke never wore cologne and that, though his nails weren't shellacked, when she looked at his strong, lean fingers, all she could think of was how they would feel on her naked body.

On the way out of the building, she stopped at the Meditation Room to get her bearings. The room's quiet serenity always had a soothing, stabilizing effect. Something had to give; her dilemma about the two men had begun to take up too much of her time, worrying her and interfering with her concentration, and her thoughts always settled on Luke. Which was nonsense? She wasn't going that way. She entered the dimly lit, peaceful oasis and sat down. Her heart pummeled her chest, and she stopped short when the only other person in the room stood and turned to leave. Luke.

He glanced her way, saw her and stopped. "Delia. I'm surprised to see you here. You alright?"

She shut down the "no" that formed on her tongue. "Just needed a peaceful minute." She left the room with him, feeling that fate had her address.

"Working overtime?" he asked.

She shook her head. "I'm leaving a reception for one of the delegates."

"Considering how exuberant you are, it must have been an exhilarating experience."

She never cared much for Luke's sarcasm; it was too pointed and too close to home. "It was." Let him chew on that.

He seemed to scrutinize her, but the softness in his wonderful eyes said he was satisfied with what he found. "Care to finish that date we had last Sunday? How about this Saturday?"

"I can't. I'm leaving Friday night for Nairobi."

"Give the Masai my best." She wondered at his mocking tone. "By the way," he added, "how's your grandmother?"

"Better, but she's not out of the woods."

He stepped closer and his right hand resting lightly on her left arm gave her comfort, and she welcomed it. "If there's anything I can do, Delia, let me know."

"I don't know how to get in touch with you."

He jotted down his address and phone numbers including his cellular number. "Call me if you need me. No matter what time. Make it collect. And Delia, take care of yourself: don't go out alone at night, protect your valuables and be careful about what you eat and drink."

Could it be that he cared? She couldn't deny that he acted as if she was important to him. And where did that leave her, feeling as she did about him? "Thanks. I... I'd better get going." He dusted her cheek with his thumb, half-smiled and followed her gaze to the elevator bank where Craig stood with his colleagues from the United States Mission to the UN. It shamed her that her thought was of Craig seeing her in an intimate conversation with someone dressed as a maintenance worker.

Luke nodded toward Craig. "What's that guy to you?"

"Nothing," she answered, knowing she'd told a half-truth.

"Why don't I believe you?" He left her standing there.

She hurried home and got to work on her program for the NIA girls. Their first outing would be the circus and, in spite of her true reason for starting the program, she looked forward to the event. She could hardly wait to show Luke her plans. Luke. Would he be at the Center, and did he want to see her? Craig. Luke. She'd like to have one, but she needed the other.

She called home, gave her mother her address and phone number in Nairobi and stopped herself as she was about to give her Luke's number. "If there's an emergency, Mama, call Erin, my secretary. She'll be able to reach me quickly. And give my love to all."

"I'll do that, and you take good care, now. You hear?"

The next night, she met five girls at the Center, told them her plans for NIA and had the satisfaction of seeing them excited and eager to get started. She promised them they'd begin in two weeks.

"Has Mr. McKnight been in this evening?" she asked them.

"He's here almost every night, but I haven't seen him tonight," Jennifer answered. "If you wait, I know he'll be here."

Delia thanked her, gathered her things and left. That had been a mistake, because the girls would tell him she'd asked about him. And they did. She'd barely gotten into the apartment when he called. "Luke. You wanted to see me?" "Uh… I just wondered why you weren't there." "Delia. Did you want to see me? Did you?" The words seemed to rush out of him. "Do you want to see me?"

She swallowed the wetness in her mouth. "I… It's late, and I'm traveling tomorrow night, so I'd…. uh… better say good night."

His voice came at her in a breathless growl. "At least you're too honest to deny it. I hope you're just as straight with Craig Radcliff because, if you are, he'll know he doesn't stand a chance. Have a good trip, Delia, and hurry back." "I… Goodbye, Luke."

Swiss Air Flight 101 put her in Zurich at eight o'clock Saturday morning, Swiss time, and she took a day room at the airport for the seven-hour wait until her connecting flight to Nairobi, Kenya. The tiny cubicle was comfortable and almost antiseptically clean but, rest broken though she was, she couldn't sleep. Luke occupied her thoughts. She had to fight the temptation to telephone him and tell him that she had wanted to see him, that the bottom had dropped out of her when she'd walked into the Center and realized that he wasn't there. She could never let herself tell him or anyone about that awful emptiness, a feeling that she'd been hollowed out, a pain that crowded around her heart when she realized she wouldn't see him before she left for Kenya. She quit trying to sleep. No point in lying to herself. Luke had gotten to her, deep inside, and settled in the spot where she lived. Doggedly, she fought the idea, pulled out her notes on the conference and tried to put him behind her.

Admitting that she'd have as much success if she tried to swim the Atlantic, she gave in and let her imagination show her how he could make her feel.

Her flight was called at last, and she endured the seven hours of anxiety with nothing to distract her. Exhausted from lack of sleep, she checked in at the Nairobi Sheraton and, on a hunch, asked whether Ambassador Radcliff had registered. He hadn't, she learned, but was expected the next day. She wasn't certain she liked the idea of staying in the same hotel as he, because Craig was a man who took a mile if you gave him an inch. She'd have to watch it.

The elegance of the office assigned to her in the Kenyatta Conference Center, the site of the meetings, surprised and pleased Delia. An hour before the opening of the Conference, she stood at her office window and gazed at the crowd flowing across City Square and into the Center for the opening session. Women from India, Pakistan and other countries of that region glided along in their silk saris and gold jewelry, anachronistic contrasts with their leather briefcases and shoulder-strap pocketbooks. Women of Sub-Saharan Africa arrived in their colorful dresses and elegant headdress, and the region's men came in brocade togas or business suits. Every region and culture was represented among those who filed through the doors. She had never seen such a pool of cultures, not even hi the UN, because a majority of the UN staff wore western dress. How she wished Luke could have been there to see the sight!

The UN Secretary-General did not attend, and she watched, mesmerized, as Craig made the conference his own within minutes after he opened it. She didn't think she'd ever before seen the calibre of skill, patience and charm with which he manipulated the delegates, exhorting them to support *him,* to make his tour as conference S-G the most rewarding event of his life. He fed them half an hour of it. She closed her ears; whether he intended it or not, he'd blocked any gains she'd hoped to get from all her hard work on that conference. She couldn't accuse him of stealing credit, because he continuously thanked her and her staff for their invaluable service to the conference and to him. But she could have been a clerk sitting beside him, for all the interest the delegates showed in her. She resigned herself; it wasn't going her way.

"Can we go together to the reception this evening?" he asked her toward the end of the day.

She had assumed they would since they were joint hosts. "Why, I expect so," she replied with an air of indifference. "After all, we're giving it."

At their joint reception that evening, he complimented her on her long, red silk evening shift. "Delia, you put every woman here to shame. I realize we shouldn't be seen together, because the gossip wouldn't do either of us any good, but I'm staking my claim. How about going on the Masai tour with me Saturday?" His fingers grazed her shoulder. "I wished you'd saved this dress for tomorrow evening; I'm hosting a reception at the embassy, and I want you to come."

Slick devil. He hadn't asked whether she'd go with him. "How do I get there?"

"Leave that to me." His confident grin told her he'd been sure of her answer.

"No wonder so many women stay single or get single after they realize their mistake," she said, her tone devoid of humor. "Playing cat and mouse with men can take all of a woman's time."

His laugh was warm and pleasant, surprising her with his joviality. "Hold it, there. Everybody knows that you women are the ones who won't go straight to a point. Or maybe, can't."

"Are you saying you associate with airheads? I'm surprised at you."

He didn't bite. "I enjoy women's company. All kinds of women. Lightweights can be relaxing and fun, and a man needs that sometime, because women like you are a challenge. Sometimes you're absolutely exhausting. But you're worth what it takes to reel you in."

She couldn't help laughing at the metaphor, which told so much about him. Again, he'd left her to guess whether he considered all women, or only her, susceptible to being reeled in. She'd wait and see.

"Tomorrow afternoon, I have be at the embassy an hour early," he explained, "so I'll send a car for you at five-thirty."

A relaxed mood enveloped her just before she remembered Prakar's assessment of Craig. Better watch him, she warned herself.

"Why didn't you stay at the embassy, Craig?"

He shrugged. "You weren't going to be there; besides, how I spend my nights is none of the government's business."

Best to ignore that one. By Saturday, in spite of his having said that they shouldn't be romantically linked, Craig had subtly made it known that they were a twosome, and that effectively established her in the minds of the delegates as his appendage. And if socially, why not professionally as well? She didn't think he'd deliberately orchestrated it, but with half the two hundred and fifty women attendees looking on him as lush fruit, she supposed he'd had to latch on to one, and she was convenient.

Their Saturday tour took them and a large group of conference delegates to the estate of a white Kenyan, where for twenty dollars each worth of Kenyan schillings, they were treated to a Masai mating ceremony. The tours supplied the majority of the estate owner's income. In turn, the Masai, whose earliest ancestors had lived on that property—long before the advent of the English—were allowed to keep their few cattle on the land. Delia watched as the young men, wearing little more than loin cloths, formed a circle and danced, each displaying his own style. Young girls just past puberty, their hair colored red with clay, and wearing rows and rows of beads around their necks in a display of their wealth and with their bosoms bare to show maturity, walked slowly around the dancing men. Delia searched her brochure and learned that the girls were choosing their life's mate. The young men had undergone initiation rites into manhood and were ready to marry and assume the responsibility of manhood, but they had to wait until chosen.

She supplied Craig with this information and joshed, "These girls know what time it is."

"Wrong," Craig corrected. "Due to some of their strange practices, there's a shortage of women, so they get to choose."

"What practices?"

"You don't want to know. It's enough to say that certain rituals and birthing practices carry high female mortality rates."

She didn't need to be reminded of that, and she shook off the shudders that shot through her. The way he told it, you'd think he cared. Maybe he did. Still, she couldn't help being disappointed that Craig wasn't outraged at the exploitation of the Masai who lived at the same poverty level as they had for the centuries of their existence, while they provided a tourist attraction—and thus wealth—for their white Kenyan over-lords. She hated that she'd contributed twenty dollars of her good money to such an abuse of human beings.

Back at the main house, Delia took one of the orange sodas that had been placed on the table for the tourists. But she never tasted it. The estate owner's daughter stood within three feet of her talking with one of the European tourists.

"They're so child-like," the woman said of the Masai. "They're lucky they have us."

"But the Masai survived before you got here," the European man retorted.

"They were preyed upon by all these other tribes," the woman claimed, "but none of those predators would dare cross our property."

"Do you have schools and social services for them?"

"Oh, no. They couldn't handle *that*. They're very primitive, though I often think some of them do have *personalities.*"

Delia could stand no more. She dumped the soda on the table and flung the bottle to the ground, stared into the woman's startled face, turned and stumbled into Craig.

"Did you hear that… that… that—"

"Okay, I get the message. It rhymes with witch. No point in getting upset about it, Delia; this country is full of such people. The whites own the land, the Indians and Pakistanis own the businesses and the native Kenyans have their backs and the sweat of their brows just as they always did."

"But doesn't that make you mad?"

"What's the point in getting mad about it? It'll take a revolution to change it. Anyway, the Masai didn't seem unhappy about it, so why make a flap over it?"

She couldn't believe he'd said it. But she already knew he'd never rock a juke box no matter what kind of music came out of it. If you planned to be head of the United Nations or US Secretary of State, you paid your taxes, hired only legal immigrants and didn't muddy the water. But if a man in Craig Radcliff's position didn't care about the plight of those people, who would? For the first time in her memory, she questioned whether the poor and down-trodden could pull themselves up without help.

As far as Delia was concerned, the Kenyan government's reception that night for the four hundred delegates was, up to that time, the event of the conference, because the business meetings had been an escalation of Craig's star and what looked like her setting sun. She got a taste of Craig's rhumba. He spun her into it without warning, and she all but stopped dancing when he began, the provocative tilts of his hips. His moving pelvis was in her imagination. It had to be; surely he wouldn't dance like that at an official reception. Later, she was glad to stand aside while he danced with the wife of every official present, and she thought he got what he deserved when several women made it clear that they wanted another dance.

She took the opportunity to visit the seer who sat in a grass hut near the ballroom door, walked in, bowed and sat down. She supposed the man was around seventy. He wore a grass skirt and grass hat, and his bare feet protruded from the lotus position into which he'd folded his frail body. His eyes, intense and piercing, seemed to puncture her soul. His stare tugged and pulled at something in her, and she knew he wanted her mind. Tentacles of fear gripped her. She would not give him or anybody power over her mind, and she closed it, deliberately refusing him entry. The old man's saddened expression told her that he knew what she'd done and why.

"I have nothing to tell you. Nothing."

To her surprise, his soft, modulated voice was that of an educated man. She rose to leave him, feeling as if she'd been stripped bare. But she still had her soul. She knew the past, and she'd as soon let the future reveal itself as it pleased.

"No point in running from what is certain to come," the gentle voice called after her. "We don't control the future. It's been with us from the beginning of time."

Delia managed not to stumble, to hold up her head and smile as she stepped out of the hut and into the group of people waiting to see the old man. But she took her liquid bones to a deserted seat in the building's foyer and worked at recovering her equilibrium. She later learned that he was a gifted man and regretted not having cooperated with him, for she knew he would have told her where Luke fitted into her life.

"You were the man of the hour," she told Craig as they left the reception at the Kenyatta Conference Center and crossed City Square to his waiting limousine.

He shrugged, as though his performance were a commonplace with him. "I considered it my duty to dance with those women; if it hadn't been an official function, I wouldn't have spared them a glance." At her look of dismay and disapproval, he added, "How could I, when you're with me?"

She rolled her eyes skyward. "Sure, and that's why you practically devoured the wife of the German delegate."

"He has a vote I want, and she'll tell him what a great guy I am."

"You're kidding. If he was in that room, he's probably planning to call you to meet him at sunrise with your saber."

He helped her into the car, seated himself and turned to her. "I hope what I'm hearing from you is jealousy. By the way, where'd you run off to?"

She told him about the seer and added, "Any woman who lets herself be jealous of you is rowing with one oar."

He moved close, and she waited for excitement to course through her when his arm circled her waist. "Delia, love, are you saying you don't care what I do nor with whom?"

She slid out of his embrace without having experienced the slightest twinge of passion. "Craig, *dear,* I'm thirty years old, and I gave up necking in cabs before I got out of my teens. Besides, I wouldn't have thought it your style."

He expelled a long breath, and she took heart; maybe he'd go directly to his room and not make a move on her. She wasn't ready for that. "You're a tough one, Delia; standard ploys don't work with you, so I have to run while I've got the ball."

In the hotel, she walked quickly to the elevator, but he stayed with her until they reached her door. "I want to come in and kiss you good night." She thought his voice trembled a little; she wasn't sure. But she knew she was scared. She wanted him to like her, to get to know her well enough to care deeply for her, but she had the sense to realize that if he made love to her that night, she wouldn't get any further with him. She meant to have it all.

"You may kiss me right here," she parried.

"How many delegates are staying on this floor?" he asked, settling the matter. She opened the door. He stepped in, taking her with him, kicked the door closed and got her into his arms. He had a thousand hands, and all of them found every inch of her body as his lips slid over hers, begging entrance for his tongue. Praying that she'd catch fire, she took him into her mouth and he tested her with an expertise that she'd never known. One of his many thumbs found her left nipple and teased it. Maybe if he'd take it into his hot mouth and suckle her, she'd want him like she'd wanted Luke. But when his hand plunged into her low-cut bodice and found her breast, she stopped him. She didn't know why, but it didn't feel right.

"What is it, Delia? Why are you fighting me? You feel it; you have to, because you're human, and I know what I've been doing to you. Is there another man, or have you decided not to like me?"

Shaken, she found her voice with difficulty and skirted the first part of his question. "I'm the type that needs more time, Craig. Bear with me."

"Alright. I'm on uncharted ground here, Delia. I've never mixed business and pleasure, because I don't think it wise, but I'm honest with myself, and I know I'm not going to stop here unless you make me. I don't want to leave you, but I won't pressure you. And I'm not a patient man but, for now, I'm waiting. Join me on safari tomorrow?"

She nodded, turned and opened the door. "Good night, Craig."

His smile would have won a prize, but her heart kept its steady rhythm. "I'm not used to women like you, and that's one reason why I won't stop before I get you. Meet you downstairs tomorrow morning at eight. If you have any bug repellent, put it on."

She leaned against the closed door. His hands had owned her, but she hadn't felt one thing. But was that so awful? Throughout most of Asia and Africa, marriages were made for business and social reasons; parents chose their children's mates or had an astrologer or other expert do that; people married for the good of clan, tribe and family. Divorce was a rare thing. Not so in the rest of the world where marriage was presumably based on love— except for the rich, most of whom managed to find mates as wealthy as themselves, love or no love. So who could censor her for seeking a man who had status and potential power—a man with whom she could have a secure, comfortable life for her children—and going after him?

It's more than that, her conscience nagged. You're in love with someone else; that's what's wrong with it. She dragged herself to the bed and sat down. Why had she let Luke McKnight sink so deeply into her being?

The next morning, Craig waited for Delia in the hotel's lobby, hoping she'd show up soon enough for them to get good seats in the tour bus. He hated sitting in the back, and he disliked waiting even more. She'd thrown him for a loop the night before, and he hadn't lied when he said he'd move mountains to make it with her in whatever way he could, because she didn't respond to his normal approach. Alright. So she was a high powered executive in a powerful job; she was a woman, wasn't she? He turned his back and walked rapidly to the men's room; the last thing he needed was that German woman hanging on to him.

He intended to make it with Delia; he had to. Besides the fact that he wanted her, he needed what she offered.

Right then, he wanted his name on the front cover of that conference report. Irregular, he knew, but he wanted it, and she could do it. He glanced out of the men's room, let out a deep breath in relief when he saw that the German delegate had joined his wife, and walked over to face the elevators. The door opened, and she stepped out, glowing in white linen slacks and a silk, orange-colored vest. He checked himself; falling for Delia Murray wasn't on his calendar.

CHAPTER 8

With the conference over, Delia returned to New York to resume her regular duties and to maneuver herself into the AS-G post. Long, lithe strides took her to her office for the first time in two weeks, and in the familiar surroundings, she had once more her feeling of power and of accomplishment. The debacle that the conference had been for her personally lessened hi importance as she set her cap for a higher goal. She didn't let her thoughts dwell on the pleasure she'd get if Luke stuck his head in her door right then and showed her a white paper bag that had coffee and a banana in it. Luke wouldn't continue his sweetness unless he knew she welcomed it, and she couldn't encourage him.

Every time she was tempted to tell him she cared and wanted to be with him, she would remember that awful day in Payne General Hospital, or her feelings for him would be tempered by childhood memories of her mother measuring the day's ration of flour or corn meal or rice. The painful remembrances would flash in vivid pictures through her mind, and she'd shrivel inside. She had encouraged Luke more than enough. She opened a letter from the WAD Foundation and let out a shriek. The foundation would fund for the NIA project. At once, she emersed herself in its plans. The money would buy uniforms for the girls, hire a music teacher, a tutor and a crafts specialist for the group and would support cultural and fun outings.

Humming softly, she wrote out their pledge and outlined her program. She would begin with the junior high school graduating class and, after getting their commitment to remain in school and graduate without getting pregnant, they would be asked to guide the juniors who would, in turn, help in recruiting girls in the grade below them. The girls would call themselves the NIA sorority and would elect their own officers. Maybe this would be the wrecking ball that turned the tide of teenage pregnancies among African - American girls in that district and begin an increase in the percentage who graduated from school. She hoped abstinence would be their method of choice but, to be on the safe side, she planned to enlist the help of the school nurse. She didn't consider herself competent to counsel health matters. Though tired from her long flight back and nursing the effects of jet lag, she decided to spend an hour at the youth center that evening.

Erin arrived with coffee and a file of newspaper clippings about the Nairobi conference. She understood Erin's subdued response to her effuse thanks when she looked at the *Times* coverage of the opening day's activities. She plowed through the lot, anger and disappointment gripping her with mounting intensity as she recognized that her toils for that meeting had gained her nothing. Ambassador Radcliff's picture graced every story; the four hundred delegates might well have stayed at home, because only Craig's words found immortality in print. She read of his genius as a negotiator and his smoothness as a chairman; editorials described him as dapper, handsome and elegant. One editor went so far as to describe him as "a breath of fresh air in a sick and troubled world." A fox in the hen house was more like it. He'd done what he went there to do, had courted the press and the delegates and won it all. She staggered into her private bath room and lost her coffee.

She knew she had to deal with Prakar, and he didn't keep her waiting. She leaned back in her chair and watched the door as he slithered through it.

"What happened?" he asked, his face cloaked in a serious, caring expression. "I thought you were going to Nairobi. No problem with your family, I hope. Radcliff sure was there. He's practically king of world right now. He's crooked as hell, but you have to admire the bastard. Sorry you didn't get noticed."

She wouldn't let him see what it had done to her. "Prakar, my job was to organize a great conference and, from all reports, it was the best ever. So if you'll—"

"He screwed you. It's the talk of the Secretariat. The great Miss Murray shackled by the devious Mr. Radcliff. Told you so." He sauntered out.

When her furor threatened to explode, she telephoned Craig and confronted him.

"But Delia, darling, I hardly expected this from you. I'd as soon hurt myself as do anything to displease you or make you unhappy. You know I care for you, so how could you accuse me of duplicity?"

He made a strong case for himself, but she knew he hadn't gotten that much attention without working at it. On occasion, she'd done as much herself. "It didn't happen by accident, Craig, that my name isn't mentioned in a single one of these reports, not even in reference to our joint reception."

"I was interviewed about the reception a couple of days after we held it, and I assure you I sang your praises to every reporter who approached me. But, Delia, I didn't write these stories. I'm sorry you're disappointed."

She didn't know what to believe, because reporters were interested in the dramatic, the sensational, and an African American ambassador presiding over a conference in Africa made better copy than she. Still, some of it didn't add up, but it would. As her Granny always said, "Murder will out."

Eleven of the twelve girls at the youth center that night sparkled with enthusiasm for the NIA project, lifting Delia's spirits. They clamored for more information and wanted to take the oath immediately. But Marine scoffed at it, saying she wouldn't let Delia or anyone else manipulate her. Delia sat huddled with the nucleus of the NIA Society, as the girls wanted to be called, and wondered at the warmth she felt for them as they laughed and regaled her with tales of their boyfriends and what the boys' reactions would be.

Jennifer stopped laughing. "Miss Murray, Mr. McKnight just walked in."

Delia glanced up and into his fierce, knowing gaze. Not a sound could be heard. She did her best to gather her composure, because every girl there had to sense the electricity flowing between her and Luke.

He advanced toward her, his gait rhythmic, animal-like. "How'd it go?"

"Uh… Hi, Luke. It went okay." She tried to shift her gaze from his, but the passion in his eyes yielded to warmth and tenderness, and she couldn't shake their hold on her.

"We can talk later," he said, having recovered first. She nodded and was glad she didn't have to answer.

"She made us into a sorority," one of the girls exclaimed, "and we're going to call ourselves *The NIA Society.*"

She read approval on his face. "I suppose you know the Kwaanza meaning of *Nia.*"

"Purpose," they shouted in unison.

"It means we aren't going to drift and let life happen to us," Jennifer elaborated. "We're going to give purpose to our lives and set ourselves some goals."

Luke nodded, and his eyes seemed to hold a new brilliance. She'd never get used to looking at them, and it scared her that they might some day drown her, that she'd surface to find him deep inside of her. She shook her head as though to unfetter herself from his spell.

"You're on your way," he told the girls, though he didn't take his gaze from Delia's eyes. "See you later." The girls looked at her, but she pretended that his message had been for them.

"Okay, where were we?" They giggled, and she couldn't blame them. Luke was sex in motion.

Luke leaned against the door as he waited for Delia. Didn't the woman go anywhere on time except the office? And another thing. She'd been back from Nairobi two days and hadn't called him, but she'd found time to see Craig Radcliff. He'd seen her stroll out of the building with him after work that evening. Maybe… He shook his head; he didn't want to think it, but how much did he know about her?

He turned when her cologne wafted past his nostrils and her fingers tripped along his shoulder. "Promises. Promises."

"I'm not promising anything," she said in a voice that he thought unusually seductive.

"Tell me about it. That's the problem. Ready to go?" They hadn't greeted each other, and he knew that was because they couldn't say and do what their needs dictated. He wanted to take her into his arms, but she hadn't given him the right to do that in the presence of others, and he wasn't sure he wanted that right. He locked his fingers through hers, walked to the corner of One-hundred sixty-ninth street and the Grand Concourse and hailed a taxi.

"We're not taking the D train tonight? Feeling flush?"

He squeezed her fingers, helped her into the cab and got in. "I want to shorten the time I have to wait to get you into my arms."

"Luke, we... we're not going to start that up again. We had two weeks to cool off, and that sort of thing is finished."

He would have laughed if he hadn't hurt so badly. She was into denial again, but he meant to show her a few things before he left her. "Whatever you say." He slouched into his corner of the taxi, but he didn't let go of her hand.

He stared right back at Pinski when they passed the man in the lobby. "Let me have your key, Delia."

"Luke, no... I—"

He let his gaze speak for him, let it torment her with its message of what he'd give her if she let him in that apartment. "Nothing will happen between us that you don't want. You only have to ask me to leave, and I'll go."

"But, Luke—"

"Don't you want to be in my arms?" he whispered. "Didn't you miss me? Open the door, Delia. I need to hold you."

A shot of adrenalin sailed straight to his groin when he heard her key turn. His hand rushed out as though of its own volition and pushed the door open. He didn't know how he got her into the apartment or how he got her coat off of her. He told himself to slow down, that he was moving too fast.

"Where do you hang this thing?" he breathed, harnessing his desire.

"I... Oh, Lord, I don't know."

The coat dropped to the floor. An indefinable, gut searing sensation shot through him, and heedless of his own warning, he pulled her willing body into his arms and fastened his mouth on her open lips. He was hard and hurting, and her soft moan fired him as would an electric current. He lifted her until her womanly cradle anchored his hard arousal. Her legs went around his hips, and he let the wall take his weight.

"Delia. Delia, look at me. If we're not going to make love, say it now."

Her feet hit the floor, and she seemed to step out of a dream. "You don't want this to happen when I'm as vulnerable as I am tonight, Luke." He watched her step away from him. "If we do this, Luke, I'll be mad with myself tomorrow, and maybe with you as well. I don't want it to happen."

"You don't want it to happen? Woman, I'm thirty-four years old; you want this more than you want air." He brushed his palm across her breasts. "Both of your nipples are rock hard, and they don't lie; a sixteen-year-old boy knows what that means. I'm no fool, Delia. Deny it all you want to, but it won't let you go. And, baby, you'll hurt. Pain? You haven't felt it."

"Talk what you know," she shot back. "I've had pain enough for legions. I don't want that kind of pain ever again."

Luke raised his hand in salute to the doorman as he left the building. He stopped. Pinski had smiled at him. What did that mean? He stuck his right hand in his pocked and headed for Central Park West and home. Delia would one day want to take him for a lover and, if he had any luck, he'd no longer be interested. She'd spoken of great pain; perhaps she had alluded to the thing that drove her, because something propelled her with a powerful force. A force so strong that she pushed aside her need for him.

A tightening of his loins startled him. Hell. He wasn't giving up. Not after the way she'd crawled all over him, pulling on his tongue as though her life depended on it, wrapping her thighs around his hips and pulsating against him as if she'd been in the grip of ecstasy. Oh, no. It might happen only once, but he'd get her, and she'd never forget it.

Delia finally slept at four o'clock the next morning. She would need strength and determination to stay out of bed with Luke, but she had enough reminders to make her stick to her goal. And that meant getting a husband and father for her children who guaranteed them all a life of comfort. A man to whom she could give her cares while she raised their family without worries as to how they would survive. She flitted away most of her precious Saturday morning in a half-real world until he called and gave meaning to her being.

She loved the circus, and it didn't occur to her to tell Luke she wouldn't go with him when he invited her. They left the Youth Center earlier than usual on Saturdays, because Luke's tickets were for a late afternoon show. "You ought to be flying high, considering the success you're having with the girls, so why are you gloomy?" Luke asked Delia.

"My mother wants my kid sister to come up here and spend some time with me, but it's a lousy idea." She couldn't tell him the truth, that knowing they'd never be more to each other than they were then made her morose.

"Why?"

"Because Bitsy—that's what we call her, though her name is Esther—Bitsy is so unsophisticated that I wouldn't know what to do with her. She'll walk around the yard with no shoes on, and she won't read anything but true confessions. At sixteen, she ought to be interested in *something.*"

"You could help her; you're a great role model for young girls. They see what you are and know what they can be. Look at the way your NIA girls have taken to you. Let her come up for a few days; see how it works."

"I don't know, Luke." She ignored his accusing stare.

Luke had refereed a basketball game and pushed the boys through several exercise regimes. "I'd better go home before we go to the circus, Delia. I don't think I could sit for two hours in this sweat shirt after a morning of basketball. It won't take long. Stop by with me?"

She hadn't wondered how he lived, but she didn't mind knowing. Her surprise began with the imposing building in which he lived, but not even the doorman's deference to Luke prepared her for his apartment. She couldn't say it was spectacular; it wasn't. But she had rarely encountered such consistently fine taste. Taste that cost money. Lots of it. She could tell that everything there was something he liked and wanted, that nothing was for show. How like him, she thought, to ignore decorating conventions and cater to his tastes.

She controlled her surprise, for she knew his gaze was on her. "You didn't have a decorator, did you?"

He shrugged. "I wouldn't know what to do with one. I didn't go looking to fill up an apartment. If I happen upon something I like, I buy it. I've never thought of decorating."

"Then you're either a lucky man or you have taste for things that are compatible. This place is lovely; feels comfortable and homey. Yet, it's elegant. I doubt a decorator could have managed this."

"Thanks."

She let her gaze roam over the spacious living room, linger on the raised dining foyer visible beyond a Gothic arch and settle on the butter-soft leather sofas and chairs and the hand woven Persian carpets. Wealth everywhere she looked. "Is this a co-op?"

"Yeah. Why?"

"Frankly, it has never occurred to me that repairmen lived so high on the hog."

"I can imagine there's a lot more you don't know. 'Scuse me while I change."

"Something's wrong here," she told herself while she waited for him. "But I'm not going to let myself think, because I want to like myself. I'm not going to change my opinion of him just because he spent money on his apartment. Just because he has some outward trappings of wealth. Anyhow," she told herself, "he could have hit the numbers or made a killing on the horses, because he didn't make it repairing office machines on a UN salary. The Lottery. Maybe he won the lottery." Well, she wasn't going to ask him how he got the money to furnish his apartment.

"Ready?"

She could imagine that her eyes rounded. He'd changed into a beige cashmere jacket, dark brown slacks, a green silk tweed-patterned shirt and matching tie. She hoped the sistahs stayed away from the circus, because he looked good enough to bite, and they wouldn't be shy about crowding him. Don't stare, girl, she told herself.

His grin brought flashing lights to his eyes. "Like something around here?"

"Yeah. Your apartment's terrific."

His dark, suggestive laughter sent a gush of longing through her. "You can have anything in here that you see. Anything." She buttoned her jacket, but the shivers that plowed through her had a more chilling effect than she'd get from the late March wind outside. "Let's go, Luke. The circus will start in forty-five minutes."

His grin seemed to have taken up permanent residence on his wonderful face. "Scared? Well, the way things look, you have i every right to be."

Outside, he hailed a taxi. His living style had impressed her, but she didn't intend to let him know it. She realized she had no idea who he was, that all she knew of him was where he worked, what he did and that she cared more for him than was good for her.

He gave the driver instructions, turned to her and said, "You're awfully quiet."

"I get like that sometime."

"You always have a lot of mouth when I'm around you. What's the matter?"

She took his hand, turned his palm over and looked at it. His fingers weren't calloused as she would have expected of a man who used tools all day. She turned it over. Smooth, strong fingers and clipped nails. She looked up, and his hot gaze drew her to him the way a lighted candle draws a moth. He used his free hand to caress her cheek, and she checked the moan that wanted release.

"You're quite a man. I was in your apartment with you for almost an hour, and you didn't touch me. You didn't so much as hold my hand."

His stare unnerved her, and she wished she hadn't spoken. "It didn't occur to me to behave differently. I want you to know that \ you can trust me, Delia. I'll never give you a reason to be afraid of me, and I won't take advantage of you."

He could afford to be magnanimous, she thought, mean spirited; in their relationship, she was the weak one. But she knew he'd spoken the truth. She patted his hand, leaned back and closed her eyes. Craig's image flashed across her mind. If she had been in his apartment, he would have pressured her to go to bed with him. What a mess!

Once inside the circus, she remembered that half the acts scared her to death. The aerial acts began, with people throwing and catching each other, defying gravity. She closed her eyes when she thought a young girl would miss a hoop and land a hundred feet below rather than in her partner's outstretched arms.

"Are you scared?"

"N… N… N… No," she answered, capitulating to her raw nerves and clutching Luke's arm. When she began visibly to shake during a man's bicycle ride on the high wire, Luke pulled her into his arms and buried her face against his shoulder. Later, she explained, "I love the circus, except for that part. I'm always scared somebody will get killed."

He kissed her cheek. "That's nothing to be ashamed of. What surprises me is that they aren't afraid. If they were, they probably wouldn't be able to do it. You're an amazing person, Delia. Almost every time we're together, I see evidence of your gentleness, but you don't want me or anyone else to know that side of you. Why?"

She didn't want to talk about herself. "You're seeing something that I'm not aware of, Luke. I don't spend much time thinking about myself."

"No, I don't suppose you would."

Walking across Seventh Avenue after leaving the circus, Luke looked up at the clear, starlit night, unusually balmy for early spring. All of his siblings would soon be on their own. He'd support them until they finished their education, but he needed to get started with his life, and he heeded to know how Delia fitted ; into it. He took her hand and walked into a coffee shop a few doors from New York's Hotel Pennsylvania imagining, from her demeanor, that she expected a bombshell. But he didn't speak until the waiter brought their coffee and left them.

"Delia, I'm going home next weekend. Will you go with me? You mean something to me, something special, and I want you to know who I am."

"Luke, I shouldn't encourage this."

"Then, how about going along for the change. We have to deal | with this, Delia."

He hadn't expected her to grab at the chance to meet his family, jv but he knew her visit to his apartment had raised his status with \ her, even though she tried to hide it. He hoped she'd be less "I certain that a romance between them had no chance. He hadn't decided that she was his future, but he knew she could be, that he wasn't likely to feel any more deeply for another woman. He could tell her he was an engineer who owned a prosperous business, but if she came to him then, he'd never know her motive.

"I'll think about it, Luke. Okay?"

"Sure. But don't think too long."

Luke brushed Delia's lips with his own, and was waiting for her to go into her apartment when Kate struggled down the hallway with an armful of packages. Seeing Luke, she stopped and appraised him with frank admiration.

"Kate Hamilton, this is Luke McKnight."

"Sorry, my hands are full," Kate said, "or I'd shake. Glad to meet you, Luke."

"Same here. Need any help with those packages?" '

Kate looked at Delia for permission. "Thanks, but I can manage. Delia, would you stick your hand in my bag and get my keys."

Luke bade them good-bye, and Delia walked with Kate to her apartment next door, opened the door for her and turned to go.

"Hey, girl, you're not going anywhere 'til you tell me who that hunk was. Looking at that man elevated my temperature. Sit down. I'll get us some coffee."

"I just had coffee, Kate."

"Then drink some more, or don't. I want to know who that man is. Are you sleeping with him?"

"Friendship doesn't cover everything," Delia said, though she'd long accepted that Kate said whatever she wanted to.

"You'd better tell me unless you want me to hang around the lobby like Pinski, wait 'til he comes home with you and snatch him after he leaves you. I never saw such eyes in all my twenty-five years."

"Come off it, Kate. Thirty-five is more like it. I'm not sleeping with Luke, but I don't want you or any other woman to lay a hand on him,"

Kate's eyes seemed twice their normal size. "Whoa, girl. I smell danger. You've fallen for him."

"Looks like it."

Kate rested her coffee cup on the table beside her chair and sat forward. "He isn't married, is he?" Delia shook her head. "He seems to have all his buttons plus some manners. Are you sure you're thinking right? Luke McKnight is one great looking man. And with that much self-confidence, he's got to be somebody. Girl, get off your high horse and go after the guy. Either that or move over."

"Life is never that simple, Kate. I'm trying to sort out things."

"Well, you'd better hurry. I could make that guy my life's work, and I'm not the only smart gal in this town. I'm surprised he's single."

"Me, too," Delia said. "Thanks for the coffee." Delia's three-hour struggle with the choice of Craig or Luke wore her thin mentally and drove her to physical exhaustion for, when she let herself think of the way in which she respond- ed to the two men, it always came back to Luke. She loved him, but how long would that last if she joined her life with his and a run of bad luck left him destitute and unable to support a family? She let out a tired breath. If she'd mis- judged his status, she'd regret it. She didn't think herself mercenary, because she was prepared to live alone. She sup- ported herself well and could do the same for a family, but she didn't plan to work, have babies and keep house simul- taneously. She gritted her teeth. A life of poverty wasn't for her; she couldn't face it. She forced back thoughts of his up- scale apartment; anybody could hit the numbers or the lot- tery. But if there was a chance for her and Luke... At ten o'clock that night, she dialed Luke's number.

"I didn't expect your call so soon."

"What time do you want to leave?"

"Delia, if you go with me, are you making a commitment?"

Her lower lip dropped, and her voice deserted her. After a moment, she could speak. "A commit... I hadn't... No."

His long pause made her anxious. "Okay. I'll pick you up Saturday morning at eight."

"Oh, I can meet you at the airport, Luke."

His irritation sprang at her through the wire. "Delia, I'll pick you up, and I'll pay for your ticket and everything else until I get you back to your place on Riverside Drive. My spending a couple of bucks on you won't obligate you one bit. If you can't handle that, let's forget the trip."

"Alright. Don't get your dander up."

She looked at the neat, white bungalow set among a grove of trees, surrounded by blooming forsythia, colorful tulips and myriad shrubs and other flowers, and her heart sank to the pit of her stomach. Luke's folks weren't as poor as her own, but that was as much as could be said. But she was there, and she wouldn't let Luke down.

"Mom, this is Delia Murray. Delia, my mother, Patsy McKnight. My dad's at the store; we'll get over there right after dinner."

She liked Luke's mother at once and greeted her with honest warmth. Patsy McKnight stepped back and looked into Delia's eyes and, apparently satisfied, told her. "You're the only girl my son's ever brought to me. Come on in."

Delia whirled around and looked at Luke, but he immediately hooded his eyes, and she knew her assessment

of his family's status and its significance hadn't escaped him.
She liked Luke's siblings, though she wanted to throttle
Dolores when she told Luke that he couldn't give her away
at her wedding because their father was entitled to that
honor.

"But can't I stand with him?" Luke asked her.

"Did you ever hear of such a thing, Della?" Dolores
asked.

Della didn't want to be drawn into the argument, but
she couldn't stifle the urge to support Luke. "I don't know
about here, but in New York, a bride has whatever kind of
wedding she wants. Sometimes the priests or ministers of
both the bride's and the groom's church officiate; I've
known brides who entered the church alone and weren't
given away. Some walk to the altar accompanied by the
groom. You can do whatever you like. It's your wedding."
She waited.

"Luke, I guess I'm old-fashioned; I want Dad to give me
away. Okay?"

"No problem." He turned to Delia. "Want to run over
and see my Dad? He's waiting for us. We'll take this Chevy;
it's old, but it runs."

Delia would have picked Rudolph McKnight from a
police lineup; his similarity to Luke was so great that it
made her nervous. Luke laughed at her expression of
stunned disbelief.

"I know what you're thinking, Delia. It's eerie. I look at
him these days and see how I'll look when I'm sixty."

"And won't you be lucky?" She could see that Luke's
father liked her, and she admitted to herself that his was an

attractive, loving family. But she didn't think she wanted to join it; she had problems enough with her own, and she'd better cut ties with Luke as soon as they got back to New York. Her father didn't own a store, but worked with his sweat in the lowest of jobs. Still, she could see that very little, other than literacy and education, separated the two men. Both would die poor.

"I don't think I want to come in," Luke told Delia that Sunday night as they stood at her door. "I'm glad you came with me, because now we know where we stand with each other. Yes, I'm disappointed, because I didn't want to believe you'd chuck this powerful thing between us for some snobbish... I don't... Look, it's not worth discussing. See you around."

He didn't wait until she went inside, so she stood there and made certain that he didn't look back. He'd finished it. They were two of a kind, from humble origins, who had made something of themselves. Luke had done it with his bare hands, and she had climbed up with her brain; both had been determined. His family needed his support and so did hers. She wasn't falling back into that. Never. Love didn't cover everything. A picture of that flame she'd seen between her parents surfaced in her thoughts, but she pushed it aside.

Luke had finished their relationship, such as it was, and she knew he meant it. For hours, she paced the floor. "I'm thirty, and if I want children, it's now or never," she said aloud. "Scarlet didn't die when Rhett walked out on her. Neither will I. She'd made up her mind.

CHAPTER 9

Five weeks after her split with Luke, Della stood at her office window looking at nothing. Luke hadn't been in her department since he'd said, "See you around." She could stop hoping; he meant it. Erin's voice came over the intercom. "Mr. Radcliff on one."

"Hello, Craig."

"Greetings, Della. I've been in Switzerland for a few days, or I'd have been in touch. I called you at home. Did you know your answering machine isn't working?"

"Sometimes I forget to turn it on. Anyway, if anybody phones when I'm not in, they'll call again. I was out of town, too." She didn't want him to think she'd sat around wondering why he didn't call. From now on, she couldn't afford to make a single mistake with him. "How are you, Craig?"

"Great, now that I've spoken with you. I missed you, Della, and I'd like to see you."

She could hardly believe her ears when he explained why he'd been away and what he'd done and finished by asking her to attend a reception and have dinner with him that evening.

At five-thirty, she met Craig at the delegates' entrance to the General Assembly Building, and he kissed her cheek at the exact moment that her eyes caught Luke's gaze as he left the Meditation Room. She smiled and tried to treat it as a casual incident, but her heart dropped to the pit of her stomach, and she had to fight the darkness that threatened to engulf her. She pasted a smile on her face, sucked in her breath and took Craig's hand.

He released her hand and put his arm around her. "I've wondered whether anything was going on between you and that guy. You know which one I mean, but I didn't see how that could be possible. He's a laborer, isn't he?"

"He repairs office machines," she replied, and her heart sank further with her nagging sense of guilt that she had betrayed Luke. Craig must have sensed her dejection, for she hadn't known him to be so gentle and considerate. A different Craig from the one she'd known. Warm. Caring.

"This is Della Murray, the brain of the Nairobi conference," he told every person to whom he introduced her. When she said she wouldn't drink on an empty stomach, he brought her a small plate of hot hors d'oeuvres, and when she declined another drink, he got a cup of coffee for her.

"Where'd you get this?" She didn't see any coffee, other than hers.

"I just stepped into the pantry and asked the waiter for coffee."

"You're resourceful."

With not even a hint of a smile, he stared down at her from his vantage point of six feet four-and-one-half inches. "You wouldn't believe how resourceful I can be. I'm a master at it."

Hot coffee spilled down her throat, and she looked around for cool water. She wasn't used to being knocked off balance that way. Even as she wished for the water, Craig seemed to have read her thoughts, for he handed her a glass of club soda.

As she sipped from the glass he'd given her, he continued his onslaught. "Anything you need, I can supply, and you'll get it exactly the way you want it."

"Don't tell me you're a magician," she bluffed, after failing, in her flustered state, to find a more cogent retort.

But he hadn't finished. "Nothing magic about it. Just skill. Masterful skill." She dragged her gaze from his, but not without difficulty, because she had the sensation of being hypnotized. He took the glass of water from her fingers, placed it on the tray of a passing waiter, and grinned at her. "For two cents, I'd kiss you right here."

A soft gasp escaped her, and she shook her head to release the shock of his words. "If you're not well, Craig, maybe we'd better leave."

When he stopped laughing, he said, "If I've ever felt better, I don't recall it. In any case, it's time to eat."

She didn't know what to make of it; Craig was behaving with Luke's sensitivity. And if he didn't stop it, she'd cry. But he kept her close to him, catering to her until she began to feel precious.

"We could have dinner in the Ambassador Lounge, if you'd like."

This was too much. He usually chose the restaurant without regard to her tastes. "I'd love it."

Where had her appetite gone? She pushed the medallions of veal, fiambed wild mushrooms and asparagus almondine around on her plate, unable to taste them. Frantic to calm her nerves and regain her equilibrium, she gulped down the last half of her glass of Chateau neuf du

Pape but would have spit it out if a receptacle had been handy.

"Are you alright, Della?"

His hand on her arm offered a tentative caress, as though he feared distressing her, and she knew that his voice, deep and soft, was meant as a comfort. *Get your act together, girl,* she admonished herself. *If you fluff this chance, you —won't get another one.*

She sucked on her bottom lip. "I'm okay. Why?" she said, knowing it wasn't true. She was about to turn a corner, and she didn't know what awaited her.

Craig stood and extended his hand. As she took it, it occurred to her that she hadn't previously noticed that hard-edged, determined demeanor nor seen his expression more serious. They walked out onto Forty-fourth Street, and he hailed one of the taxis that waited in front of the UN Plaza Hotel.

"My place?" he asked, as he opened the door.

She'd known he'd say that, so she nodded and got in. During the short ride to his apartment on East Sixty-third Street, she didn't speak, because she could scarcely breathe. He held her hand, but he didn't crowd her and, for that, he earned her gratitude. Whatever happened between them had to be her decision, because she wanted it, and not because he pressured her until she acquiesced.

She hardly spared the simple but elegant furnishings in his apartment a glance. He turned on a table lamp in the living room and, standing at least three feet away, spoke in soft tones.

"Della, if you don't want to stay, I'll take you home right now. I've wanted you a long time, and an unconsummated, heavy petting session could make a maniac out of me." He stepped closer. "Will you stay? Do you want to?"

She didn't know how she found her voice. "I want to."

Immediately, his face shone with anticipated pleasure, and he held out his arms to her. She walked into mem and asked herself why it pleased her that he hugged her but didn't kiss her.

"Sit here," he said pointing to the sofa. Seconds later he returned with two long stemmed champagne glasses and a bottle of Moet and Chandon. He gained her admiration when he eased the cork out of the bottle without its having made a sound. That wasn't an easy trick. They sipped the cold, bubbly liquid in silence for several minutes, before he placed her glass on the coffee table and cradled her head against his shoulder. His kiss was soft, lingering with slowly rising passion. How different from his previous kisses, she thought.

She had never *submitted* to a man because lovemaking was mutual, but he seemed to want quiescence.

"May I undress you?"

She nodded, because she'd rather not talk. She wanted to lose herself in him, to find in him the answer to her prayers, and she wanted to banish the ghost of Luke that had sneaked into her head. Encouraged, he stripped her, turned back the bed covers to reveal tiger-patterned linen, and laid her in bed.

"You still alright?" he asked.

She put a smile on her face and willed herself to wrap him in her arms.

Forty-five minutes later, Delia emerged from the bathroom looking exactly as she had when they'd met in the UN building earlier that evening. He examined her for a softening in her demeanor, for evidence that she'd melted inside, that she belonged to him, but he didn't see it. After sated lovemaking, a woman was supposed to be a lump of sweet mush, but if she felt differently toward him, she hid it well.

"Since you insist on going home, I'll take you."

Her smile didn't convince him. "You don't need to. Your doorman can get me a taxi."

He wasn't used to the strange feeling of incompleteness that had settled in him, and something hurt deep in his gut. "Della, I'm taking you home."

She didn't snuggle up to him in the taxi, and saying good night to him at her door didn't seem to bother her the way something tore at him because he had to leave her. When he stepped out in the cool air, the world looked new, and the realization that the chickens had come home to roost hit him hard. He'd always loved women, felt nothing but sexual relief after taking them to bed, and left them. But not this time. She had rocked his world; cannons had exploded in his head; and he couldn't have given his name if his life had depended on it. She had zonked him. He knew he faced a battle, but he was damned if he'd let his penis run his life.

He hailed a taxi at the corner of Broadway and Seventy-fourth Street, ducked in and gave the driver his address, still unable to shake the gloom that had settled over him. It wasn't his penis that hurt; it was his heart. He walked into his bedroom and looked at the place where she'd clobbered him, stripped the bed and threw the linen into the hamper. It was enough that he remembered her scent; he didn't want it to torment him all night. He undressed, stretched out on the bare mattress and flicked off the light.

He didn't like the way he felt. He had expected to enjoy her body, to make the kind of impression that would ensure him a welcome if he wanted to return, but what he'd done was guarantee himself the *need* to go back to her. He reached for her and realized that she wasn't there beside him. Though he might be some things of questionable morality, he didn't think himself a cad, so he couldn't give her what would prove to be a one-night stand. Yet, if he made love with her again, she'd be wedged that much deeper in him. But he couldn't have her creeping into him like that. Top diplomats didn't encumber themselves with UN staff members, no matter how high up they were. And besides, if he was going to make the career he'd set for himself, he needed a woman who had political leverage, and money wouldn't hurt her. That left Delia out. But… He flipped over on his belly. What had he done to himself? He'd never get enough of this woman. He squeezed his eyes shut. What the hell was he going to do?

That conference had catapulted him into the big league, and he couldn't afford to trash the opportunities coming his way by going head over heels for Delia. He could have his pick of women, and he had sense enough to know that he'd better go for the one who would put him in a position to get what he wanted. An appointment to Director-General of one of the specialized agencies, or Secretary-General of the UN would cure any kind of heartache. He fell over on his back and begged for sleep.

Della got into her apartment and let the artificial smile fade from her face. The experience hadn't been unpleasant, but she hadn't felt anything. She'd faked a response. Craig hadn't lied when he'd said he was a master at resourcefulness. Half of his moves should have sent her into the stratosphere, but they had served only to prove the lack of chemistry between them. She hadn't been turned off altogether, because he was skilled and patient, but the urge to explode had never come. Instead, Luke's face had mocked her.

Luke had finished their relationship, and she had to get over him. Craig was her man. "I'll be alright," she told herself. "With some men, chemistry has to develop." But what was she going to do about Luke?

A little over a week after she'd made love with Craig, Delia put in her formal application for the post of Assistant Secretary-General in charge of SCAG, and was told that Prakar had also applied. She outlined her work with the

NIA society as evidence of her ability to do the job, fighting guilt as she signed the papers. She called in a few debts from colleagues who owed her allegiance, but without her government's support, all of her efforts would probably be wasted. At that level, competence didn't always count; the winner was guaranteed to be a master at playing hard ball, and government support was the power that cracked the bat.

That evening at dinner, she mentioned to Craig her drive for the AS-G post and the competition for it. "Why didn't you tell me about it earlier? I'll take it up with the Ambassador tomorrow. We may have to check with State down in Washington, but it ought to be a cinch. You have a commendable record."

Thank goodness, she hadn't had to ask him, that he'd volunteered. "I didn't want to ask you, because I know you have to guard your position with the Mission, but I appreciate it."

She hadn't expected that he'd be attentive, though he'd shown her many sides of himself. At times, he mystified her. Before the conference, he'd appeared self-serving and, at least once, she'd had to remind him of her status. But that had changed, and he treated her as though he cherished her. It did bother her that he seemed to prefer that they not be seen together on the UN premises. However, he wanted her in his life, so she'd deal with the rest when she had to.

Craig thought about his promise to Delia while he wrestled with sleeplessness that night. He'd meant it when he offered to get government support for her promotion, but what would he say when the Ambassador questioned his motive? The man had seen him with Delia any number of times, and he couldn't afford the charge of seeking favors for his lover. And with things boiling for him right then, he stood to gain plenty if he watched his step. He consoled himself with the assurance that Delia would win the post on merit.

Several weeks after Craig made his magnanimous offer, Della walked past Kate in the hallway of the apartment building in which they lived, and her friend grabbed her arm and swung her around. "You almost knocked me down, girl; what's happening?"

Delia blinked. "I forgot to put in my contacts. Come on in for a few minutes."

Kate walked in and dropped her basket of laundry on the floor in the foyer. "Delia, something tells me you messed up good with Luke... What was his name? You know. I haven't seen you with him since that night."

"We'd never cemented anything, but we broke up what we had, sort of by mutual agreement."

Kate stared at her. "Delia, that was a nice man. It'll be a hot day hi January before you find another brother like that one." She pretended to pout. "Thought you were going to give him to me if it didn't work for you."

Della didn't want to talk about Luke. "I'm seeing some-one else."

Kate looked toward Heaven and then shook her head. "Not that polished glass I saw you with Friday, I hope. I thought he was somebody you worked with."

Delia left her chair, moved to the sofa beside Kate and studied her face. "Why do you call him polished glass?" She wished Kate would quit that habit of letting her gaze dig into a person's psyche.

"My Lord, don't tell me you're sleeping with him?";
Della squirmed.

"I'd laugh if it was funny," Kate told her. "He's not the one you want, and you're doing yourself a disservice. A month ago, you told me you didn't want any woman to have Luke, and I dare you to tell me you don't care what he does." Her tone softened. "Why didn't you go after him, honey? He wanted you."

A deep sigh of longing poured out of Della. "I wanted more than he offered."

"And you need more than this other fellow's giving you, too. It's written all over you. Girl, you're short-changing yourself."

Della's shoulders slumped in resignation. "It isn't his fault. It... it's just that there's nothing there."

Kate rested her elbows on her knees and looked down at the floor. "If it doesn't swing right in the hay, Delia, leave it. You can't force it, and there's no point in even praying for it to get better. I've been there. You're sure he gives all?"

"As much as he can. Yes."

"And you're still going to try and make something out of it? I admit he's a great-looking guy but, girl, cave women didn't put up with that. What does he say when you don't respond?"

She rubbed the back of her neck, ill at ease. "He didn't know it."

'*What?* Faking is stupid. You're going to regret it. Wait a minute. You don't know what you're missing, do you? It hasn't ever happened to you, has it?" Delia shook her head. "No wonder.

Girl, you just wait 'til you find out. I gotta go iron. Drop that charade, Delia. It's not worth it, not even if the brother owns the whole Internet."

"It wasn't his fault, Kate. The problem is I'm not in love with him."

Kate pulled a lot of air in through her teeth and looked toward the sky, "For goodness sake, Della, you don't have to be in love for the earth to move; I've never been in love in my life. Your problem is Luke. Later, girlfriend."

Delia sat like a catatonic staring into space for a full half hour after Kate closed the door. How right she was! All Luke had to do was put his hand on her, and she was a ball of fire. No other man had drawn that response from her. What would loving be like with Luke?

The depressed state in which Kate left her persisted until the next morning, and she roamed around in her office. Restless.

"Call on line two, Ms. Murray." Erin told her through the intercom.

"Don't tell me that, Papa," Delia cried. "When did it happen?"

"Just now. Hold yourself together, and come as soon as you can. Alright?"

She went into her bath room and washed her tear-stained face. She'd known it was coming. They had all known it, but it still hurt. She straightened her desk, got her brief-case and pocketbook, told Erin her grandmother had died and left her office.

Luke walked toward her as she headed toward the elevator. She averted her gaze, but tears stung her face, and he stopped her.

"What is it, Delia? What's happened to you?"

"My Granny. She's gone."

His arms drew her into the warmth, the comfort of his body, and she clung to him. Nearly three months had passed since she'd seen him. Months that now seemed like years.

He hugged her to him. "Come on. I'll take you home."

She wanted to hold him close to her, to kiss every part of him that she could reach. Not even her grief dulled her need of him or abated her hunger for him.

There in the corridor, he held her to him with one hand while he punched out a number on his cellular phone with the other.

"I have to leave the UN, Bill, and I don't know when I'll be back. Get a man over here, and tell him to start with request number six. Got it?"

They passed Pinski in the lobby of her building and, depressed though she was, she noted an unusual belligerence in the man, but shrugged it off. Luke phoned the airline, reserved a limousine in Wilmington, and while she packed, he threw out of her refrigerator anything that would spoil.

"I'd suggest a rental car, but you probably shouldn't drive right now," he told her, adding, "we'd better call your folks and let them know you're on your way. What's the number?"

She gave it to him and took the phone after he dialed. "I'll be in sometime tonight, Mama. Around seven or so, I guess."

"Do you want me to go with you, Della?"

His question didn't surprise her. "Thanks, but I can manage alright. Luke, what about your work? The way things have been with us recently, why would you do that? Why are you…?

"Because I love you, Della. I love you."

Her breath gushed out of her as she gazed at him in utter astonishment, while her mind fought to reject the significance of his words. She couldn't imagine what he thought, as she stood before him speechless. Unnerved. She hid her shaking hands behind her, but he moved to her and wrapped her in his powerful arms,

"I didn't expect you to know, Delia, because I didn't; I knew I cared deep down, but I had to miss you to know how much."

"Oh, Luke. Luke. What have I done to myself? And to you?"

"Shhhhh. It'll work itself out. Time to go." He picked up her suit case, handed her the umbrella that hung on the inside of the hall closet door and took her arm.

An hour later, they stood at the boarding gate for US Airways Flight 443 with barely an inch separating them. She knew she had to deal with the sensations swirling in her as his beloved fingers stroked her cheek, and he stared into her eyes.

"Flight 443 to Wilmington now boarding."

The voice of the flight attendant brought forcibly to her what she was leaving and what awaited her. He must have sensed her brief moment of trepidation, for he locked her in his arms and, at last, let her feel the wonder of his mouth on hers. She knew no shame, as her lips begged for all the sweetness he could give her.

"...now boarding," she heard again..

"Take good care," he said, his demeanor gray and solemn.

Luke watched Delia pull herself up the ramp. Her carry-on was light, so it had to be her heart that weighted her down. He supposed Providence was at work; for the past eleven weeks, he'd assigned one of his employees to take care of Erin's orders. He'd headed toward Della's department that morning to appease his hunger for the sight of her and, when he'd seen her, the urgency of her gut level need for him had shattered his defenses. He hadn't meant to speak with her, only to treat his eyes to a feast. But she'd touched him, deep down, and he'd told her he loved her because, at that moment, what he'd felt had transcended in importance everything else in his life. He walked out of the terminal and got in the line for a taxi. The earlier drizzle had developed into a torrential rain. He noticed his damp brogans and shrugged. Getting wet was the least of his concerns; unless Delia had undergone a metamorphosis, he was looking at a long stretch of gloom.

Della found her seat, stored her flight bag, and tried to get her bearings. Pain ravaged her head, and she leaned back and closed her eyes. She had to admit it wasn't accidental that every molecule of her body had welcomed his nearness. She was attuned to him. He'd only looked at her there in the UN corridor, and her blood had flown hot and free through her veins. Her nerves, dead as it were for weeks past, had stood at attention waiting to dance to the tune he'd play. But she'd made her bed, and she'd sleep in it. Girding herself in determination, she wiped the tears that cascaded down her cheeks, took out her department's *Information Bulletin* for the month of May, and started editing it. But it didn't surprise her that the work failed to distract her thoughts from what she'd left behind and what she faced in Pine Whispers. In recent weeks, something had been eating away at her perspective on life. She pitched forward at the change in the engine's sound, jittery with fear of what she faced at her parents' home. The plane's wheels had dropped for landing at Wilmington's New Hanover International Airport before she realized she'd left New York without saying one word to Craig. She hadn't remembered that he existed.

Della looked at the familiar old house, less depressive in the sunshine amidst the now green trees and profusion of spring flowers. Tate Murray stepped out on the front porch and welcomed her. Only then did she notice the black ribbon on the front door, and sobs wrenched out of her when she walked into her father's arms. The vision of a similar scene decades earlier— when she and her mother had returned from Payne General Hospital without little Mark—flashed through her mind, deepening her pain.

"I'm so sorry, Papa."

"Now, now, Child. We have to accept it. Your Granny didn't want anybody to be sad about her leaving. Come on inside and pay your respects."

Della didn't want to go in there. She didn't want to see her Granny mute, unable to give her a devilish wink or to hug her. She thought about the opportunities she'd missed, the weekends when she'd chosen to work or do something else instead of spending a day with her sick grandmother.

Her father took her arm. "Come on, Daughter. I know it'll be hard." He held her hand and opened the front door.

The bottom seemed to drop out of her when she walked into the front room and her gaze fell on the bier. Yellow spring flowers and gladiolus bedecked the gray casket, and her grandmother's hands held a small white bible. She turned away, unable to tolerate the scene.

In the kitchen, her mother and half a dozen neighbors prepared food for the evening wake.

"Della, honey, come here." She took comfort in the warmth and reassurance of her mother's arms.

"Your Granny wouldn't want you to be sad," Lizzie cooed. "Somebody open the kitchen door."

Neighbor after neighbor arrived with food. Some brought flowers, and all gave a few dollars. The Reverend arrived, said a prayer and hurried away. Soon the house teemed with well wishers, and Delia had to admit she'd rarely heard such beautiful singing—even in the Metropolitan Opera House. Hymns and spirituals poured from untrained but elegant voices. It saddened her that many of them could have enjoyed a singing career if they'd had the opportunity. Periodically someone would volunteer a eulogy. Delia wasn't certain that her granny would have appreciated Miss Mary's hysterical shouting.

Of similar mind, Mariah pulled at the woman's skirt. "Sit down, Mary. Ain't nothing wrong with you. Besides, you're wasting your time; the Reverend's already gone home. All that shouting and carryin' on just to get attention." Mary shouted a few seconds longer and sat down.

It occurred to Delia that very few of her New York friends and acquaintances would mourn her. She couldn't imagine that more than half a dozen would attend her funeral. The singing had comforted her, but when thoughts of her desolate life intruded, a cloud darkened her spirits. Mariah stood to give out a hymn, as they did in the old-fashioned, local prayer meetings, and soon the sound of *Amazing Grace* soared through the emptiness. Delia smiled through her tears. Granny would have loved every second of that. She left the room and met Mark in the short hallway.

"What's the matter, Ludell? Can't you take it? Too countrified for you? I don't suppose they do this kinda thing up there in New York."

"Oh, Mark. Granny wouldn't want us to snipe at each other this day of all days."

Chastened, he shrugged. "Yeah, I suppose you're right. She left a message for you."

"What message?"

He took a piece of yellow note paper out of his pocket. "Let's see. She said, 'Tell Ludie, you know, honey, everybody is somebody to somebody'."

Chills crept through her body, making her shiver. "I don't believe you."

He lifted his left shoulder. "Suit yourself. But you can ask Papa. He was sitting right there when she said it. One of the last things she said."

Della raised her head and fought the tears. "I hate that sight in there. You make sure nobody does that to me."

"Right. I'll look after your interest if you make sure a gang of people don't walk around staring down at me and shaking their heads."

A smile drifted over Delia's face. "Sometimes I forget how funny you can be. If you look after me, that means I won't be here to take care of your interests. Oh, Mark, why do we spend so much time hurting each other?"

"We don't approve of each other, Ludell. Strange. When we were little, we were thick as thieves." He pulled her to him, held her in a long, tender hug, and she thought her heart would break; Mark so rarely showed her affection.

Only Della wore black to the funeral. Other family members wore a black arm band or a black scarf on their heads. "Folks down here don't get special clothes for funerals," Rachel explained. "We wear whatever we have."

She didn't know how she managed to sit through the funeral in the little Baptist church in which she grew up. The straight-back, hard pews; bare, white-washed walls; the mournful sound of the organ; the stark gray casket; Matthew and Bitsy's quiet tears; and the soulful a-mens and yes-Lords plunged her into deep anguish. She wanted to run, to stop her heart from breaking, to stop the pain and banish the awful presence of death. There seemed no end to it.

After the ceremonies, Dela joined her family at the home of one of the church leaders, where they were taken for a meal and prayers. The hospitality and good will of the people flowed around her and should have comforted her, she knew, but she couldn't help reflecting on their impoverished lives and her gnawing fear of sinking back into it. The people sang, laughed and told long tales of Granny that explained her endearment to them. Delia stood it for as long as she could hold back the tears. As they cascaded down her face, she walked outside and leaned against a chinaberry tree. She needed air, privacy and a moment in which to try and accept what the friends and neighbors around her offered.

"You disappeared for a while there, Ludell," her father said when the family was at last home and alone.

"It got to me, Papa."

"Your Grandmother left you a message." He repeated what Mark had read to her. "You could say she meant for you to stop looking down your nose at people," he added, startling her.

"I wasn't—"

"I say you did and you do. Not every nobody's had your advantages, Daughter. We're proud of what you've di... done, but not how you act."

"What do you expect, Papa? You don't see what I see. The people in this town hum through life as though they all live on Park Avenue, when they're barely existing. How can they be so contented with their lives? And you, Papa, why don't you go to school and learn to read so you won't have to spend the rest of your life cleaning up after people? School's free, but you haven't taken advantage of it."

Her mother's flat palm burned the side of Delia's face, nearly spinning her around. "How dare you speak that way to your father? If you had taken the pains to find out, you'd know your father's dyslexic. When he was in school, the teachers said he was stupid, but he's not, and they punished him, because he couldn't learn to read. Well, he's done as well with what he had as you have with your brilliant mind. I've taught him grammar and helped him learn to speak well." She stared into Delia's eyes. "He suits me, Ludell."

"I... I'm sorry, Papa. I didn't know."

"Proud of yourself, Ludell?" Mark asked. She hadn't seen him leaning against the doorjamb. "How many of your New York cronies would go to your funeral and follow you to the cemetery? I bet you can count 'em on your two hands. Better get your ducks in a row, kid."

It didn't escape Della that neither of her parents had ever slapped or hit her before, and she knew she had hurt her mother deeply. "I'm terribly sorry, Mama. I am. Papa, I'm going to send Mama some information about dyslexia and remedies for it."

Did her father stand straighter than before? Certainly, he radiated pride. "It's alright, Daughter. You want to improve me and make me into something you think you can respect. Well, I like my job as a janitor. I keep my school neat and clean. It's the model for the county. I can't read, but I take pride in doing well what I gi… get paid to do, such as it is. I hope you do the same."

CHAPTER 10

A note from Luke awaited Delia when she returned to New York. At that first glimpse of his handwriting, her adrenalin geared up to race, but his message slowed it to a crawl. She hadn't known how badly she wanted to see him. She read it for the second time.

"I'll be down in Polk Town, North Carolina, for a while running my father's business while he recovers from a fall. I don't know how badly he's hurt, so I can't say when I'll see you. If you need me for anything, call my beeper number. You can also do that if you miss me. Luke"

If she missed him. She didn't want to miss Luke McKnight. And doggonit, she wouldn't. She kicked off her shoes, stuck her feet into a pair of sneakers, and knocked on Kate's door.

"Hi."

"You got company?".

"Wish I did. Come on in. Anything wrong?"

"No. I don't know. Ever feel like your life's getting out from under you?"

Laughter spilled out of Kate. Her hands went up and she looked toward the ceiling. "Getting out from under me? I've never been in control of it. What's the matter? Oh, oh. That man, I'll bet."

(missing page pg. 173)

anyone else."

Delia went home, made a sandwich, got a glass of milk, took it to her living room and turned on the television. Anything to get her thoughts off Luke. Maybe if he stayed with his folks a month or so—not that she wished his father a long illness—he'd lose his appeal for her.

In Polk Town, Luke dealt with similar thoughts. He risked losing his way if he didn't pull back and get Delia out of his system. She intrigued him. Fascinated him. He hadn't met a greater challenge. What he felt sometimes, when he looked at her, was tantamount to emotional strangulation, his only thought being to have her, no matter what. And if he got her, the rewards would outshine any he'd reaped. But if he invested himself in her and lost, he'd sink deeper than he'd ever been.

He parked his father's old Chevy in front of McKnight's General Store and was about to lock it when he remembered that no one in Polk Town would steal a car. He entered the old building—a town landmark—and pride stole over him. His family lacked wealth, but his parents enjoyed the respect and esteem of their fellow citizens.

"Ellie! What a surprise." He rounded the counter in his father's grocery store and grasped the hand of his first girl. She'd gone off to Spellman College and gotten involved with a Morehouse man, but he'd disappointed her, and she'd wanted to regain her place in Luke's heart. He'd already closed the door.

"How're things going with you?"

"Luke!" Her hand went to her chest. "I had no idea… no idea. Are you back to stay? I heard you were doing well. What happened?" He explained about his father's fall, and her face lost its eagerness. He couldn't believe that, after so many years, she still harbored an interest.

"Would you... I'm sure Papa would love to see you. He still plays a good game of chess, and not many people around here can keep up with him like you could."

He'd love a game of chess, but not at the expense of his freedom. "I have to stick pretty close to the store, so—"

"I make a mean pot roast, if I do say so myself, and you're more than welcome."

He mustered what had to be a lame smile. "We'll see how things go with my dad." She lingered longer than he thought necessary and purchased more than she probably needed, and he figured he'd have to be pretty slick to avoid her. Still, she was more beautiful at thirty-five than she'd been at eighteen, and... "Not on your life," he told himself. Relief poured over him when the door closed behind her. No use trying to escape into something he didn't want just because Delia had screwed up his mind.

The morning passed without incident; those who came to buy had enough money for their purchases. His father gave credit to anybody who asked for it, but Luke thought that was bad business practice. Still, in his father's store, he had to honor his father's directives. But it galled him.

Early in the afternoon, Roy Lassiter came in for two loaves of Patsy McKnight's homemade bread, his bloodshot whites of his eyes giving the blue of his irises a ghostly hue. "Put it on my bill."

Luke couldn't find the man's account, so he took a dollar and a half from his pocket and put it in the cash register.

"You're a real sweet boy," the man said, and Luke had to turn his head to avoid the blast of whiskey air. "Chip off the old block."

"Sure thing," Luke replied, remembering that he stood in his father's store in a small town.

He closed the store at six and drove to the train station to meet his sister, Wanda, who was coming home from college for the weekend.

"What do you mean you're taking ROTC so you'll be accepted hi the Air Force?" Luke demanded of Wanda at dinner that evening.

"I want to be a pilot, and the Air Force will train me if I'll stay in for five years."

Oblivious to the hush that filled the room and the worried looks of his parents, and of Irene and Nelson, Luke rested his fork on his plate and turned to his favorite sibling. "Run that past me again, Wanda. You want to drop out of college and join the United States Air Force. I don't believe I'm hearing this. Why the devil did you waste time and money going to North Carolina Central? You could have gone into the service right out of high school. And why on earth do you want to be a soldier and put yourself at the mercy of a bunch of bullies? You know the trouble girls are having in the service."

He got up from the table, paced around it and sat back down when he caught his mother's censoring gaze. "Look, Wanda. This is absolutely unacceptable. Of all the things…" His voice trailed off. "Dad, you don't go along with this, do you?"

When his father cleared his throat, Luke knew he could expect a lecture. "Son, we all know you want the best for your brother and sisters and that you've sacrificed a lot so they'll have a good foundation. But Luke, we can't live their lives for them. Nobody told you that you couldn't be an engineer. Suppose I had insisted you go to work in the store when you finished high school.

Wanda would be miserable teaching elementary school, or sitting still doing any kind of work. You know that. Let her be."

Luke turned to Wanda. "I know you'll do what you want, but I'm disappointed, and I hope you'll change your mind."

"Don't count on that, Luke. It's all I thought about for years."

"What? Why didn't you tell me?"

"I didn't tell you, Luke, because you had your own agenda for me. I tried to follow it, but I just can't."

"I wish that was the only thing I had to worry about. Think it over long and hard, Wanda, before you sign any papers."

"I will."

He didn't want anything else to eat. The thought of his sister at the mercy of some brutish soldiers took his appetite. He had to get out. Away. He excused himself, got in his father's car and started driving to nowhere. When he stopped, he looked up at Ellie Robinson's front door. He slumped against the back of the seat. What the heck was he doing? He started the engine, switched into drive and poised his foot over the accelerator. The front door opened, and Ellie walked out on the porch. Too late. She saw the car and ran down the steps to him.

"Oh, Luke. Luke. I'm so happy you came. I hoped, but I didn't dare believe…"

What, for Heaven's sake, could she be talking about? He had the sensation of being a wild animal ensnared in a hunter's trap, and he didn't move until she knocked repeatedly on the window of the front passenger door.

"It's been ages since I had a game of chess, and I thought I'd see if your father wanted to play. If he isn't home, I'll stop by another time." He didn't look at her, but he hoped she'd gotten his message that he wasn't seeking her company. It didn't work.

"I don't care why you're here, Luke. You're here, and you come on in." From the street- light across the way, he could see the gleam of happiness that lit her face. Well, he'd asked for it. He'd struggled with the pain of Wanda's asserted independence from him and his family's support of her stance, and his ego had needed a boost. But not this big a lift. He got out of the car and, as he'd known she would, she grasped his hand and led him into the house. He could truthfully say he'd just eaten and that he didn't drink when driving. And after one game, he rose to leave.

"Sure was good to have you, Luke," Ellie's father said, "and I know Ellie's tickled pink to have you back here. You drop by any time. Any time."

He thanked the man and made his way to the front door, glad to escape, but he hadn't counted on Ellie's determination nor her boldness. She stilled his hand when he reached for the door knob, reached up and kissed him on the mouth, her own open and her breath hot. Stunned at the distaste he felt, he grasped her waist with both hands and moved her gently away from him.

"There's someone else, Ellie."

"I didn't think all women were crazy, Luke. But whoever she is, she's not here right now when you need her, and I am. I don't think you came over here to play chess without first calling my papa. You'll be back, and I'll be here for you."

Luke stared down at her. No longer the frivolous school girl darting from boy to boy, but a woman willing to fulfill a man's needs, honest about what she wanted and not afraid to go after it.

"Good night, Ellie." ' "Night, Luke. See you again soon."

He sat in the car in front of his parents' home, thinking about what he'd done. He didn't fool himself; he needed Delia, and he'd turned toward Ellie, because he knew she wanted him, that she'd be salve for his bruised soul. Delia wanted him, cared for him, but was ashamed of it. And for years he'd walked as a giant amidst his family, but first Dolores and now Wanda felt strong enough to make plans and see themselves through without his help or counsel. It was their right, but it pained him. He loved them and wanted to be important to them. He'd told Delia that it was over between them, but with each passing second, the pain inside of him deepened, jabbed at his insides until he wanted to scream. It would never be over for him.

He got out of the car and walked toward the center of town, conscious of being alone, meeting no one, and his loneliness intensified. He ducked into Wilkins Drug Store just as the man was about to close the door.

"I need about ten dollars worth of quarters, Mr. Wilkins."

"No trouble, Luke."

He dialed Della's home phone number. "This is Luke." Her silence told him that he'd surprised her.

"Hi. I didn't expect you to call, but I'm glad you did. How's your father?"

"Strapped in a back brace. If he doesn't improve soon, we'll probably hospitalize him. His spirits are good, though." He wanted to lay his cards on the table, tell her what he felt, that he needed her, but he couldn't. He couldn't risk rejection.

"How are things with you? You haven't used my beeper number; does that mean you haven't missed me?"

"'Course I miss you. They gave me a special intercom box that's supposed to link me to the General Assembly and the Councils, but all this thing does is blast noise whenever I turn it on. If you were here—"

"I see you're into denial, Delia. I didn't call you to talk about your office machines, and you know it, but if that's all you've got to say…"

"What do you want to hear, Luke?"

"For starters, you can explain the way you kissed me when I took you to the airport. We hadn't been near each other in months and, with a few hundred people looking on and you full of grief for your grandmother, you parted your lips and kissed me with all the urgency of a rushing river breaking a dam. You nearly ate me up. You'd missed me then, alright. So what's happened since?"

"Things aren't what they ought to be, Luke. I… I need a little space. I…"

"Do I mean anything to you beyond the fire I build in you? Do I?"

"Luke, you're asking a—"

"Tell me now or forget it. I'm not a top you can spin at will. *Do you* care?"

"Yes. *Yes!* Now, will you please leave me be." Her sobbing bruised his eardrums.

"Delia." The dial tone almost deafened him.

He stared first at the receiver and then at his five remaining quarters. Mr. Wilkins stood by the front door, ready to lock up. Luke shrugged, put the change in his pocket, told Wilkins good night and started back home, uncertain as to whether he'd won or lost. She cared, alright, but so what. Many strong men didn't have her fortitude; she could walk away from anything and sacrifice anything—except her ambition. With luck, they'd all be in bed when he got back to his parents' home and, right then, he wasn't sure he'd welcome the company of an angel. He stood on the porch, gazing at the moonlit night. He had a business that netted him over half a million dollars a year, loyal employees and a wonderful family. If he had the woman he loved, he'd be sitting on top of the world.

Luke let out a deep breath. Three days had passed, and Ellie hadn't been back in the store. He wouldn't say he wasn't tempted; she could be what he needed to cool his fever for Delia. Ellie Robinson's beauty rivaled that of some Hollywood queens, but her price was too high. He got home from his father's store as Irene and Nelson, his other siblings, arrived from their local choral club practice.

Patsy came in from the back porch with a bunch of purple bearded irises. "You children come on back in the kitchen. I made pecan brownies, and you can have some sassafras tea." She sat with them, her pride in her children obvious.

"How's college life?" Luke asked Irene, who was a sophomore and commuted daily to North Carolina Central in Durham.

"Great."

His head snapped around. Since when did long-winded Irene give an answer of that brevity. "If there's a problem, Irene, you should tell me. You know I'm committed to seeing you through for as long as you want to go."

"I… Uh… I'm going to study voice."

"No problem, so long as you get your degree first.

Her long sigh alerted him to expect the unwanted. "Luke, I'm in the school of music, and my teachers say it's time for me to start voice lessons. I have to do what my advisory teacher tells

me."

"*You're in the school of music?* I thought you went there for elementary education."

"I did, but my tests showed I didn't have an aptitude for that, so I went for what I really wanted. I never wanted to teach, anyway."

"_Deja vu._ What else is going on here that I don't know about?" His mother's neutral expression told him he'd get no help from her.

"What about you, Nelson? Are you planning to walk to the moon?" If he sounded sarcastic, he didn't care. His three sisters had once huddled around him, drinking in his every word. That was then.

"Well?" he said to Nelson.

"I'm planning to be an engineer like you so we can go into business together. It's only four and a half years away. We could be partners."

At least his kid brother needed him. "We'd better talk about this, Nelson, so we're certain you know what you want."

"Dad, Luke says all I have do is make my grades; he'll do the rest," Nelson announced at dinner. "We're going to send applications to the ten top engineering schools. My straight As may get me into MIT."

"MIT is expensive," Rudolph told him. "Where's all this money coming from?"

"It's okay, Dad. Luke says he'll send me all the way through, even graduate school."

Rudolph locked his gaze on his eldest child. "You've done well, Son, and I'm proud of you. You've succeeded beyond our dreams. But you worked hard for it, and it means something to you. I still remember how you struggled to get to college and how hard you worked to stay there. I used to worry about you delivering papers five o'clock in the mornings in zero temperature before going to school, running errands for people and taking anything they'd give you. Pennies. You chopped wood. You shoveled snow until I feared you'd lose your fingers from the cold, and you must have gathered a ton of pecans for people. Your mother and I couldn't believe you picked a hundred and twenty quarts of strawberries one day, and you hadn't gotten to your fourteenth birthday. Luke, Son, you appreciate what you've accomplished, because you worked hard and studied hard. You earned it. Give Nelson a chance to be as much of a man as you are. You can help him with books, transportation, things like that, but I don't want you to do it all for him."

Luke ran his fingers over his tight curls. Frustrated. He wasn't in the habit of arguing with his father. "But Dad, why shouldn't he have it easier than I did? You don't have a guarantee that my helping him will spoil him."

"I didn't say you couldn't assist him some. We'll lay down the rules, and you'll stick with them. Help him choose the courses he needs. Tell him what to expect, and how to handle problems. That's help he needs."

"But if he needs financial help?"

"If he knows there isn't any, he's less likely to need it, and that's my position."

Luke didn't pretend he couldn't see his father's point; he preached that philosophy to the boys he counselled at the youth center. He stayed with his mother after dinner, helped her clear away the remains of dinner and washed the dishes.

"Did you and Della break up, Son?"

"Mama, Della and I have been on a seesaw for months, almost from the time we met. We can't seem to get it together."

"That's strange. I've never been around two people who were more strongly attracted to each other."

"The chemistry's strong, so much so that it rules out anyone else. But physical attraction alone won't suffice for the long haul, Mama. We have plenty in common, but... heck, I don't know what the problem is. I... We can't get together and we don't stay apart. It beats me." He threw up his hands, kissed his mother on me cheek, and started to walk out of the kitchen.

"What about Ellie? She called here just before you got home."

Both of his eyebrows shot up. "Did she say what she wanted?"

"No, but I expect she wants you."

"I thought about that, Mama, but I'm pretty certain she's wasting her time."

"Della?"

"Della." He left the kitchen and went to find his father. "When's Dolores coming home? It's strange her not being here, but I suppose when she gets married, things won't be the same anyway."

Rudolph leaned back in his chair. "She said she'd be here Saturday afternoon, but Dan won't make it this time."

Luke jerked forward. "You telling me they're living together?"

Rudolph waved a hand, as though the subject was of no import. "No, I'm not telling you that, because I don't know that. And if I did know it, I wouldn't consider it worth mentioning. Dolores is twenty-five and engaged to Dan. Period."

"Touché. I stand corrected. How do you handle watching us make our own way without going berserk, Dad?"

He loved the sound of his father's deep, rolling laughter. "Who told you I handle it? Your mother and I did our best when you were under our control; you know what's right. No point in worrying now."

Luke wished he'd inherited his father's brand of equanimity; Dolores put him to the test the minute she got home.

"What would you like for a wedding present?" he asked her.

"I don't know, Luke. It's up to you?"

"But what do you need?"

She shrugged, almost as though unconcerned. "Surprise me."

"Okay. I will. I hope you and Dan plan to live somewhere near Mom and Dad. They're getting older, and having you nearby would be a comfort." She didn't respond. They'd once been so close, but... well, he supposed it was to be expected that she'd take her fiance's advice. Maybe their mother could talk to Dolores.

"Mom, I hope Dolores and Dan are going to settle somewhere near here, " he said, when he was alone with her. "Irene and Nelson will be off at school, and you and Dad will be by yourselves."

"Oh, that's not necessary, Son. Anyway, they're planning to live near Dan's mother. She's recently widowed, you know."

He walked around to stand beside her at the stove. "Doesn't she have other children?"

Patsy turned to face him. "Maybe. But so do I."

Luke sat on the woodpile, gazing absentmindedly at the green logs he'd sawed and stacked for the family's winter use, unable to banish the feeling that his brother and sisters no longer needed him, that his life had changed when he hadn't been looking. He needed to put his house in order. Delia didn't know who he was, and he still wasn't comfortable telling her. He didn't want her to love him and accept him for what he'd accomplished and what he had, but for himself. He suspected she needed status, and he could give her that, but he wouldn't offer it until she confessed to love him and was willing to share her life with him.

CHAPTER 11

Della fidgeted. Restless. Why had he telephoned her and pressured her into telling him she cared? He hadn't needed her words. She grabbed the report she'd been editing and tossed it across her living room. She hated it. Hated her work, her career, everything that stood between her and Luke. She dragged herself to the corner and retrieved the scattered papers. She had to go on with her life. She started toward the ringing phone, turned and went back to her desk. Let it ring; it wasn't Luke calling. She heard Craig's voice on the answering machine, and her immediate reaction was to dash toward it. But she stopped: that was something else she had to deal with—the lie she had lived when she allowed Craig to touch her. Maybe if she leveled with him, she'd feel closer to him. She couldn't remember having been so indecisive and unsettled.

Maybe what she needed was a good workout with the girls at the youth center. If she hurried, she'd have at least an hour with them.

When she got to the center, Marine sat at the counsellor's desk smoking and didn't stop when Delia walked in.

"Marine, you know that's against the rules." Delia didn't have to be told that every girl present had stopped whatever she'd been doing to watch them.

"So are a lot of things." She blew a series of smoke rings.

"Marine, either stop it or leave." She hadn't expected a fight, but Marine advanced toward her, and the other girls crowded around to watch.

"Think before you act," she warned Marine. "You're to leave this building at once, and don't think I won't defend myself if you get foolish enough to lay a finger on me."

"Don't be a fool, Marine," Jennifer cautioned. "You'll get beat up, and then they'll kick you out of school."

"And who'll beat me up?" the girl asked.

A voice from the back of the crowd announced, "If Miss Murray can't manage it, we'll do it for her." Delia glanced at the girl who had never said a word to her. Marine glared at Delia for long minutes before tossing her head like a thoroughbred in the winner's circle and strolling out. Delia didn't know she'd been perspiring until Jennifer handed her a tissue.

"Thanks. I'd thought we could discuss our excursions today, but I'll wait until we have more time. How about Wednesday night?"

They all nodded assent, seeming to look upon her with a new respect.

"I sure would've loved to see you give it to Marine, Ms. Murray. She so tough, and she's mean, too," Jennifer said in an attempt to console Delia.

"I wouldn't have enjoyed it," Delia corrected. "Ladies don't brawl. See you all Wednesday."

She hailed a taxi on the corner from the school, and slumped into the back seat. Drained. Shaken. She hadn't known whether Marine carried a knife, but she suspected it. If she'd had a fight with a student, that would have been the end of her chances for the SCAG post; she could even have gotten fired.

When Craig called later that evening and wanted to see her, she agreed without hesitation. Thinking it over before he arrived, she could only attribute her eager response to her unraveling experience at the youth center and a need to be grounded in the familiar. Anxiety threatened to unsettle her, and she knew she was uneasy because she hadn't come to terms with her feelings for Luke. Yet she didn't want to scuttle what might be her one chance at the life for which she yearned: comfortable living with a husband and children.

Tension gripped her when the doorbell rang, and she tried to shake it off, but when she opened the door, she saw that Craig wasn't his usual impervious self. Her anxiety intensified as they faced each other, not speaking, until he suddenly opened his arms and enveloped her.

"You're looking at a needy man, Delia."

"What's the matter?" He needn't have told her that he was out of sorts; she sensed it in his subdued demeanor.

"I don't know. Everything. Mostly I… You… Della, I need you."

He'd never used those words to her. Want had been the extent of his interest. She looked at him, appraising him. Was he offering more? And if he was, what would be her response?

"You looked peaked," she bluffed. "Let me get you a drink of… what would you like?"

He spread his arms out on the back of the sofa, leaned back and stretched out his legs. "Scotch whiskey and soda." She spun around, and he couldn't miss what she knew was a shocked expression. Craig never drank.

"You sure?".

"As I am of my name."

She brought his drink and a glass of wine for herself and sat across from him.

He patted the place beside him. "Sit over here with me."

She moved over, but she couldn't understand her attitude, her reticence, the clutch of what seemed like cold thongs around her heart. He took her hand, turned it over and looked at it.

"My sister used to read palms for sport." He folded her left palm until her thumb touched the base of her little finger. "Sensuous. A dazzling lover." He looked into her eyes when he said it, but guarded his expression. "A daughter of Venus and a disciple of Aphrodite. A man's woman." He glanced up, stared into her eyes and tremors raced through her. Not of passion, but of nervousness. Did he know?

He sipped the liquid, taking his time, savoring the last drop, and she could only await his move. What would he ask of her? Still holding her hand, he stood.

"That drink didn't put out the fire, Della; only you can do that." His heavy sigh sent tremors roaring through her. "But I doubt it'll be that easy. I need you something terrible." She followed him to her bedroom, wondering whether she had died inside. He closed the door and within seconds, his hungry, tortured kiss told her that he hadn't overstated his need, that whether or not he said the words, he was after more than her body. His fingers gripped the zipper of her dress, but her right hand shot over her shoulder and clamped down on his flesh.

He stepped back. "What is it? Are you having... is there some reason?"

She shook her head. "It's just me, Craig. I shouldn't have let things go so far. I...I can't."

He straightened up, and didn't attempt to shield his face, ; though pain clouded his fine features. "What do you mean?"

"I can't do it. I... I have to terminate our relationship, Craig. I'm sorry I let it get this far, tonight, but I didn't know my feelings until this minute. I... I hope you'll forgive me."

He shoved his hands into his pants pockets and started back to • the living room. She couldn't believe it when he took a seat.

"Who is he? There is a he, isn't there?"

She nodded.

"All this time there was someone else, wasn't there?"

She couldn't speak. So she inclined her head.

"I'm waiting."]

At last she managed to say, "I wanted to make it with you Craig, and I tried. Perhaps harder than I should have. But Providence evidently has its own agenda. I'm sorry."

He raked the back of his fingers through his hair, and draped his right foot over his left knee. "I've weathered a few hurricanes in my life, Delia, but not one of this magnitude. Why did you wait until you knew you had me at your mercy to tell me to go packing?" A laugh, rough and ugly tumbled out of him. "This is a first. I've always been the one who checked out. Never looking back. I wanted you as soon as I met you, but I hadn't planned to invest any of myself in a relationship with you. Somewhere along, that changed, and I suspect you were aware of it." He got up and walked toward the door. "It doesn't feel too good, Della, but it isn't going to kill me. If we're together again, you'll make the call." He ran his thumb down the side of her face, let it linger on her jaw, turned the door knob and walked out.

Delia told herself not to think about the implications of that parting gesture, but it nagged her. With her, at least, he'd lost the streak of callousness that had concerned her in the early days of their friendship. She sat in the darkened room battling the truth: she and Craig had much in common. He'd wanted to use her, and he'd managed that to an extent, as least in respect to the Nairobi conference. But he'd fallen for her. If she'd been more experienced, she would have recognized it in his changed behavior when he began to court her. She'd bet he'd rather have fallen for a woman of higher status, one who could help him reach his goals.

And what had she done? She'd led him to believe she cared, that she enjoyed their one coming together in the hope that he'd propose marriage and guarantee her the life she'd always wanted. And she'd done this knowing that her heart lay elsewhere. What she wouldn't give if she could take back every one of the few minutes spent in his arms.

She didn't need a man to take care of her, and motherhood didn't depend on having a husband, but she wanted her children to enjoy the love and guidance of a father, one who could support them while she nurtured them. That meant finding an eligible man and marrying him. And from her experiences, eligible included financial security. For the nth time, she made up her mind to get over her driving need for Luke.

She began her working day the next morning with a trip to the bulletin board maintained by the Volunteer Services—a group of volunteers who planned recreational activities for the UN staff— to collect free tickets or discount coupons so that she could plan some outings for the NIA girls. The day crept along until she was at last sitting on the floor in the youth center with the girls huddled around. She offered the New York City Opera, the Stuttgart Ballet; a Mostly Mozart concert and a trip to the Brooklyn Museum.

She rocked back on her heels, unsteady, when it appeared that the girls were near revolt. Even Jennifer censored her. "Why can't we go to a basketball game, or a Central Park concert this summer? Even something in the jazz festival. Ms. Murray, all this high class stuff is for show, and what good will it do us to go once? We won't be able to afford it ourselves."

"Alright. Alright. Since nobody seems enthusiastic, we'll try something else."

As she left, Jennifer stopped her and placed a tentative hand on her arm. "Don't be disappointed, Ms. Murray. You would have been there all by yourself with that handful of tickets. You have to get suggestions from the girls, and let us decide what we want. You can veto anything that doesn't meet your approval. I know you want us to be like you, and I wish I was like you, but some of the others don't. Why don't you get some tickets to a fashion show or a *hair* styling show so we'll learn how to look good?"

"Oh, Jennifer, I don't know what I'd do without you. I'm a little hurt, but I suppose you're right." She hugged the girl, whose eyes widened in surprise before she returned the embrace.

"You'll do okay, Miss M; you just need a little seasoning," Jennifer said and dashed off in obvious embarrassment.

Pinski met her in the lobby of her apartment building, grinned at her and bowed from the waist. Startled, Delia asked the doorman, "Did you see that?"

"Yes, ma'am. He seems very outgoing today, but he still doesn't say anything."

"Has he been grinning at everybody?"

"Not that I saw, ma'am."

She hoped Pinski wasn't getting unhinged. From just looking to grinning and bowing was a big step, and she hoped he'd reached his limit of communication, at least with her.

The next morning at work, she asked Erin's views on the lecture she'd gotten from Jennifer. "Ms. Murray," Erin replied, "you're dealing with girls who may not know what an opera is. You want them to learn uplifting things, but maybe you'll have to start with what interests them. After they learn to trust you and like you, they'll probably do anything you ask them to do. I think Jennifer's right. Unless kids know you care about them, they won't cooperate with you. And Ms. Murray, you're a formidable figure. Trust me. I love you 'cause I know you're super; they don't know that."

Back to square one. Maybe she should have stayed with her idea of taking the girls to the circus. Luke would have some ideas. Luke. She couldn't let herself think about him or she wouldn't get anything done.

Erin stuck her head in the door. "Your sister's on line two."

Apprehension gripped her, and she steeled herself for bad news; Bitsy rarely called. "Ludell, I was thinking I could spend weekend after next with you in New York. Mama said she wouldn't mind if I went."

Della stood and paced around her desk. "Bitsy, honey, that won't do; I have some plans that I don't want to cancel. We can arrange this for another time, but give me a little more notice."

"You never want me to visit you," Bitsy said, her voice rising in uncontrolled hysteria. "Every time I ask you, you got something else to do."

"It isn't because I don't want you to come see me, Bitsy, but weekend after next is a bad time. That's all."

"That's what you always say," was the sharp retort before the dial tone struck her ear.

"Come in," she called, absentmindedly, her thoughts lingering on Bitsy's sharp words.

The sound of keys and tools clanking brought her head sharply around, and she grabbed her chest to still her dancing heart. *"Luke!"*

He advanced toward her. Slowly. Rhythmically. Seductively. "Hello, Delia."

"Hi. When did you get back?" What did it matter? She didn't care when he got back; all she wanted was the warmth of his arms. "This is some surprise."

"Did you miss me?" He didn't smile, and she couldn't read his face.

"I'm glad to see you, Luke."

"Still playing games, I see." He walked as close to her as propriety would allow, since they were in her office. "You're kinda down. What's the matter?"

She shrugged. "My sixteen-year-old sister wants to visit me weekend after next, but that's the date I've set aside for the NIA girls' outing."

A frown clouded his face as though he disapproved of what he'd heard. "I'd have thought that would be the perfect time for her visit. You could take her out with the NIA girls. They told me last night after you left there to suggest a basketball game."

"You were at the youth center last night?"

"A couple a minutes after you left. I went there directly from the airport."

"I missed you, Delia, and I'd like to see you tonight. How about dinner?"

She was tired of cheating herself, of pushing him away when what she wanted more than anything was his nearness. "Okay."

His left eyebrow quirked. "Okay? That means I come to your place at around seven and get you?"

"Alright." Hot particles seemed to flit through her blood stream as his gaze burned her. "Seven is fine," she added.

Della brushed her hair down around her shoulders, lathered her body with Opium perfumed skin creme, clipped a pair of pearls to her ears and dressed in red silk from her skin to her dazzling dinner suit. She dabbed Opium perfume in strategic places, picked up her black patent bag and thought better of it. She trusted Luke. She took out her door keys, and when he arrived, handed them to him.

He stared wordlessly for what seemed like minutes, a look of disbelief shadowing his face. "What's this, Delia?"

"If you carry them for me, I won't be burdened with a pocketbook."

He looked first at her and then at the keys, before a rueful grin claimed his face. "For a minute there, I thought you might have decided to get down to business." He winked. "Hold it a second while I float back down to earth."

"Cut out the melodrama. I figured my keys are safe with you."

"Did you, now? You wouldn't trust a destitute man to hold a million bucks for you while you went on vacation, would you?"

"You're not destitute."

Just as she'd begun to luxuriate in the laughter that flowed out of him, his face settled into bleakness. "I'm human, Delia. I'll do my best not to let you down, but I've got limits."

She didn't want to begin their evening in a solemn atmosphere, though she didn't know how she wanted it to go or what she hoped would come of it. As he locked the door, her only thought was that, at its end, he'd take her in his arms. She itched for the feel of him.

Luke laughed. "Straighten out your mind, Della." He threw her keys up and caught them. "Unless you want me to open that door, take you back in that apartment, and let my senses have their way."

She had to remember that Luke read her as though she were an open book. There was comfort in that but, at times, it annoyed her.

She let the comment pass. "Where're we going?"

"If you like Italian food, and I hope you do, there's a wonderful cozy little restaurant in Little Italy. How about it?"

"I'd love it." She could see that her enthusiastic reply pleased him.

Luke gazed at the woman who sat across from him. Elegant and lovely, at home in the softly romantic ambiance. For so long, he'd wanted to be there with her, uplifted by the calming beauty of the place. He ordered white wine, which she preferred, and studied his menu.

Della ordered marinated wild mushrooms for a starter followed by veal scaloppini with tiny new potatoes and a green salad. Her antenna stretched when Luke gave his order.

"Prendo, prosciutto di parma con melone, e come secondo, saltimbocco con riso. Grazie."

"Prego, Signore" the waiter replied.

"Where 'd you learn to speak Italian?"

"Bumming around Italy." If she didn't judge him on it and find him wanting, it would be a first.

""Bumming around. Care to explain that?" she asked.

"Doing my usual, right?"

He suspected she caught the injury, the pain that had to be mirrored in his eyes. If only she could see beyond her narrow vision of him as a repairman. If she'd give him the smallest indication that she didn't care about his status, or that she was willing to overlook what she thought it to be, he'd open up to her. He longed for her to know him as he was.

Neither her words nor the soft, caressing tenor of her voice were what he'd expected to hear. "Luke, you're an enigma. What were you doing bumming around Italy and when did you do this? That's a direct question. It's not an innuendo, and nothing unkind is intended."

He sipped his wine and looked deeply into her eyes. "I never know with you. I thought once that I wanted to be an architect. Schooling is far less expensive in Italy, and their graduate faculties have a good reputation. I worked my way over there on a freighter one summer and got to see several master builders working in different parts of the country. Since they didn't speak English, I studied Italian and found I had an aptitude for it. I also discovered that what I wanted to build wasn't buildings but machines and appliances. After a year of apprenticeship with several builders, I decided to quit wasting time and came back home."

"You just gave up your dream? Just like that?"

"Della, before you get judgmental, remember I found myself. A year out of a young person's life is nothing compared to the value of knowing who you are when you're still young enough to take full advantage of that knowledge."

"What *did* you do with it?"

He wasn't going to tell all, because she still wasn't ready for it.

"I've been able to send three of my siblings to college and to plan for my younger brother's university schooling."

A sadness pervaded him, and he paused, questioning the wisdom of going further. "They've always looked up to me as their big brother, and our parents have always seemed proud of me for what I've been able to give my sisters and my brother. But during this last visit, everything seemed to fall apart. It's as though I've done too much, or I'm attempting to control their lives. I don't think they mean it, but that's how it seems to me right now. I know I can be tenacious, but I hadn't thought I forced them to do anything."

His pain seared her heart, and she wrestled with her desire to hold him, to comfort him, when she knew he needed the truth. She didn't want him to see her remark as disloyalty, so she spoke softly and rested her hand on his wrist. "You mean Dolores's wedding plans? Luke, she was right in asking you to give way to your father."

She released a sigh of relief when he turned his palm over and took hold of her hand. "I know, but it's more than that and more than Dolores. Look, that's a topic I don't need right now, and anyway, this probably doesn't mean much to you. I don't suppose your folks need your help."

She should have known he'd get around to digging into her. She wouldn't lie, but she couldn't open up. She just couldn't. She eased her hand from his, because she knew her fingers would shake and betray to him her nervousness. "I'm the oldest. My older brother's working, and the younger one's in junior high. My sister's in her third year of high school."

"They're a lot younger than you."

He was getting too close. He didn't have to know about little Morris, the other child her parents had lost or her mother's miscarriages. "I'm two years older than my brother, Mark, and there are two years between Matthew and Bitsy."

"We're both the oldest child in our family. How interesting. The oldest is supposed to be self-centered. Are you?" he asked, and she hoped he'd lose his train of investigation.

"In some respects, but you'll have to figure that out yourself. The dinner was wonderful, and I don't know when I've enjoyed a restaurant so much."

He seemed to concentrate on her, measuring her. Saying nothing. She observed the inherent strength of his face, marveled at his eyes intent upon her. Eyes that could mesmerize her. She leaned back in her chair and let him look. What else could she do? He'd speak when he got ready. His gaze roamed over her. Searching. Appraising. Excitement swished through her body and she grasped her shoulders as though to contain the wildness that leaped in her when his eyes darkened and he swallowed heavily.

"You've enjoyed this time with me," he said at last. "Even my questions that you didn't answer? Is that what you're telling me when you say you enjoyed the dinner and the restaurant? And you'll have dinner with me again, or we can just be together enjoying each other's company?"

Her uneasiness returned, because she knew he wouldn't consider half a loaf, that he'd settle for nothing less than her whole self. "Luke, you traveled pretty far in that sentence. I have to take my time here. You're asking me whether I'm willing to turn a corner with you. I don't know, Luke. Can't we just... just see what happens?"

He leaned forward and something akin to anger glittered in his eyes. "You want to string me along, or what? You know you want to be with me, but you can't make up your mind to accept me. Are you willing to give us a chance, or not?"

"You're not giving me a choice. Try using a softer glove."

He laughed. "Sweetheart, that's all I've used with you. Eat your *gelato,* and let's go. I think I'd better show you what strong arming means."

"It's delicious. Don't you want a little bit?" She offered him a spoonfull, and he grasped her wrist and held it while he savored the ice cream, his gaze boring into her.

He rimmed his lips with his tongue. "The thought of my strong arming you doesn't seem to have made much of an impression."

She couldn't help grinning. "Luke, once it's been established that a man is honorable, nobody will pay attention if he pretends to be debased. Besides, I've never experienced strong-arming; with you, it could be… who knows?"

He threw up his hands. "I've ruined my reputation. I can't even act ugly." He paid the bill with his gold MasterCard and hoped she didn't notice. Taking her hand, he growled, "Come on, woman. You're about to atone for your sins." She couldn't have held back the giggles if her life had depended on it.

He took her hand as they walked along Thompson street, where senior citizens sipped espresso coffee and chatted in the outdoor cafes in an air perfumed with the mingled odors of ripening cheeses, garlic and baking bread.

Luke stopped at a lamp post. "Look up, Delia. What do you see?"

She followed his gaze skyward. "Moon, stars, a white cloud here and there. Why?'

His smile nearly brought her from her feet and into his arms. "I want to ride through Central Park in a Hansom. I've wanted to do that for years. Have you ever done that?"

She gazed into his eyes, conscious that he was locking her to him as surely as a welder forged steel. She thought of her longing for a life free of money problems, of her desire for children and the pleasure of being at home with them until they went to school and tried to back off. But his pull, his lure, was too strong to resist.

"No, but it sounds wonderful."

His smile enveloped his face, and new life seemed to pulsate in him. "Great. Come with me."

The star-spangled night had brought many tourists to the Fifty-ninth street Plaza but, after a short wait, they got a Hansom cab. The softly haunting music *of Love Walked In* that flowed from the driver's radio and the rhythmic clickety-clack of the horse's hooves wove a dream-like spell, and she didn't resist, didn't want to resist when Luke put an arm around her and brought her close.

"When I was a boy, I'd stand at the edge of our back porch on nights like this and dream my life, my future. I had my own special stars; I knew the dogs far away by their howls; and I imagined friends among the white clouds. I'm the great grandson of a slave, Delia. I didn't start with much. Growing up, we had what we needed, but not much more. My father saved every penny he could for our schooling. For recreation, we gathered around our old piano and sang hymns and folk songs while mother played. I don't think that piano was ever tuned. Some Sunday afternoons in the summer, Dad would take us to the fair, if there was one, and we'd get a ride on the merry-go-round, some cotton candy, and if business had been good that week, a book.

"The next Sunday afternoon, one of us kids would be asked to read the book aloud. Then, we'd all talk about it, add some more to the story, change it around. We all enjoyed that. The love in our house was so thick, you could almost slice it. I missed them when I went away to school, and I still do. I talk with them all once a week and get to see them as often as I can. Nobody can tell me you need money in order to be happy. It helps, but it isn't essential. My youth was a time of joy."

He looked up at the sky that soothed him still and took a deep breath. "I suppose it was inevitable that those ties would loosen as we go our separate ways, live our lives as we need to. But I can't get used to the idea that my sisters don't need me and that their boy friends and, soon, husbands are more important to them. I know I don't make sense, but I'm not ready to give them up." He hadn't intended to open up to her as he had, but when she'd relaxed in his arms, it had poured out of him. The music changed to *The Days Of Wine And Roses,* and he felt her snuggle to him. He tipped her chin with his index finger and looked into her eyes.

"Kiss me?"

The tender expression in her eyes sent his stomach plummeting, and when she lifted her arms to his shoulders, he knew his lips trembled and that she could feel it when she parted her own and welcomed him. Passive. He'd never had a passive kiss from her. The sweetness of her surrender fired his desire and sharpened his need to possess her forever. He didn't want to respond to her tenderness with full arousal, but the sensation of her hand gently skimming his face and her open lips begging for more drove him to complete hardness. Perspiration dripped down his face, and he had to set her away from him.

"You know what you mean to me, Della. I've told you, and that hasn't changed. It will never change. When you're soft and sweet with me like this, I could tame a bronco, bare-backed. You and I are not going to leave each other alone, Delia, but if we don't resolve this, we'll spoil something beautiful. I never thought I was a masochist, but I'm beginning to wonder."

"I... I love being with you Luke; that's not a secret. My problem is that I don't know what to do about you. I know you may be losing patience with me, but you shouldn't, because I'm just beginning to sort out my life."

He saw that the Hansom had returned to the Plaza, helped her out and paid the driver. "You've taught me a lot about myself, Delia, not the least of which is an ability to persevere in the face of tough odds. Let's walk up to your place."

Absorbed as she was in Luke and all he'd told her, Delia nevertheless noticed that Pinski's newly acquired smile was not in evidence. A scowl covered his face. Thank goodness he didn't get on the elevator with them. Luke took out the key she'd given him earlier that evening and handed it to her. She wanted to give it back to him, but fear curled within her. Fear of crossing a line over which she knew she'd never return. *And what would be so bad about that?* her conscience needled. Luke hadn't had much during his youth, but he'd known a better life than she, and he hadn't experienced a tragedy that would eventually distance him from his family.

"What'll it be?" he asked, giving no hint as to what he'd like.

She opened the door without glancing his way and stepped inside, but he didn't move. "Want to come in for a minute?"

He leaned against the doorjamb and lifted his shoulder in a shrug. "For a minute?"

She swallowed hard, her gaze sweeping his healthy male form and settling on the spot where she fantasized most about him. Nothing could have kept her from him when his need became a pool of fire in his gaze, and the heat in him swirled around her.

"Delia. Hell, baby, you can't do this to me." Swept up in his arms, she clamped her legs around him, and he walked with her into the apartment and kicked the door closed. He let the wall take his weight, slid his hand inside her jacket and found her taut nipple as she parted her lips beneath his. Spiraling heat claimed her whole body, and she wanted to rip off her blouse and jacket and feel his mouth on her breast. He held her away from him and, frustrated, she tried to pull him to her.

He resisted. "I don't want to leave you. If you're going to send me packing, say so now. Do you want me? Tell me. Della, tell me."

She slid down to the floor and made herself look him in the eye. "Yes, Luke, I want you. You can't know how badly."

"But?"

"For tonight, at least, you'd better go. If we take the next step, there's no turning back. We both know that. I want to be sure, Luke."

She could almost touch his frustration, and she hurt for him, for them both. "If I didn't wear brogans to work, would making up your mind be as difficult?"

He needed the truth, but she couldn't share all of it. Perhaps she never would, but he deserved something. "Your brogans are not the problem, only a symptom of it. My past experiences beginning as far back as the tender age of eight are what's between us, Luke. I'm trying, but I have to be true to myself."

"Alright. You're not going to tell all, and I've known for sometime that you're lugging around a burden. When you finally share it with me, you'll be free of it. His kiss drugged her. "I'd better go."

She watched the door close. Could she be happy with him if he lost his job? If she lost hers? If they had three children and not enough food? She'd wanted desperately to make love with Luke, but she'd only recently broken off with Craig, and she couldn't easily move from one man to another. She had settled one thing, though. She couldn't marry Craig or any other man as long as Luke possessed her heart, her thoughts and dreams. As long as she loved him.

The next morning, Erin walked in Della's office bringing coffee. "Where'd that come from?" she asked, pointing to an empty cup. "You bringing your own these days?"

"A friend brought it," she hedged.

"I'd better get in here early and look this friend over," Erin joked. "You want this one?"

"I sure do." In an unusually personal revelation, she added, "I usually get two cups, but not this morning."

"What time of morning does this coffee usually walk in here?"

"Oh, around the time you're leaving home."

The girl's eyebrows shot up. "I'm not sure I'll get up at five o'clock just to be nosey, but don't dismiss the possibility."

"It's only coffee, my dear," Della told her.

"Oh, I know that," Erin shot back. "It's the messenger I'm interested in." When the phone rang, she picked up the receiver at Delia's desk. "Ms. Murray's office. May I help you? Yes, sir. She's right here." She passed it to Delia. "It's your father."

Della waited until Erin had left the room. "Hello, Papa. How's everybody?"

"We're doing as best we can. Seems awfully empty here without your grandmother."

"I know, Papa. I feel it, too. I guess it'll take tune before we get used to not having her."

"If we ever do. When can you come down to sign the papers for Mark. He said you're giving him what you inherited from her. I want us to straighten out these things, so come soon as you can. Remember, now. The county offices don't open on Saturdays."

"Would Friday be alright? I can get down there Thursday night or Friday before noon."

"That'll be just fine, Daughter. Just fine." He hung up, and she realized that he began calling her Daughter after she changed her name from Ludell to Delia.

She wasn't obligated to tell Luke her whereabouts, but she couldn't make herself leave town without his knowing where she'd gone. She telephoned Luke at home that evening and got his answering service. The phone rang at around ten, and in her dash to answer it, she skidded on the highly polished floor and had to grab the table for balance.

"Hello."-,

"This is Luke. How are you?"

"I'm... uh... okay."

"Why are you out of breath?"

She ignored his probe. "I wanted you to know that I'll be home in Pine Whispers this weekend. I haven't decided whether to leave Thursday night or early Friday morning. Just thought I'd tellyou."

She listened to the dead air for nearly a minute. "Thanks for letting me know. I... I'd like to take you to the airport."

"Thanks, but that isn't necessary."

"Delia, it's necessary. You hear me. It's absolutely necessary that you let me do things for you. Seeing that you get on the plane won't constitute an infringement of your independence. Can't you decide now when to leave?"

"Well... Friday morning. I hate driving two-lane highways at night."

"And you're right. I'll be at your place with a taxi at a quarter to seven if you're making the eight o'clock."

"I am, and thanks."

"It's my pleasure, Della."

"Well, th... thanks. I uh... good night."

"Woman," he growled, "why can't you tell me what you feel? If your walls ever come down, they'll make Jerico look like alphabet blocks. Sweetheart, confession is good for the soul. Don't trust my word. It's in the bible. Check it." His merriment reached her through the wires.

"What are you laughing at?"

"Laughing? Baby, those are tears you hear in my voice."

"Luke, stop making me feel guilty."

"What do you feel guilty about? Not telling me you love me? I have no sympathy for you, taking my heart and batting it around. But you just wait. My day will come."

"And what'll you do then?"

, "Sitting down? *Then,* I'll make love to you every way I can think of. Delia, I plan to love you 'til the hair stands up on your head and you're a live wire, a human ball of electricity. A living vortex of ecstasy. After that, you'll be able to write your own Kama Sutra. Woman, don't get me started on this topic."

When she could breathe again, she said in barely audible tones, "I asked a question, and you answered it."

His roar of laughter was what she needed after his recitation of what he had in store for her. "You're priceless. I'll see you Friday morning, Delia. Good night, Love." He hung up before she could respond, and she didn't mind for, though he was her love, she wouldn't have told him so.

Della had to struggle to keep her mind on the task before her as she drove the rented Taurus over thirty miles of monotonous highway from Wilmington, North Carolina, to Pine Whispers. Luke crowded her thoughts. His kiss at the airport had been brazen and possessive, teasing and titillating her senses from her scalp to the bottom of her feet. But he could stop the onslaught now, because he'd done his work well. All she could think of was how he made her feel. Even her work had less appeal than he, and she rarely remembered the AS-G post that she coveted.

She reached her parents' home at about eleven-thirty, and her father came out to meet her. "Your mother's at the grocery store," he said, after hugging her. Until her granny died, she hadn't thought much about what she meant to her family. *You've been so busy criticizing them,* her conscience reminded her. She drove Mark and her father to the County Court House where she signed papers transferring Ludell Jones Murray's property to Mark.

Mark got her alone, and she knew a reprimand was in the offing. "Why can't Bitsy spend a few weeks with you when her school term is over, Delia? There's nothing here for her to do except hang out with the questionable characters that live around here. In New York, she could at least go to a library and read, learn something. She could visit the UN, take a short course in computers; most anything would be better than sitting around here or meeting a bunch of kids down the road and doing I don't know what."

"I won't have time to supervise her, Mark, and letting her loose in New York could cause greater damage than anything likely to happen here. You can't imagine how men, even women, can prey upon naive girls. I couldn't let her out of my sight."

"Okay. But you're not fooling me. You'd have to get rid of her dreadlocks, straighten her hair, buy her a new wardrobe and teach her how to walk, sit, eat and breathe according to your standards. Where do you think *you* learned those things? Definitely not in New York!"

"Alright. As soon as I know whether I have to go overseas and for how long, I'll make some plans for her."

CHAPTER 12

Craig paced the floor of his office in the US Mission to the United Nations, ignoring the ringing phone. He ought to be in the clouds, because few men had his options. If it were only a matter of choosing between jobs, he wouldn't hesitate, but if he left the scene, he'd forfeit the small chance that Delia might walk away from that repairman and turn to him. He sensed that she didn't want to throw her lot with the other man, and that spelled bad news for him, because he suspected she'd fought her desire for his competition and lost. Still, she'd cared enough to be his lover—at least that once. His attention focused on the three sets of papers on his desk—*a* promotion to senior ambassador, an appointment that would take him to Europe and his resignation from the US Department Of State.

He stared at the picture of his grandfather, a Barbadian sugarcane cutter, a man who'd had no options, but who had loved his grandson above all else. If he'd had Martin Radcliff's sense of morality, maybe he'd have stood a better chance with Delia. But he'd gone through women, treating them as though they had no feelings, using them for his own purposes, never thinking he'd pay for it. Never dreaming he'd fall so deeply in love that he'd give anything to have that woman for his own, a woman who didn't respond to him, because she loved another man. A woman he'd take on any terms she posed. If anybody had told him three months earlier that he'd go head over heels for Delia Murray, he'd have laughed. He put the papers in his top desk drawer, locked it and headed across the street to the UN Secretariat

Building. He had to give it one more shot, had to know for certain that he didn't stand a chance with her. He only hoped he could rope in his pride long enough to make a case for himself.

Craig had never visited Della in her office, and Erin's announcement of his presence floored her. She watched, speechless, as he strode in and took a seat beside her desk without her having invited him to sit down. He studied her for seconds before speaking.

"You're looking very well," he said without the formality of a greeting. "Does this mean you've settled things with that guy?"

She turned fully to face him. His words had been delivered in a light, airy fashion that his somber expression belied. Guilt that she'd led him on surfaced within her and toyed with her conscience. She could only speak the truth.

"No, I haven't settled things with him, Craig, but I've settled them with myself."

"Meaning?"

"I didn't expect to have another personal conversation with you. I—"

Sheer agony streaked over his features before his face creased into a smile. "Delia, Love, there's no reason to be so serious. I only came because I wanted to know how things are with you. Whether you're happy with your job, that sort of thing. If you're aren't, or even if you are, how do you feel about transferring to the new International Institute For The Child?"

She jerked forward, pulling in her bottom lip lest its tremors betray her. "You're in a position to fill a senior post in IIFC? It was only chartered last week. How...?" His smile bordered on evil, and she knew. He'd come to make certain of his chances with her, but he wouldn't leave empty-handed; he'd have the pleasure of announcing his escalation to the top. Balm for his wounded ego.

"I've been elected Director-General of IIFC, Delia. It isn't a top post I'm offering you, more of an assistant to me, but since we worked together so well at the Nairobi Conference, you're the first person I thought of hiring."

He could appear to gloat, but he didn't fool her. He'd known she'd refuse his offer; he'd phrased it vaguely to make certain that she wouldn't take it. His pride wouldn't let him tell her what she meant to him, nor allow her to see his disappointment. Instead, he chose to try to humiliate her by offering her a job beneath her level. And to think of the lengths to which she'd gone to secure a permanent relationship with him.

She leaned back, resting her chair on its hind legs. "Craig, I don't know your reasons for offering me such a low-level job, but in doing so, you've succeeded in relieving me of the guilt I had about my association with you. I'm sure you'll tower over every other D-G in the UN system."

His glistening teeth against his smooth brown skin showed his pleasure at her remark. "Thanks. I just wanted you to know. Glad I have your good wishes."

Surely he hadn't missed the sarcasm of her words, but she could make it clearer. "Considering you're six-feet-four, towering over those elves is a snap."

She'd wasted her breath. His ego wouldn't allow him to be diminished. "You're a big tease, Delia." He stood, his face somber once more. "Hang in there, Love, and don't let anybody get on your blind side."

"Ms. Murray, Mr. McKnight is here," Erin announced over the intercom. "Should I ask him to wait?"

"Please," she replied to her secretary, glad to put Craig on the back burner of her life. "I wish you the best," she told him.

"Please excuse me. I have an appointment."

Craig eyed Luke as they passed each other in Delia's office doorway. She had attempted to belittle him, but he wouldn't let her see his pain. He had it coming, but he'd take his medicine and get on with his life. A repairman. Only weeks earlier, he would have asked himself what a woman in Delia's position would want with a repairman, but now he knew. If that person lived in your blood, occupied your every waking thought and troubled your dreams, you didn't care what she did or where she did it. He'd thought he wanted a woman of wealth and status, an aristocratic anchor for his working-class heritage, not someone of Delia's ilk whose ambition constantly betrayed her origins. Until he'd fallen in love. And he'd fallen hard. He had to rethink his priorities and straighten out his values, but

nothing he did now would put Delia in his bed every night
for the rest of his life. At the US Mission, he signed both
his resignation from the State Department and the papers
that gave him the title of Director-General.

Luke didn't pause until he was inches from where she
stood enveloped in fury at Craig's brazen announcement.
Although she'd worked hard for that conference, he'd
reaped all the benefits and hadn't had the decency to say so
or to apologize.

"You got something going with that guy?" Luke asked,
bringing her back to the present. "This must be the third
time I've asked you this. What is he to you?"

Della didn't want to discuss Craig. As it was, tears over
her folly in attempting to maneuver him into her life while
her heart remained elsewhere, threatened to spill down her
cheeks.

"Well?"

She pasted a smile on her face. "We worked together on
a conference. There's nothing personal between us.
Nothing at all." She didn't mention the relief that the truth
of her statement gave her.

"You broke up with him?"

"What? You're saying there was something between us?"

He threw his baseball cap up and caught it without
removing his gaze from her face. "I don't suppose I have a
right to ask such questions," he said, and she breathed
deeply. Relieved.

"I'm taking my boys to a hockey game tonight. Could you come with us?"

"Hockey's so rough. Somebody's always getting half-killed."

His grin sparkled against his dark skin and brought lights to his eyes, dazzling her. "I know you're scared of anything that gets the least bit turbulent or threatening, but not to worry, I'll keep those big guys out of your lap."

Her right hand went to her hip, but she quickly removed it, "Did I ask you to keep anybody out of my lap?"

He ran his hand over his hair and rubbed his nose. "Some of those guys weigh a good two hundred pounds, but—"

"But so do you. I'll ask for your help when I need it."

He bunched his right shoulder and lifted it carelessly. "Well, that's something. You going?" She nodded. "Okay. I'll pick you up at six."

"See you at six."

That grin again. "You don't get rid of me so easily. Want me to kiss you now… or later?"

She looked at the blatant sensuality that faced her in the person of Luke McKnight and licked her lips. "Now."

"Della."

In a half daze, she let her gaze travel from his brogans to his eyes, lifted her shoulders and advised him, "But I can wait if you can." She watched, fascinated, as his left hand curved itself into a tightly-balled fist, and glanced up to see his pupils dilate. She didn't deliberately rim her bottom lip with her tongue, because he was already on fire, and they were both in her office. When her gaze went to his muscled thigh and started upward, she had to force it not to linger at his center of male power. Air hot and heavy crackled between them, and his narrowed eyes and accelerated breathing told her she'd better calm the charged atmosphere.

Her search for something clever to say proved futile. So she told him, "You'd better get to work, otherwise you might get fired for... uh .... fooling around on the job."

His hand shot out toward her, but he pulled it back before touching her. "Witch. You may find you have more to lose than I have, Delia. Close your door and lock it, and I'll show you how scared I am of losing my job."

"I never thought you were reckless."

"I don't take foolish dares, Delia, but I'd risk a lot to get you where I want you right now."

She sucked her bottom lip. "I'm not going to win this one, am His fingers warmed her cheek in a gentle caress. "I don't think you want to. See you at six."

He was through playing cat and mouse with Delia; if she didn't know what she wanted, by damn, he'd show her. She could start a fire faster than any woman he'd met without any thought as to how or, for that matter, *whether* she'd put it out. "The bell tolls for thee, baby," he heard himself mutter. He checked his appointment list, crossed off the two basement jobs and phoned Bill.

"Get a roller for that color copier in 18-3B, and order some ink for those two laser printers in 111-3B." He called the head of the printing section and moved the appointment for repairs up a week. Inconvenient, maybe, but somebody would get some much needed exercise using the copiers and printers on another floor. That gave him a couple of free hours. He went home, showered, dressed and picked up a van from Avis. He'd promised the boys at the center a special night, and he meant to see that they enjoyed it. A glance at his watch told him that he had to wait another hour and twenty minutes before he'd see her. A whole lifetime.

Della finished dressing and got the day's *New York Times* to pass away the time while waiting for Luke. A warm feeling settled over her as she anticipated the moment when he'd walk into her door and she'd be in his arms. Six-thirty. No point in being alarmed, though Luke was punctual to a fault. She recalled Craig's behavior that morning. He'd never admitted it, but he'd come to care deeply for her. In the beginning, she hadn't fitted into his future plans, just as Luke hadn't been what she'd wanted for herself, and she suspected that, like her, Craig had been after bigger game.

But fate had tricked them both, and Craig had fallen in love with her, as she had with Luke. Nothing else could account for the gentleness and sensitivity with which he'd courted her after his return from Europe. Still, she had it on good authority that he didn't support her application for the AS-G post as head of SCAG, obviously out of concern for the damage he might do to his own chances for promotion. And yet, he must have realized she'd need her government's backing. And that morning, when he'd satisfied himself that he had no chance with her, he had covered his hurt, reverting to the old cunning Craig, and had sought to humiliate her with an offer of a post below her rank. He'd gloated about his promotion to the second highest level in the international community, using it to protect his ego; only the UN Secretary-General out-ranked a Director-General. His vaunting had stung her; she had paid a high price for her affair with him.

At seven o'clock, she turned on the television for company, turned it off and paced the floor. Eight o'clock arrived and she could no longer contain her anxiety. The hockey game had already begun. Her fears turned to anger, and she called down to her doorman.

"If Luke McKnight comes here for me, tell him that I am not to be disturbed."

"But Miss Murray, Mr. McKnight went up to your apartment two hours ago. I didn't buzz you, because you told me you were expecting him. He has to be in the building, because I haven't moved from this door since he came in."

"You can't be serious. I haven't seen him. He never came to my door."

"All right, Miss Murray, don't worry and stay in your apartment. I'll have the building searched."

Fear curdled her blood when she heard the knock on her door; Luke usually rang the bell. "Who is it?"

"Police, Ms. Murray. We'd like to speak with you." Tension gripped her as she opened the peep hole, saw the uniforms and opened the door. "What is it? What's the matter?"

"I'm Officer Collins, and this is Officer Montgomery. Mind if we step inside, ma'am? We've sent Luke McKnight to the hospital. Steady there," he said, when she gasped and clutched her chest. "Seems he'd been hit on the back of the head with a heavy object. Knocked him unconscious."

Della grabbed the officer's shoulders as though to shake him. "I don't believe you. Where's he? Is he alright?"

"I'm sorry ma'am, but I have to get some information from you, so would you please—"

"I'm not telling you anything 'til you tell me how he is. Talk to me. Is he… is he all… alright?"

"Get her some water, Monty," the officer told the other policeman. "He wasn't conscious when the ambulance left here. Where's your phone?"

She pointed to the nearest one. "In the kitchen beside the door."

He used the phone, walked back to her and took the empty glass from her hand. "Your name Della?" she nodded. "He's conscious and asking for you, but he took a dangerous blow to his head."

"Will he need an operation?"

"They didn't say. Be thankful he's conscious."

"Where'she?"

"St. Luke's."

"Thanks." She got up and started for her bedroom to get her pocketbook.

"Wait a minute. Where're you going, lady?"

"Where do you think? That man is my world. My whole life. So excuse me."

After looking steadily at her for seconds, the officer must have decided that if he wanted her cooperation, he had to accommodate her. "Alright. We'll run you over there, and you can talk on the way. To begin with, who in this house would have attempted to kill McKnight."

Breath hissed out of her. "Try to kill him? I... I don't know. Where was he?"

"In the stairwell.""

"That's strange. He wouldn't walk up to the eleventh floor. He always took the elevator."

"Yeah. Somebody slugged him and then dragged him in there."

She shrank from the sight of a policeman guarding Luke's room. Officer Collins' hand at her elbow was a reminder that she had to pull herself together, because Luke would sense her anxiety.

She recoiled from what she saw. Bandages swathed his head and a large knot protruded from its side. She hated seeing him helpless, and anger boiled up in her.

When she would have rushed to the bed, Collins restrained her. "He may not be awake, so don't be alarmed if he doesn't respond to you right away."

Ignoring the warning, she walked to the bed and grasped Luke's hand. "Luke. Darling, can you hear me? It's Della, Luke."

"Easy, now," she heard Collins say.

"Luke. Honey, talk to me."

Tears streamed down her cheeks when he opened his eyes. "Luke, it's me. Delia. Are you all right?"

He blinked and regarded her quizzically. "Della?" The happiest smile she'd ever seen sent her pulse racing. "Hey, baby." His head fell back on the pillow, and he moved it as though clearing away debris. "Something hit me? My head's killing me. The last thing I remember is getting on the elevator in your building. Any idea what happened?"

"Let me talk with him, Ms. Murray," Collins said, pulling up a chair. "Somebody hit you on the back of the head, Mr. McKnight, dragged you into the stairwell and left you there. Did anyone get on the elevator with you?"

Luke frowned, and she got an uncomfortable feeling, a sense of foreboding. Mtf *that,* she prayed.

His frown deepened, and anger flashed in his eyes. "That fellow, Pinski, followed me into the elevator and rode up with me, but I didn't think he got off when I did."

Collins stopped writing. "Who's Pinski?"

"A harmless guy who's always loitering in the lobby," Luke said.

"I didn't think he'd hurt anybody," Delia interjected, marveling that, even in a barely conscious state, Luke was able to wield sarcasm. "He never spoke, just looked. Well, recently, he grinned," she added.

Collins folded his notebook. "I'll probably be in touch with both of you again, but right now, I'm gonna have a talk with this Pinski fellow—if I can find him." As he left, he spoke with the guard on the door, but she couldn't understand their exchange.

"Are you comfortable?" she asked Luke.

"Except for this headache. Do you know what happened to my boys? They were waiting for me in the van."

"I haven't seen them or the van, so I guess the authorities took care of them."

"I'd ask you to make a couple of calls for me, but you'd have to drop my hand. You see my cellular phone anywhere?" She shook her head. He gave her a number and asked her to call Bill Levy when she left, and tell him what had happened. He didn't tell her who Bill Levy was to him, and she didn't ask. At eleven o'clock, a nurse told her she'd have to leave, and she stood over his bed looking down at him, trying to hide her anxiety.

"Why are you blinking your eyes?" she asked him.

"It's hard to focus. You leaving me?"

"The nurse said I have to."

"Sorry I didn't get to give you that kiss. I owe you one...."

He drifted off, and at her look of alarm, the nurse assured her, "He's tired and the medicine makes him drowsy. Come see him tomorrow."

Delia leaned over Luke, pressed a kiss to his lips and caressed his jaw. "I will."

The next morning, Friday, she phoned Erin, explained that she had an emergency and wouldn't be in. She was walking the corridor toward Luke's room when it occurred to her that she'd left her briefcase at home. Well, she didn't suppose she would have opened it anyway. Her shoulder lifted in a quick shrug. If her heart had begun to overrule her mind, she wasn't up to fighting it. She greeted the guard on duty at Luke's door and thought it strange that he didn't stop her. Luke sat up in bed with the aid of numerous pillows at his back and sides, and she walked directly to him and placed her lips against his as though she had the right, "Hi. Feeling better this morning?"

His lips moved beneath hers and clung when she would have broken away. He reached toward her. "I tried to convince myself that you'd been here. My head's better, but that's probably these pills they're feeding me. I told them I didn't want any more drugs, but there's some swelling up there." He pointed to his head. "The nurse said you kissed me last night. Did you?"

Della sat down, crossed her knees and took his hand in both of hers. "Sure did, and this morning, too."

"I thought I dreamed it. I told that guard I didn't want to see anybody but you and Bill?"

"Who's Bill?"

"One of my… uh… we work together."

A tall, familiar man of uncertain ethnicity and the build of a linebacker walked in wearing a somber look.

"Bill?"

He smiled at her and extended his hand. "Yes, ma'am. How are ya, Ms. Murray?" She stepped aside while the two spoke. It had to be her imagination that Luke gave Bill orders and that the man deferred to Luke. They talked amiably for a time, before Bill shook hands with Luke and left them. She noticed his limp and remembered that the man who had brought her coffee at Luke's behest had also limped.

"Luke, did you ask him to bring coffee for me one morning when you had to go to the Oldenhaus Building?"

"I might have. Yeah. I think Pinski's the one who bashed me in the head. What have the police found out?"

"Nothing yet. If he *is* the one who did that, I'll have to move, otherwise you won't come to see me any more."

He cocked an eyebrow, and seeing glimpses of his wicked self brought a smile to her face. "Shouldn't be a problem. I've got a fairly decent place, and it's reasonably spacious. You can bunk with me. Stay as long as you like." The color of his voice changed and she heard a Southern lilt that betrayed the depth of his feelings. "If you stayed forever, that wouldn't be long enough for me; I'd never be ready for you to leave me."

She could sense that special magnetism darting around them, tightening the tension between them. He was asking for something, but she had no answer, not until she knew she could accept whatever he offered. Yet, she loved him more with every passing second.

"Don't say anything Delia. Not one word. Nothing. Unless you're going to say you belong to me now and for as long as we both live."

"You don't know what you're asking, Luke, because I've never told you who I am, and I don't think I can right now."

"Is there a man any place on this planet who has a claim on you?"

She shook her head. "Only... No. There's no one."

His smile of pure male satisfaction sent rivulets of heat shooting through her veins. "No one, huh? Wait'lll get back on my feet; we'll settle that once and for all."

Her surprise at his brazen, confident remark sent words dripping from her tongue that she'd as soon had remained unsaid. "Fine with me. Nobody hates uncertainty more than I.."

His eyes darkened in spite of his obvious discomfort. "You're a trial, Della, but you're also at a crossroad, and I'm willing to make whatever effort it takes to see that you take the route that leads to me."

Collins' knock saved her an answer. "Glad to see you've improved this morning, Mr. McKnight." He looked toward Delia. "'Morning, Ms. Murray. This fellow Pinski admitted he landed that blow on your head with a metal bookend, Mr. McKnight.

Said he'd been saving it for months. Claims you were after his woman. Ms. Murray here."

Della jumped up. "What?"

"It's alright." he told her. "We know he's mentally deficient. You won't have to worry; his folks are sending him to some posh place in Arizona so he won't be tempted to go near you or your building." He turned to Luke. "That is, unless you want to press charges. His family is offering to pay the expense of your full recovery and any time lost at work."

Luke's hand went to his head as if to soothe a pain. "They can pay my medical bills, but that's all."

"Are you crazy?" Delia exploded. "Pinski's family is rich."

"That's my decision," he told the officer. "They can send him to Australia for all I care." She knew why he didn't look at her, that her interference hadn't set well with him. But she couldn't understand his cavalier attitude about money and success.

No sooner had the door closed behind Collins than Luke let her have the weight of his displeasure. Annoyed though she was, she felt herself squirming under the intensity of his stare. Not even when they had been at loggerheads in the early days of their association had he shown her a modicum of hostility. She should apologize for interfering, but she doubted anything so simple would soothe his ire.

"You're angry," she ventured after experiencing several minutes of his silence.

"I'm disappointed. If you want to make me over to suit you, Delia, forget what I said back there. I have no intention of putting myself in a position to be constantly harangued about how I run my life. I certainly wouldn't presume to tell you how to run yours."

She bristled as much at his testiness as at his words. "No?" she sputtered. "You have a short memory. This whole thing between us started with you telling me how to run my life, and every time I'm not running it the way you think I ought to, you dash right over and point me in the direction you think I should go."

"I haven't done any such—"

"You have so." She leaned toward the bed, shaking her finger at him. Good Lord. She was fighting with Luke while he lay in bed injured and with a killer headache. Had she lost her mind? He wouldn't think it funny, maybe, but laughter bubbled out of her. She must be losing it.

"Please let me in on this joke. I could use a good laugh."

"The joke's on me. You did meddle, and you were right every single time."

"Of course I was... You say I was right?"

She reached for his hand and folded it in hers. If she tried to explain her outburst, she'd only exacerbate an already touchy situation. "Luke, I'll always be grateful to you for my last visit with my Granny. I... I'll try to... to be less judgmental."

A tingling warmth spread through her when his wonderful eyes sparkled, and a smile began its slow journey over his face.

"You'll try, but let's be thankful that your life doesn't depend on your succeeding."

"You talk up a storm, because I can't lambast you while you're helpless in bed."

His white teeth sparkled against his dark skin. "Come on. You didn't have any trouble raising hell with me a minute ago."

"I forgot you were defenseless." She gazed at him sprawled out in the bed, and it occurred to her that until the night before, she'd never seen him lying down. Her tongue started to rim her top lip and, abruptly, she stopped it, her eyelids lowering in embarrassment.

He shifted his hips. Restless. And then the fierce want in his eyes changed to a mischievous sparkle. She wasn't surprised that he didn't spare her, but let the mirth roll out of him. When he could stop laughing, he told her, "You and I are going to have one damn good time one of these days."

She opened her mouth… and bit her tongue as the words, *hurry sundown,* nearly tumbled from her lips. She whirled around at the sound of a throat clearing.

A label on the white coat identified the intruder as a Dr. Morgan. "How's my patient?" he asked matter of factly.

"Ready to go home," Luke told him. "Except for this headache, I'm fine."

"Your headache is symptomatic of your condition. You've sustained a serious concussion, and you can't leave here until this internal swelling's gone. I want some tests sometime today, and as soon as the nurse gets here, we'll change these bandages."

Della didn't want to see that. "I'll run down and get a snack."

Abruptly, Luke sat up, supporting his head with his left hand. "You coming back? Are you?"

Della walked back to the bed and took his hand. "I won't leave without telling you."

The doctor looked from one to the other. "This heavy duty romantic stuff has been known to floor men who didn't have the added trauma of a concussion."

Della's gaze flew to the doctor's expressionless face. "You mean it's not good for him to… for me to…"

Laughter rumbled in the doctor's throat. "Whoa now. You're way ahead of me. I hadn't gotten past soulful eyes and clinging hands. Anything else will have to wait a while. And a pretty good while, at that." He glanced up at her and grinned.

When a hole failed to open in the floor, she glared at him, putting every ounce of venom she could in that stare.

"You're risking the brunt of a razor sharp tongue, Doctor," Luke warned, hardly stifling the laugh that seemed to envelop his whole self.

"I'm getting out of here," Delia muttered.

"Hurry back," the doctor called over his shoulder. "You're part of my patient's recovery program."

Delia made her way to the cafeteria, hating the bleak walls, the smell of antiseptics and the parade of gurneys carrying human forms, often with IVs hooked to their veins. She had nearly panicked when she'd walked up to the receptionist's desk earlier that morning and asked for permission to visit Luke. For a moment, the figure at the desk had become that heartless woman of long ago who had refused her little brother admittance to Wilmington's Payne General Hospital.

"Is something wrong? Are you alright?" The woman had stood and gestured as if to help her, bringing Delia back to the present.

"I… I'm fine," she'd managed. Then she had reached for the pass and gone on to Luke's room.

She found a seat in the cafeteria and sipped her coffee. What kind of food did they serve, she wondered, if none of it emitted an odor? She rose to go, glanced at her watch and sat down. Scarcely fifteen minutes had passed. "And all this time," she said aloud to herself, "I haven't once thought about my office." Somehow, without conscious thought, she had begun to reorder her priorities. Fate or Providence, call it what you liked, had taken a hand, a strong one; she wondered what the end would be.

CHAPTER 13

Days later, after his release from the hospital, Luke headed home to Polk Town. At La Guardia airport, he turned back and waved at Delia, who stood as he'd left her before boarding his American Airlines flight to the Raleigh/Durham airport. She hadn't offered to take the trip with him to his parents home' in Polk Town, and why should she? She hadn't been enamored of his home environment on the one occasion she'd been there, and her reaction had made him walk away from her— for good, he'd thought. Her luminous smile urged him back to her, but he knew he couldn't let Delia take care of him. He waved once more, headed around the slight bend of the walkway, and she was no longer visible. He seated himself, adjusted the tiny pillow beneath his head and closed his eyes. With luck, he'd sleep all the way to Durham. Because if he couldn't sleep, Delia would roam around in his head, and he'd believe that her attentiveness during his two weeks of hospitalization had been an expression of her love and loyalty.

He hadn't thought anything would distract her from her single-minded drive to reach the top. She'd once considered herself too busy to visit her sick grandmother, but she went to see him daily—before, during and after work. He wondered if she'd noticed the difference. She read poetry to him and confided that, as a volunteer, she not only recorded poems for the blind, but also read to hospital patients. With his eyes closed and his fingers wrapped in hers, he had listened to classic love poems— Browning,

Shakespeare, Dunbar—that he knew by heart, but which became new, thrilling, even powerful when the words flowed from her lips. And he had never loved her more. His mother hadn't told him what she thought of Delia, and he hoped that didn't indicate a dislike for her, because he was rapidly approaching a decision, and he didn't expect that he'd voluntarily put her out of his life.

He got out of the taxi at his parents' house, inhaled the fresh June air, and did his best to walk up the front steps without drawing attention to his grogginess and unsteady gait.

His mother rushed through the front door to meet him, stopped and looked him over. "Are you alright now, Son, or do you need a little more time?"

Exhausted from the trip, he smiled as best he could, put his arm around her and walked into the house. "I have to remain quiet and get some rest, but I'll be fine. The doctors don't expect any permanent damage."

"Here," she said. "Stretch out on the couch. You'll get some nice cool breeze, and I won't bother you. Sleep if you want to."

He knew she wanted the details of what had happened, so he told her about Pinski and his peculiar fixation on Delia, and it didn't surprise him that Patsy sympathized with the man and with his family.

"Since he knows where Delia lives, shouldn't she move?"

He told her about the arrangements that Pinski's family had made, though he couldn't say they'd been carried out. "Mom, did you like Della?" He'd told himself that he wouldn't ask her, but knowing suddenly became urgent. "Tell me. I can take it."

She patted his hand. "I didn't want to influence you, so I kept my peace. But since you ask, she'd be wonderful for you, and all of us liked her. I wasn't sure whether she loves you, but professional women may not wear their hearts on their sleeves the way simpler women... you know, less sophisticated ones, sometimes do. You love her, don't you?"

He had expected that. "Yes. Yes, I love her."

She sat quietly, staring at her hands. "You need a lot of love, Son. You always did, and you always picked strange ways of showing it. I hope. Well—"

"She loves me. If she denied it, I wouldn't believe her." • "Hasn't she told you?"

"In many ways." He let his eyelids drift shut, signaling to her that he'd say no more about Della. She'd given him what he wanted, the joy of knowing that his family wouldn't interfere in his relationship with Delia.

"Telephone, Luke," his father called to him after supper that evening.

"How are you, Luke. It's Della."

He stared at the receiver, stunned, because it hadn't occurred to him that she'd call.'This is a pleasant surprise. How'd you get my number down here?"

"Easy as falling off a log. I just called up Gene at Jojo's Kitchen, and he told me."

"You're resourceful. I'm glad you called." He glanced at Irene leaning against the door eavesdropping, covered the mouthpiece and told his youngest sister to go mind her own business.

"Gene sends his regards."

"Yeah? I'll bet. How long did he talk?' "Not long."

"How long is 'not long'?"

"Half an hour."

"Hmmm. I knew he was slow, but he's getting worse if it took him thirty minutes to repeat ten numbers.

"Well, he had to ask how you were and what you were doing in Polk Town."

"Are you going back there for brunch? Or is he sending you a carry-out?"

"He gave me the recipe, remember? By now, I'll bet I'm as good at making jerked chicken as he is."

"Why didn't you tell me?"

"Well, I was going to take some along to the hockey game, but you know what happened."

"Do I ever? Any news about Pinski?

"Not much. They brought him here to pack his things, and when I saw him, two men who seemed to be paramedics and a policeman were taking him out. He didn't even look my way, thank Goodness. I hope the trip down didn't tire you."

"In fact it did, but I'm going slow. You can imagine I have no choice with my mother hovering around."

"Please give her my regards."

"If I do that, she may want to know what's going on between us, and I wouldn't know what to tell her."

"You'll think of something," she replied, a bit testily, he thought.

"Wait a minute there. After the tenderness you've been ladling out to me for the past two weeks, your tart tongue "is a dagger in my heart." :

"Did you go to drama school? If you did, I'll bet you led your class."

No point in lying, he told himself, but he didn't have to be candid and tell her he'd belonged to the University Players and traveled the university circuit with them in his junior and senior years at the University of North Carolina at Chapel Hill. "Whenever there was a class play, your man here was in it."

Her seductive chuckle sent hot pinions of desire skittering through his body. "And I'll bet you conned the audience the minute you walked on stage."

"Why do you say that? I haven't succeeded in conning you?"

"What makes you so sure of that?"

"Look, baby, don't get frisky with me just because we've got five or six hundred miles between us. I've got a long memory and plenty of time to anticipate something that occupies my mind half the time."

"And what's that?"

He drew a deep breath. "Delia, if I was within a city block of you, you wouldn't be so reckless."

"Me? Reckless? No, sir. I think before I speak."

He could hear the thumping of his heart, and in his mind's eye, he could see her lolling on her bed, her pale negligee falling away from her body. He sat up from his reclining position, reached in his pocket for a handkerchief to wipe the perspiration that streamed down the side of his face.

"I'm glad to know that. What keeps my mind busy is imagining myself locked in your arms with you loving me. Want me to go on?"

"Uh... Sorry... I..."

He twirled the telephone cord around his wrist. "But you're not brash. Remember? You wanted to hear it from my mouth, though you knew what I'd say if I was honest. Delia, a rising temperature will not help this head that Pinski gave me. Don't forget that."

"I think I'd better hang up. I don't want to tire you out." "Will you call me again?"

"Of course I will. Goodnight, Luke." "Hey. Not so fast. Don't I get a kiss?"

She made a kissing sound. "I put that right smack on your bottom lip. Good night."

The dial tone screamed in his ear. He'd meant to tell her he loved her but... Well, hell. He hung up.

Two weeks of doing practically nothing had begun to tire on him, but the doctors had said that as long as he had headaches or dizzy spells, he was not to exert himself. He no longer had the dizzy spells and the headaches occurred less frequently, but any loud noise or sudden movement triggered one. In the past few days, he'd gotten an itch to do something creative and being away from his apartment, where he worked on designs, frustrated him. He watched his brother, Nelson, and his father weed his mother's garden and saw the discomfort it caused his father, who hadn't fully recovered from his early spring accident. Ideas filled his head, and a feverish desire to design gripped him. He drafted three different types of gadgets for pulling weeds, looked at them and threw up his hands. He had to find a way to open his design and manufacturing studio and still help his family. He wasn't ready to risk hundreds of thousands of dollars as long as his folks needed him. And what if he got married? He put the drawings in his luggage and vowed that he'd someday reproduce them.

From his mother's end of a phone conversation, Luke deduced that Wanda would be home that evening to spend the weekend. But when his mother went to another part of the house without mentioning the call to him, he figured that he might not want to know what Wanda had to say. That much was confirmed for him at dinner.

"How's school?" he asked Wanda. "Still in ROTC?" Cold marbles danced around in his belly when the import of the silence at the table hit him. His parents, Wanda, Irene and Nelson suddenly found something in their plates that required their undivided attention.

"Well?" he persisted. "If you dropped out of it, I sure wouldn't care. How's it going?"

"I... uh... I'm out of it, but I—"

"Great. So why is everybody so somber?"

When Wanda took a deep breath and laid her fork on her plate, he braced himself. "Luke, I've joined the Air Force?"

"*What?* Run that past me again." He breathed deeply and slowly. The dinner table wasn't the place for an argument.

"I said—"

"I know what you said, Wanda. You mentioned that you were thinking about it, and I told you what I thought. You went ahead, anyway, so it seems my views don't matter."

"They do matter, Luke, but I want to fly airplanes. I don't to sit in a classroom and pretend to enjoy teaching. I'm sorry, Luke."

Everybody had stopped eating and focused on their painful dialogue, and he knew they hurt for Wanda and him, the two siblings who had always been closest. Inseparable. Only he could restore the warmth and joviality that had preceded Wanda's declaration.

He made the effort. "I hope they at least gave you a decent rank."

How could he begrudge her this opportunity to realize her dream when her face held new lights and sparkles he'd never seen flicked in her eyes? Well, since he had to accept it, he'd be graceful.

"Tell those guys that if they don't treat you right, your big brother will mow 'em down." He couldn't maintain the strength of his voice, and they all heard its wobbling. He would have left the table if Irene hadn't blurted out the biggest surprise of all. "Well, since it's time for unwelcome announcements, I might as well throw in my firecracker."

Rudolph McKnight's head snapped up, and his gazed focused on his younger daughter. "Can't this wait?"

She shrugged. "It's not worse than what Wanda's done. I've got a full scholarship to study at Julliard, and I've already started packing."

I'm not going to react to this, Luke told himself, as he watched his father beam, his pride evident. "This is wonderful. When did you learn about it?" his father asked.

"This afternoon. I got a phone call, and I was waiting 'til now to tell you. I didn't know Luke was going to react like that to Wanda being an *Air* Force officer."

Luke sat forward. "You're an officer, Wanda?"

"I've got a commission, but I have to win my wings before I can put on those bars. Not to worry, Luke, I'll also finish my bachelor's degree."

"Well, that's something." He congratulated Irene, but his heart wasn't in it. How was she going to make a living singing? She didn't enjoy pop music, and if she had an operatic voice, he hadn't heard about it. Still, a scholarship to Julliard meant something. He pasted a smile on his face, got up and hugged each of his sisters and assured them he'd always be there for them. He asked his parents to excuse him, started out of the dining room, stopped and looked back. When had it happened? His sisters were women. Dolores was weeks from becoming the wife of a man he didn't know. He shook his head. Nelson was nearly as tall as he. Sometime when he hadn't been looking, they'd stopped being his little brothers and sisters.

Later that evening, as he shoved his pawn across the chess board and captured Nelson's king, he asked his brother, "How is it that you didn't have any surprises for me? I'm beginning to think I don't know my own family."

"I didn't have anything to tell. You already know I'm going to engineering school. I've decided to focus on electrical design just like you did. Then we can work together."

But when Luke began to outline his plans for Nelson, which included a considerable allowance and complete payment for Nelson's education at a prestigious school that he would help him chose, Rudolph, who had been watching the game, objected.

"I thought we'd settled this, Luke. You're a successful man, but did you ever wonder why? I'll tell you. You worked hard to get to school and to get through it. You appreciated what you had and didn't squander it. When a man earns what he gets in this life, he values it more. Give Nelson a chance to be as much man as you've become."

Luke wondered if he'd gotten off at the wrong stop, if this was where he usually stayed when he came to Polk Town. But he respected his father's judgment. "Alright, Dad, what if the three of us sit together and work it out?"

"Yes, and we'll let Nelson decide where he wants to go, because he's going to work and pay for at least half of it."

Luke shrugged and took great satisfaction in capturing Nelson's queen. "Decide what you want to do, and let me know," he told his brother. Their raised eyebrows was all the evidence he needed that they recognized he'd acquiesced to their wishes and changed his tune with his siblings.

He walked out to the back porch and sat on the top step, and it didn't amuse him to recall that he'd always sat hi that exact spot when, as a child, he'd felt misunderstood. He swore under his breath. He wasn't being peevish; he'd had his place in his family pirated, and not one of them seemed to understand what had happened. Even Nelson had readily agreed with their father to accept limited help with his college education. Maybe that was as it should be, but he hated feeling as though he wasn't needed in his own family. For what reason had he foregone the pleasure of a satisfying private life, if not to help his parents and siblings? He thought of calling Della, but resisted; he didn't dump on women, but on a night like this one, he'd give anything to have her with him.

After a time, he joined his parents on the front porch where the family usually congregated on summer evenings.

"I see you mended that hole in the screen door," Rudolph said to Luke. "It was a little too high for me, since I still don't get on a ladder. And I'm not sure you should have done it and risked another dizzy spell while you were up there."

"They come less frequently, Dad." He watched his father limp over to the swing to sit beside Patsy. Since his fall, walking had become a chore and negotiating the front and back steps exhausted him. When Nelson left for college in September, his parents would be alone with no one to help with difficult tasks. They'd struggled long enough with meager comforts.

"You know, Dad, it's time you and Mom had an easier life. You don't have to work yourself to death in that store twelve hours a day, six days a week. We can hire somebody to run it for you."

Rudolph cleared his throat, as was his habit when he was about to disagree. "But in that case, I wouldn't see my friends and get to chat with them."

"Oh, you could go in from time to time. And another thing, I'm going to build you two a house with every modern convenience. No more stacking wood, cold rooms all winter and that kind of thing, and Mom will have an ultra modern kitchen. I can—"

"You already give us more than enough Son, and I appreciate what you want to do, but we're comfortable like we are."

He wanted more for them. He hated the difference between his living standard and theirs. "You think that, but wait 'til you see some of the plans I'll send you."

"Luke, we appreciate all you do, and I know you mean well, but we're comfortable, like your father said."

"But Mom—"

She reached for Rudolph's hand. "Luke, my husband's head of this house, and I'm happy with whatever he provides for me. I don't want anything that he can't give me. I will not allow you or any of my children to usurp his place, no matter how well meaning you are. Son, you have to stop trying to control our lives. You're a wonderful son, and I thank God for you daily. You're generous with us, and your intentions are good, but Luke, well meaning doesn't always produce the best results.

"Just think," she went on, "Dolores is unhappy, because she feels she disappointed and hurt you by marrying the man she loves and granting your father the honor of giving her away. Look at Wanda and Irene, in their room right now instead of out here with us, because they feel they've let you down and don't know what to say to you. Luke, I've thought long and hard about this. You have this drive, this… this strong need to be needed, because you're such a giving person. As a child, you protected every kid smaller than you. You fed your dog before you would eat. You're full of love, and you need so much of it. Your brother and sisters worshipped you when they were little, drank in your every word. They still adore you, but they will also love other people.

"The woman who loves you will need you, and your children will need you, as you will need them. But no one should try to control another out of personal need. When you go back to New York, think about what I'm saying and move on with your life."

As though in a dream, he watched his mother walk over to him and put an arm around his shoulder. "You're my firstborn," she said, her voice soft and gentle. "You're my heart, and no one will ever mean more to me than you do."

He patted the hand that lay on his shoulder to let her know he'd heard her, but his mind had taken him far away. She'd said he should move on with his life, but she didn't know the hurdles before him. He either had to make Delia a permanent part of his life or get over her, and neither would be easy.

A few days later, mended and rested, Luke relaxed in his first class seat on American Airlines Flight 1127 from Raleigh/Durham to La Guardia airport in New York.

"Orange juice? Coffee?" the flight attendant asked.

He declined both and closed his eyes. Had his acts of kindness to his family been self-serving, born of a hunger for love? And had he attempted to control them all, to force their dependency on him so that they'd never desert him, as his mother had suggested? Oh, she hadn't used those words, but what else could she have meant? He had a hard time believing that of himself. His joy had come from knowing they'd succeed in life. And didn't he know better than Irene how singers lolled around New York's casting studios and agents' offices waiting for scraps, for bit parts in musicals, for a chance at the Met, for a record contract?

He knew he should be happy if they thought they no longer needed him, but he wasn't convinced that they were ready to jump out on their own. Remembering his exhilaration when he saw his first paycheck as an engineer, he wondered if his mother could be right? No matter. He felt estranged from all of them, even Nelson, and it hurt.

Della waited at the baggage carousel, impatient to see Luke. 1 She'd stopped asking herself whether she could settle for him, and whether she'd risk the threat of poverty for herself and her children, though she hadn't gotten further in her thinking than the admission that she loved and needed him. He walked through the gate, and her heart started a jerky dance in her chest when he looked around. Searching. Happiness flooded her and she rushed to him, but he passed her and headed for the baggage carousel. She prayed that the blow to his head hadn't impaired his vision.

Luke stepped through the arrivals gate at La Guardia Airport and looked around. Where was she? He'd told her what time his plane landed in the hope that she'd meet him. He picked up his luggage, and an arm snaked between his hand and the bag. His breath quickened, and he locked his gaze in hers.

"Hi. I was wondering if you'd make it." He kept his voice neutral so as not to give away his feelings.

"Try getting rid of me."

He didn't want that. He needed her. All or nothing. "No more teasing, Delia."

"It isn't what I say; it's how you take it."

He didn't want to match wits, either. "Delia, don't mis-understand me. I'm through with this come-here-go-away act. I need more, and I'm sure you do, too." He hadn't wanted to offend her, but she stopped walking and her facial expression didn't communicate joy.

"I'll go home with you and see if everything's in order. I want to do it, Luke."

He accepted her offer, because he wanted to be with her. "I...alright." He took her hand when a taxi stopped for them. "I'm glad we can have some time together."

Della fought back a sense of alarm. This man showed signs of being depressed, of having lost something vital about himself. At his apartment, he declined all her offers of help, dropped into a chair and stretched his legs out in front of him.

"Nothing's the same," he said, primarily to himself.

She pushed a hassock to his chair and sat beside him. "What is it, Luke? What's happened to you?" She longed to comfort him, but she'd had little experience as a nurturer, and she fumbled her way. Luke took the hand she offered. "My family made it clear that they don't need me anymore, that I have to stop giving advice and offering help." He repeated his mother's assessment of himself and asked her, "Do you think she's right? Is that why I work so hard for the boys at the center, to fulfill a need to have people dependent on me? To control them?"

"She didn't mean that, Luke."

"Then what? I don't have a family of my own, because I wanted my sisters and my brother to have an easier time of it than I had, but she suggested that I want to be the eternal big brother. Look, I did every dirty job you can think of to put myself through college and graduate school. I lived in a tenement over a greasy spoon on a hundred and thirty-third Street in Harlem to save money so I could start my business, and I've succeeded beyond anything I imagined. They know that. I don't want them to struggle as I did, and I want my parents to live comfortably. I can afford to give them anything they want, but why should I beg anybody to take my money."

She'd stopped listening. His words droned in her ear leaving her stunned. Luke was a wealthy man. Educated. Successful. And all this time, she'd thought...

He was staring at her. "How far back are you, Delia? Somewhere back there you stopped listening, and I suspect that was at the point where you learned that I work for myself and that I'm not a high school drop-out. If you hadn't been so sure that I didn't rate your serious concern because of the way I work, if you'd had any doubt, you'd have bothered to find out that the RPM in RPM Electrical Repair and Engineering Co. on my jacket stands for Rudolph and Patsy McKnight. You only had to look closely at the logo. I'm tired." He closed his eyes, and she knew she'd lost him.

"I'd better go, Luke. I have to design a good conduct certificate for the NIA girls."

"You don't need an excuse to leave, Delia."

"I know." She wanted to hold him. If she could only touch him somehow. But it was too late.

Luke watched her walk down the hallway to^the elevator. There went his dreams. He'd opened himself up to "her, let her see his naked soul, but she was more impressed by his status and what he'd accomplished. He loved her, and he probably always would, but as his mother had advised, he had to move on with his life. But could he do it without her?

At home that evening, Delia stared at the telephone. Bitsy was pregnant, and the news had given her father an angina attack. Mark's rage still swirled around her. "You didn't help her," he'd said, "and now it's too late. Nothing here for girls to do, and as soon as their breasts start bouncing around, these men and boys take off after them. If she'd been up there with you, it wouldn't have happened. Mama's sitting hi a corner crying, and I have to take papa to the hospital." Tears streamed down Delia's face, and she couldn't control her sobs. Maybe she could have done more, but was it her fault? She dragged herself into the bathroom and washed her face.

She had a mind not to answer the phone. After the tenth or so ring, she picked up the receiver but said nothing.

"Delia." Shaken by the unexpected sound of his voice, she was momentarily speechless.

"Delia. I want to talk with you."

"I can't… I don't want… please, let me be."

"What's wrong?"

"Nothing. Everything. Good-bye." She hung up.

Half an hour later she opened her door, knowing that her caller was Luke.

Her misery had reached him through the telephone wires, and he hadn't been able to shrug it off. He'd come to her because he had to. "I came over here because you need me, and I couldn't stay away. What's the matter?" He pulled her into his arms, knowing what that would do to him.

Words tumbled out of her, and he carried her to the sofa and sat with her in his lap. Her mother and Mark blamed her for Bitsy's mishap, she cried, wrenching sobs spilling from her throat.

"Della, don't. No matter what they said, it isn't you fault. You aren't responsible for your sister's behavior." He wiped her eyes with his finger, but when her body shook as though tortured, he tightened his arms around her and rocked her.

"Sweetheart, don't." Her fingers clutched his chest, and her heat, her woman's scent began to tease his nostrils until water accumulated in his mouth. He swallowed and attempted to put her away from him, but she clung tighter, the way a squirrel clings to the bark of a tree. He didn't want to put her from him, but he couldn't bear another trip to the brink of lovemaking with all his senses filled with her and his body near the point of explosion, only to have to cool down alone.

"Della. Honey, We can't go on doing this. I need you. I'm starved for you." He got out his handkerchief and wiped her tears. "Talk to me, baby."

She shifted in his lap, laid her head on his shoulder and let him feel the soft, warm pressure of her parted lips on his neck.

"Sweetheart, don't pick this time to test my control, because I'm not sure I have any. What do you want from me?"

Her words came to him thickly, unsteady, and as though from afar. "I need you, Luke. I need you so badly."

He feared for his sanity. Had he heard her correctly, and what did she mean? "What are you saying, Delia? Give it to me straight. Do you want me?"

She nodded, but he demanded that she say it, tearing the words out of himself. If she said no, he didn't think he could survive. "Tell me if you want me."

Her warm lips caressed his jaw, and the fingers of her right hand trembled when she gripped his left biceps. "I want you."

"Now? Right now?"

"Yes. Yes! *Yes!*"

He squeezed her trembling body to him, as the shock of her answer sent hot pinions racing through his nervous system and heat pooling in his loins. "Slow down, man," he told himself, as her hand at the back of his head guided his mouth to hers. The feel of her lips quivering beneath his nearly sent him into a tailspin; she hadn't lied. He could taste her hunger as her lips opened wider in search of his tongue. But he had to hold back, to pace her slowly, because he needed her total surrender and her complete satisfaction. He meant to love her until she'd be blind to every man but him.

He rimmed her lips with his tongue, and her squirming body told his she needed more, but he meant to take his time. And when her knee touched his arm, he knew her hunger had made her cross her legs. He pulled away from her mouth to plant soft kisses on her eyes, her cheeks and the tip of her nose, and his fingers skimmed tantalizingly along her bare arms. Wanting the feel of her nipple between his fingers, he stroked one to ripeness and groaned aloud at the speed with which the little bud hardened. He gloried in her gasp and the quick movements of her hips as she shifted in his lap. But suddenly she faced him, and he stood and lifted her before she could straddle him and make him explode.

"Where's your bed?" he asked and breathed more easily when she pointed toward the hallway that led from the living room.

Della clung to Luke knowing that the fire racing through her signaled the beginning of a journey she'd never taken. Every spot his fingers touched burned as though he'd tattooed it before moving on to brand her somewhere else. In her room, he managed to lay back the covers while still holding her in his arms. As his gaze bore into hers, his long tapered fingers stroked from her ankle to beneath her knee. She was a burning blaze, dying for him to move on upward. He pulled off her shoes, bent over her and placed his hand flat on her belly.

"You're mine, Della. If you can't accept that—"

"I am. Oh, Luke, I've always belonged to you." Of its own volition, her hungry body undulated to him. "Hold me. Luke, love me. Just love me."

When he leaned toward her, she rose to meet him with parted lips, frantic to have him inside of her. He placed one knee on the bed and pulled her fully into his arms. She didn't understand his murmured words, but when his tongue invaded her mouth, hot arrows of desire pummelled her feminine core, and she didn't try to stifle her moans.

"Luke, please. Take me. I've needed you so long."

"It hasn't caught us yet, darling," he said, taking the necessary precautions to protect her. "Relax and trust me to give us what we both want and need. May I take these off?"

"Yes. Yes." Suddenly, knowing she'd soon feel his flesh on hers rattled her senses. He slid her bra over her head, gripped her panties and pulled them from her. He stood above her, gazing from her head to her toes, and the heat of desire rampaged through her body when he swallowed hard and jumped to full readiness. Quickly, he divested himself of his clothing, and her eyes beheld him at last. Strong. Powerful. She opened her arms to him, and he went to her, letting her lock him to her. But when she reached for him, he pulled away and began to skim his fingers along the inside of her thighs. Teasing. Tantalizing. If only he'd touch her where she ached. She burned to have his fingers caress her, but instead, he stroked her belly. His lips grazed her neck and, frantically, she moved his hand to her nipple.

His fingers toyed with her until she thought she'd go mad. "Kiss me. Kiss them. I want to feel your mouth on me."

"All in good time," he murmured. Realizing that she could exert some pressure of her own, she slid down and fastened her lips to his flat pectoral and his breathing quickened. But he moved her up, and she knew he'd chart his own course. But at last his hot breath fanned her nipple, and his lips fastened on it, drawing from her a keening cry of want. He sucked vigorously on it while he kneaded and massaged the other one. Having gotten the surrender that he must have been seeking, he moved to the other breast, twirled his tongue around its nipple and pulled it into his mouth. When she thought she could stand no more, his fingers found her feminine secret and began their talented dance. Frantically, she spread her legs, undulating with want.

"Luke, I can't stand this. I want you. I want to feel you inside of me. *Take me!* She felt the liquid flow from her, not knowing what it meant, but he stroked her more vigorously until, hi her exasperation, she grasped him. Her eyes flew open to see him staring into her face.

"Take me in, darling." How could she? He bent to her and twirled his tongue in her mouth. Then, "Take me."

With their gazes locked, she lifted herself and took him into her body. "Relax, love," he said as he slowly fitted himself within her. "Look at me. I want you to look at me." She stared into his mesmerizing eyes, and he began their dance. Immediately the heat began to build in her, teasing her, maddening her, foretelling the ecstasy to come, and she raced for it.

"Not so fast, darling," he whispered. "Move with me."

She caught his rhythm, and her eyes widened as he moved within her, stroking her. She wanted to burst, but he denied her, slowed down and then started his powerful strokes again. Her breathing escalated and she knew he could hear the pounding of her heart as hot sensations began at the bottom of her feet and shot up to her feminine core. : "What...What is it, Luke? What is happening to me?"

He gathered her to him and increased the power of his movements. "Shhh, darling. Let go and let it happen. Just feel what I'm doing to you." She thought she'd die when the clenching began and he slowed down to string it out, but she wouldn't be denied, gripped his hips and demanded all of his strength. The clutching, pumping and squeezing began in earnest, and the heat exploded inside of her. A scream burst from her throat, and then a turbulence such as she'd never known grabbed hold of her. He was in her, on her, all around her. The misery. The death. And then the unbelievable sweetness, as she broke away from herself and became one with him. She cried aloud as the hurricane of fulfillment ploughed through her.

"Luke. Oh Luke. I love you. I love you. I've always loved you. Only you."

She heard his shout of satisfaction as he fell apart, shimmering in her arms, and she gripped him to her with all her strength.

He kept his place within her, gazing into her eyes. Then his kisses brushed her cheeks and her eyes, and he locked his arms around her shoulders and kissed her lips. Her body absorbed the shock of the powerful shudders that raced through him. What a fool she had been. Tears streamed from the corners of her eyes as she thought of her meaningless relationship with Craig to whom she hadn't responded because she'd loved Luke. She knew that Luke sensed her astonishment at what had happened between them, but he would never know what her false values had cost her.

"Why are you crying, love?" Don't tell me you're already sorry. I don't want to hear it."

It was no use trying to stop the water that flowed down her cheeks. "if I'm sorry, its's for the mess I've made of things. I didn't know who I was 'til you showed me just now. Oh, Luke, I've been wrong about so much."

"And now?"

"I can't think. I'd never experienced what I felt with you. I didn't know it existed."

His lips drank her tears, and fierce hug wrapped her in a strange, unfamiliar peace. When he separated them and pulled her to his side, she had a curl into him and stay there. She faced him, drew him into her arms and asked, "Would it be bad manners if I thanked you?"

Luke's laugther fell on her ears as would the music of angels.

"Go head. A guy likes to know he's satisfied his woman."

She stroked his chest, brushing his left pectoral, and saw him glance warily at her from the corner of his eye. She loved the feel of his muscles as they flexed beneath her questing fingers, and she let her hand discover the increasing thickness of his body hair as it lead to his navel-and passed over it. Fascinated, she sat up and looked at his bare physique, only half aware that he watched her, hawk like. Her fingers itched to go further, and as though he read her thoughts, he grabbed her timid hand and placed it where he wanted it.

He was hard and pulsating with heat, and she knew he waited for something. But what? He pressed her fingers to him and taught her to stroke the he liked.

"Look at me, Della," he rasped with an urgency that sent waves of excitement rollicking through her.

She forced her gaze to his and got an inkling of her power as his eyes darkened, he clenched and unclenched his fist, and moans rumbled in his throat. Without warning, he had her on her back and quickly covered her. Skin to skin. Limb to limb. Wild fire roared through her as her libido shouted its demands. His kiss fired her body until hot darts of desire danced on her nerve endings. His tongue slid up the inside of her arm and made its way slowly, too slowly, to her waiting nipple. She held her breath, waiting for him to claim it, and he suckled until she begged him to join them. But his fingers began their wicked torture of her feminine core, demanding her total submission.

"Luke. Please. I can't bear it any more."

"Talk to me, love."

"I think I'm… Luke, get in me. *Get in me!*"

"Take what you want, baby. It's yours. *I'm yours.*"

With unsteady hands, she found him and guided him to her portal of love. He sucked her nipple into his mouth, put his hand between them and rubbed gently while he rocked powerfully within her. She writhed beneath him, grasping his buttocks until he lifted her from the bed, and she met him thrust for thrust. She heard the thunder and saw the lightning ^flash as he drove mercilessly, forcing her to erupt in spasm after spasm, sending her swirling in a vortex of ecstasy. She thought the wind had been knocked out of her, but he hadn't finished with her and, in seconds, the rhythmic clenching began again. Surely, this time she was dying. Uncontrollable contractions shook her and her cries filled the room.

"Luke. Oh, Luke, my love. I love you so."

Luke heard her screams of ecstasy as her spasms gripped him. He wanted to give her more, to stake an irreversible claim, but the powerful movement of her body, squeezing and pulling, demanded all that he had. Every ounce of him. With one last surge, he gave her his essence and splintered in her arms.

He lay above her with his elbows taking his weight. His love for her overwhelmed him, and he couldn't move. Couldn't speak. He buried his head in the curve of her neck, heard again his mother's words and acknowledged their truth. He had called her to tell her it was over, that he was giving his assistant responsibility for the UN contract and wouldn't see her again. And then he'd heard the troubled tenor of her voice, had known that she needed him—not for any land of help, but for himself. She'd needed his comfort and his loving, and he hadn't been able to turn his back on her. In spite of his reservations, he'd come to her, needing to have her need him. His mother might be right, but he didn't consider it a weakness. At least not in this case, because right then he felt as though he could force open a lion's jaw.

He wasn't sorry. How could he be? She'd given him all that he'd asked for and more. More than he'd ever had. In her, he'd found himself. But why now? Why, after all these months, had she let her heart overrule her ambitions? Because he'd told her who he was? He closed his eyes and separated from her, taking care to leave her feeling cherished. But he hurt.

He went around to her side of the bed and sat down. "Delia, you told me twice that you love me. You shouted it. You knew I loved you. Why couldn't you tell me before?"

She closed her eyes as though in pain. "I was foolish." She shook her head, and the expression of sadness that marred her lovely face tore at his heart. "I have no other excuse."

He sucked in his breath. Now wasn't the time to let something that concerned him so deeply slide. "I don't like what I'm thinking, Della."

"I know. But will you forgive me, Luke? Can you?"

He locked his gaze with hers and brushed her cheek with the
back of his hand. "I... God knows I want to, Delia. You'll never know how much." He couldn't muster more.

CHAPTER 14

What will be, will be," Della told herself the next morning, after a sleepless night. She took the NIA certificate to a printer, checked her United Nations laissez passez to make sure she had her Thailand visa, held a conference with her assistant and prepared to leave the office for a noon flight to Bangkok, Thailand, one of the world's jewelry capitols. While there, she intended to buy herself a ruby ring and name it Luke as a daily reminder of her folly. She'd kept a distance between them, because she'd thought him a man of modest means, and she'd hurt him, and she wouldn't be surprised if, in spite of the wonder of their lovemaking, he walked away from her for good. If her turmoil over Luke wasn't enough, Bitsy's condition plagued her continuously, and she didn't have an answer for it.

She completed her mission in Bangkok within the allotted two days and was checking out of the Dusit Thani Hotel when she noticed a package in her open canvas canyon that hadn't been there before. Thinking that it had fallen from the counter, she was about to give it to the desk clerk when a man approached and asked whether she had a package from Ambassador Besa.. *Besa!* The seriousness of what the man's question suggested stunned her. She had only put reading matter in her canyon bag, and since she'd slept on the flight from New York, she had barely glimpsed the bag's contents after boarding the plane. Marbles battled for space in her stomach when she recalled that a man had sat beside her briefly in the waiting lounge at Kennedy Airport. He'd asked her the time, but when she'd looked up

from her watch, he was walking away. She'd thought nothing of it—until now. Alert to the implications, she told the
man she didn't have a package from anyone, dashed outside, got a taxi to the US Embassy and related the incident
to the Officer-in-charge. When told what she'd discovered,
she sank into the nearest chair, her relief palpable, and
gratefully accepted the Embassy's protection of safe passage
out of Thailand.

When she returned to her office at the UN, she wasn't
surprised to learn from Erin that Besa had been detained
for trafficking in rubies and sapphires and was no longer a
diplomat. And no sooner had she faced the mound of
papers on her desk than Erin peeped in with more news.

"Ms. Murray, the S-G wants to see you."

Though still shaky from having narrowly escaped an
involvement in smuggling, her heart took off, bouncing in
joyful palpitation as she anticipated the good news.

"How'd you like to work for an AS-G?" she flipped at
Erin, who gaped at her.

"You asking me? I'd be two grades higher."

It had to be what she'd fought so hard fqr and sacrificed
so much for, otherwise, the S-G would have sent her a letter. But not that time. She sat immobile and in stunned disbelief as he spoke.

"Miss Murray, you're certainly one of our most capable
senior officials, perhaps the best on your level, but I'm
sorry. You were not chosen." She couldn't help being grateful that her dark complexion prevent his seeing the blood
drain from her face. "It was an extremely difficult thing to
do," he droned on, "but I had to take account of national-

ity. It would have been inappropriate for both SCAG and the International Institute For The Child to be headed by US citizens. Ambassador Radcliff's election as Director-General of IIC automatically precluded your appointment to head SCAG."

In his mind, maybe. That wasn't an intractable rule, though he could apply it if he chose. She studied his demeanor carefully and \ dared to ask, "Pillay?"

He waved his hand in a gesture of dismissal. "Pillay was never in contention.

At least he'd given her that. She left the exalted chamber with as much grace as she could summon, found her way to her office I and closed the door. *Craig.* Not only had he won it all but because his success, she hadn't achieved her coveted goal. When would her folly cease to plague her? She'd gone after Craig, driven by avarice, and she'd gotten him when she was no longer willing to pay the price of having him. She'd give anything if she had been more prudent, but you didn't get a chance to relive you life, to erase your stupidities; you had to go on.. She listened to Erin's voice on her intercom, young, untainted, by life's hazards. "The Mayor wants you to call his office." "The Mayor? Why didn't you buzz me?" "His aide sent an e-mail. Should I ring her now?" Delia agreed. She listened while the woman in the Mayor's office told her that, thanks to NIA, dropouts among girl students attending that school had declined by forty percent and that none of the NIA girls was pregnant when they filled out the end of term health questionnaire.

"That is a tremendous change, and the mayor is very proud to have this on his record," Delia was told. "You're to receive a special citation Monday morning at eleven in the Mayor's office."

Erin rushed in and congratulated her. "Aren't you elated?"

"Oh, yes. I am."

"You don't act like it," Erin protested.

How could she, when she couldn't think of anything but Bitsy? Her sixteen year old sister. Pregnant. She had opened new vistas for the NIA girls, possibly saved them from the trap into which her own little sister had gotten snared and which would forever circumscribe her life. Demoralized, she dabbed at her eyes, forcing back the tears, as she wrote a two-hundred word acceptance speech and began mentally to prepare herself for the ordeal of City Hall.

Erin opened the door, interrupting her. "Ms. Murray, Mr. McKnight has walked up to my desk three times this morning, glanced at your closed door and just walked off. I know it isn't my business, but if there's anything I can do... I mean... he looked so miserable."

Astonished at the girl's insight, Delia regarded her intently. Probably the only person toward whom she'd ever had a truly maternal feeling. "If he does that again, Erin, please tell him I'd like to see him."

She wasn't about to question the smile that burst forth on Erin's face, but she couldn't help grinning. Red hair and a smile like sunshine.

"I sure will tell him. Boy, am I glad I got up the nerve to mention it. I *thought* something had gone wrong."

Delia knew her lower lip had dropped in a most unprofessional manner. "What? What do you mean?"

Erin displayed her perfect teeth and pulled on her hair. "I'm eighteen, Ms. Murray, but you have to admit, I've got sense."

Della lifted an eyebrow. "Tell me about it. Sometimes I forget you're not thirty-five."

"I could... er... re... call him," Erin threw over her shoulder as she neared the door.

Deciding it was best to pretend she hadn't heard it and let Erin do that if she wanted to, Delia went back to jotting down notes for her acceptance speech.

"RPM. McKnight speaking." He blinked several times in surprise. "Erin, what do you mean, she wants to see me?" Anxiously, he listened to the young woman's hurried explanation.

"I might have gotten a little out of bounds there, Mr. McKnight, but I figured it was time I did something."

Relief flooded him. He'd wanted to see her so badly that he could have eaten nails, but he hadn't wanted her to think their night together had been a firm commitment on his part. Some things about her worried him still.

"Remind me to dance at your wedding, my friend," he told Erin. He got two cups of coffee, put them in a brown paper bag and headed for the middle-rise elevator. Erin nodded toward the door, but he knocked nonetheless.

"Hi. I wanted to bring you some coffee, but I didn't know if you wanted any."

Her smile burst upon him like the rising sun. It was what he'd needed. He understood now that she granted him the right to sort out his feelings about her and that she wouldn't sulk while he did it."

"Is that coffee in that bag?" "Sure is." "And you're standing there holding it when I could be drinking it?" He looked deeply into her eyes, and it was as though his soul turned over. "You mean you haven't had your caffeine fix this morning?"

The answering fire in her eyes sent his blood to racing, and he told himself to cool down. "Haven't had time."

He opened one cup and put it on her desk, and when she saw that he had another, she asked, "Do you have time to drink it here with me?"

He couldn't have been more astonished. Such a short time ago, she'd been afraid for anyone, including Erin, to find him socializing with her in her office. He sat on the edge of the chair and took a few sips.

"I'll stay a couple of seconds. You okay?"

She wasn't, but if she started to unload, there'd be no end to it. "I'm making it."

He took a long drink, closed the cup and put it back in the bag. "And this isn't the time nor the place to go into it. Right?"

"Right."

He pinned her with a stare of shocking intimacy, a knowing look that said he knew her stripped of all but surging passion. An exquisite shiver raced through her, bringing *a gasp of longing. She lowered her gaze.

He leaned over and brushed a quick kiss over her lips. "I'll call you."

Delia watched the man she loved stroll out of her office, keys and tools singing their clanking tune. She wasn't out of the woods with him yet; he'd worn his reservations like a brightly-colored banner but in his way, he'd also asked for her patience. He loved her. She didn't doubt that, but he had the mental toughness of a Goliath. Nothing would master him, not even a profound love. She'd have to wait until he found his course. And if it led him away from her?

"I won't let it break me," she told herself. Never again would she allow any event to take control of her life as had the death of her little brother. Never.

Luke stopped at Erin's desk just outside Delia's office. "Thanks, Erin. I owe you a big one."

"No problem. You'd do the same for me. Say, isn't it great that the Mayor's giving her a citation for her work with the NIA girls? He wants a chapter in every school in New York."

Luke stared at Erin, thinking he couldn't have heard her correctly. Hadn't he just left Delia seconds earlier without her having uttered a word about it? He thought of going back in there and having it out with her. Oh, what the heck? He winked at Erin and went on to his next job.

Several mornings later, Erin stopped Delia as she arrived for work. "Ms. Murray, are you alright? What happened? I can't believe this. It's twenty minutes past nine."

Della shrugged. "Erin, I suppose this means I'm human. I overslept."

Erin gaped at her. *"You overslept?"*

Della nodded and went on into her office. She could see that Erin wasn't convinced. Of course, if you were notorious for being punctual and if you reprimanded your staff when they weren't, anybody would wonder if you came in late one morning. Four days had passed, and Luke hadn't called as he'd said, and the previous night, she hadn't slept until daybreak. Oddly, she hadn't cared if she got to work late. She spend the next hour going through her mail, then left for City Hall.

The thunderous applause of twenty-three NIA girls, dressed in their NIA jackets, greeted Delia when she walked into the Mayor's press room. Some carried NIA banners and, to her amazement, Ella—one of the toughest among them—held a poster that proclaimed, DELLA IS THE GREATEST.

She thought back to her reasons for inaugurating the NIA society—to bolster her claim to the position of Assistant Secretary-General in charge of SCAG. She'd lost out on that one. But when she looked at the twenty-three proud girls who had grasped the chance for a better life, she doubted the promotion would have given her more satisfaction.

She acknowledged the Mayor's introduction but, after she looked down at the eager faces of her girls, discarded her prepared speech and spoke extemporaneously of what the young girls had given her and what they would one day give to their country. Applause droned in her ears, and the girls crowded around her with hugs, tears and smiles, gifts she'd never dreamed of receiving. Above their heads, she saw Luke leaning against the wall, his hands in his pants pockets and his face expressionless, as though he were a disinterested observer. She got away from the girls as quickly as she could without seeming ungrateful for their adulation, but when she walked outside the room, Luke had gone.

She should have been aglow with excitement, with happiness that she'd made a difference and that her work had been so well received, but she didn't feel like rejoicing. How could she when Luke had walked off without a word and when her sister Bitsy's predicament crowded her thoughts and pricked her conscience, an ominous cloud that wouldn't go away. She went through the motions of politeness and professionalism at the official luncheon that followed, but she knew a palpable relief when, at last, she could be alone. She turned back and waved the girls good-bye, but Jennifer waited for her at the door.

"It came off real cool, Ms. Murray. I never thought you'd do it. I hope you're going to stick with us; you might even get Trixie to straighten up."

She placed a hand on the girl's shoulder in a gentle caress, aware mat in the beginning she hadn't had an impulse to touch them, hadn't had an affection for any of them. They'd been stepping stones. "I hope so." She let her mind wander over the morning's events. "Marine's the only one who didn't come."

"Yeah. But don't worry about Marine, Ms. Murray. Every day that girl puts some more rocks in her bed. She's a born loser. See you Friday."

Emotionally drained, Delia didn't bother to go back to the office but went on home, not questioning the change in herself. Hours of soul-searching, self-castigation and pondering produced no solution for Bitsy, so Delia called her mother.

"Honey, I'm so glad you called," Rachel said. "You remember you promised to speak at the church fund raiser? Well, how about next Friday night?"

Friday. There was something, but she couldn't remember what.

"Alright, Mama. But what about Bitsy?"

"We'll talk about that when you get here, honey. You take care, now."

It surprised her to receive a call at home from Luke during working hours, and especially since he'd left the Mayor's office without speaking to her. Their greetings were strained, and he let her know he hadn't called for purely personal reasons.

"You remember Dr. Gray, an elder in my church?"

Disappointed at his business-like manner, she answered in kind. "Yes, of course. Why?"

"He saw you on TV at the Mayor's press conference. Says there's no reason why the NIA society should be confined to schools and girls, and he'd like you to start one for our boys and girls at the church. What about it?"

"I'll be glad to help with that, Luke, but not this weekend. I have to go home." How prophetic that she should succeed at what she'd least cared about and fail where she'd wanted desperately to triumph. It was a lesson she wouldn't soon forget.

"No new problem there, I hope."i

"No."

The silence screamed at them, exposing their vulnerability. Stabbing into their hearts. Neither one of them could say good bye.

"Have dinner with me this evening, Delia," Luke said at last.

It wouldn't be all pleasant, she knew, because so much had to be said, and that old, open wound that Luke carried still festered.

"Alright. Around seven?"

"I'll be there."

She hadn't known them to be so formal with each other. Perhaps she should have declined his invitation to dinner; their conversation pained her.

"May I please have the salt? "

"Certainly."

"Would you care for anything else?"

"No, thank you. I enjoyed this."

They walked out into the warm June evening, and she longed for him to take her hand. Why couldn't he just tell her what had happened to make him so distant since the morning five days earlier when he'd brought her coffee and brushed a kiss on her mouth before he left her? Well, let him sulk; she was doggoned if she'd ask him.

So she was taken aback when he stood at her door, his face devoid of warmth, and held out his hand for her door key. She handed it to him and waited. Luke was not sulking, she learned. He let her know at once that he disliked discussing over the telephone anything that was important to him.

"I wanted to air this out days ago, he began, but I had to wait 'til we could be together so we could see each other's reactions."

"Have a seat," she said, giving herself time to gather her composure. She had a feeling he'd go for the jugular.

He didn't bother to go in the living room but pulled a straight back chair from her dining room table and sat, as she'd asked, giving her no choice but to do the same. Her first thought was that Luke didn't want a passionate exchange and was making certain they didn't get too close to each other.

"You knew how much that youth program means to me," he began, "and how happy I've been to see those girls reform, but you hadn't the courtesy to tell me you were getting that citation from the Mayor. Did you think I'd show up in my work clothes and embarrass you?"

"How could you think such a thing?" she asked, bewildered at the accusation.

His stony face told her that an apology wouldn't mean much. "What else am I supposed to think? I got the information from Erin seconds after I walked out of your office. I suppose inviting me to drink coffee with you was as far as you were able to extend yourself in the short span of twenty minutes. And another thing, you were sanguine as all hell about what the girls have achieved, but I know your heart wasn't in it when you started that program.

You did it for yourself. For your own glory."

How dare he belittle her. She released a loud gasp. "You don't know what you're talking about."

"I'm not a fool, Della. You didn't start that program because I suggested it; you saw something in it for yourself. Not that it matters for the girls why you did it."

She could hear the thumping of her racing heart as she rushed forward and stood over him. "Who are you to talk? You claim you love me, but how do you show it? I don't need a judge-penitent in my life, Mister. If I want to confess, I'll see a vicar or a priest."

His very demeanor, casual, relaxed and seemingly unaffected, fueled the anger that sent shudders plowing through her.

"Do you think you need to confess?" he needled. "Are you pleased with yourself?" He shot up from the chair, grasped her shoulders and stared into her eyes. "Are you?"

She turned her head. "Leave me alone."

"I won't. I can't. I love you. And you love me. You told the truth about that. But you thought I didn't measure up to your standard—whatever that is—and took up with that worthless diplomat, a man who plays the field for his own gain. What happened? Tell me. Did *he* decide that a Director-General needed a woman whose status is higher than yours? Did he give you some of your own medicine?

What made you do it, Delia? Didn't you know how much I love you? Or didn't ypu care?"

He squeezed her shoulders, and her need for him shoved the anger aside. Her body heaved as sobs wrenched from her. The pain that snared her must have been mirrored in her eyes, but he didn't take her in his arms. Her lips trembled and she squeezed her eyelids shut for such privacy as she could get.

"Leave me be. Please leave."

"Not this time, Della. You let me love you. Oh, yes you did.

Every time I touched you, you lit up like lightning in an electric storm. So you give me some answers, because I'm not leaving here'til I get them."

Her breath came in short gasps and water cascaded down her cheeks. When he left there, she'd never see him again. "Oh, Luke. Luke. If you only knew. You haven't ever been to school with your toes protruding from your shoes, watching other children eating candy and fruit. I didn't want to be poor again."

"That's an excuse, not a reason. It's deeper than that, Delia."

She wrenched away from him, walked a few paces and spoke in a barely audible voice. "Did you watch your brother or sister die because there weren't any cost-free ward beds for black babies and because your parents didn't have a credit card or a bank account and no cash and couldn't afford to pay? My baby brother died in my mother's arms in the hospital reception room. I swore then that I'd never be poor. Never, Luke.

"When I went home with you, I didn't see your family, I only saw poverty. I scorned my father as a shiftless illiterate, and I've never been so ashamed as when my mother informed me that he's dyslexic and how he's suffered for it. She told me about my father's strength, his goodness, and I was so humiliated. Mortified because of my own self-righteousness. If it hadn't been for you, I might not have seen my Granny that last time before she died, because I was aiming for a promoti9n that I thought I had to work day and night to get-"

"Did you get it?"

She shrugged. "It went to someone else. I wouldn't have gotten it no matter what I did. Wrong nationality."

"Have you finished with Radcliff?" ; "I never felt anything for Craig."

He walked around her so that she could see his expression of incredulity. "Then why, for Heaven's sake?"

"I thought he could take me where I wanted to go."

He seized her arm, and she could see his pain mirrored in his eyes. "But you had an affair with him. It's common knowledge around the building."

"A one-time affair, and I'm ashamed of it. I didn't feel one thing. I thought the feeling would grow, that I'd come to love him. I even thought something was the matter with me, but when I figured out that the problem was you, I stopped seeing him. I know now that there's nothing wrong with me."

He hooded his eyes so that she couldn't see what he felt. "How do you know that?"

She didn't try to hide the truth. "You only had to touch me; sometime, a look sufficed. And… that night with you… here… when we… well, I'll never again settle for less than that. Never."

He leaned against the wall and folded his arms across his chest. "Don't try to impress me, Delia. I know what you felt, and I know you weren't pretending. I love you, Delia, but I have to think about all this. Just tell me one thing."

"What?" she asked, her voice ringing with hope.

"What are you planning to do about your sister?"

Her shoulders sagged, and he had to notice her disappointment. Determined not to let him see her down, she straightened up and replied, "I'm going to have a talk with her and see what she wants to do. And I'll help her do it, so long as she doesn't plan to break the law."

He gazed at her for a long minute, sad though resolute. "I'd better be going; it's getting late."

The next Saturday, around noon, Delia parked the rented Taurus in front of her parents' house and prepared herself for the ordeal of facing her sister. To her surprise, Bitsy met her on the front porch.

"Mama and Papa are awfully upset with me, Ludell, so for goodness sake, don't get on my case."

Della opened the front door, set her suitcase inside and turned to her sister. "I have to speak at the church tonight, and I'm going to be talking about the responsibilities that individuals have for their families and their community. Sure you want to go?"

Bitsy raised an eyebrow. "I'm surprised you know anything about that."

Delia couldn't resist a wry smile. "I do now, thanks to you. Let me know your plans, and we'll figure out how I can help."

The shock that registered on Bitsy's face was humbling, indeed. "You will?"

"That's what I said." Arm in arm, they went to find their mother.

"I'm real proud of you, Daughter," Tate Murray said as they left the church after Delia's speech that evening. She thanked her father and couldn't help rejoicing in seeing him increase in height and stature, not unlike *Orpheus Ascending*. Someone had said that a man's pride resides in his woman, his children and his work. Understanding at last one of the roles she played in his life, a sense of pride suffused her, and she leaned to him and kissed his cheek. When he batted his eyelids rapidly, she turned away.

She kept Bitsy close to her, as though shielding the young girl. "Let's go to Johnson's Chicken Grill and get some ice cream after I drop the rest off at home," she said to Bitsy."

The girl showed reluctance, but agreed when Delia said, "We have to work things out. You can't just let it happen with no plans for dealing with it."

"I have plans," Bitsy informed her when they were alone.

Delia listened to what proved to be a carefully crafted scheme.

Bitsy and her boyfriend, who would finish high school one year before Bitsy, planned to get married and live in Pine Whispers with the boy's parents. He would work until she finished school and had the baby. They would enter North Carolina Central together, share living quarters and both would work parttime.

"All right," Delia agreed. "I'll pay for your confinement and for the apartrient, but who'll keep the baby?"

"Ted's parents. They're helping us as much as they can, and Mama will make my school clothes. She said she'll take our baby when Ted's mother has to go some place. Thanks a lot for your help; we've been worrying about rent. We'll both be on scholarships, so tuition isn't a problem."

Della looked at the young girl and wondered how she could be so fearless in the face of such an awesome unknown. "I wish I could face my life with as much confidence as you're showing."

Bitsy pulled the last of her ice cream soda through the straw with noticeable noise and squinted at her sister. "What's the matter?"

Delia lifted her left shoulder. "Long story."

"Couldn't be that long."

"I love him. He loves me. I messed up. He said 'later'. End of story."

Bitsy sucked more air through the straw. "That's not so bad. At least he loves you. Just tell him you're going, off your bean, you did a dumb thing, you're having a hard time getting along without him, and you're sorry. Piece of cake."

Della stared at her sister. Out of the mouths of babes. She laughed a cleansing laugh for the first time in days.

Luke parked in the alley beside his father's general store, locked the car and went inside. At six-thirty in the evening, the place ought to be empty of customers. For days, he'd searched himself for an answer to his dilemma about Delia, and he'd concluded that he needed advice. Oh, he knew what he wanted; he wanted Delia. But did he have the right to expect more from her than she'd given him? He hadn't asked her to marry him. So wasn't she free to do as she pleased? He needed to talk to someone. Gene would agree with him, but his father would set him straight. He told his father as much as he wanted him to know.

"Luke," Rudolph began, "if you love a person, you have to accept them on their terms, not yours. Unconditionally. Nobody's perfect."

Luke leaned against the counter and cupped his chin in both hands. "What would you do?"

"I'm not sure you want to hear this," Rudolph told him. "I've never mentioned it to anybody. In the early years of my marriage to your mother, I started to walk away from all of you on at least half a dozen occasions. Marriage isn't all hot loving, Son. The bills came in; problems arose with the job before I got the store; you children needed everything under the sun, and I never had enough. Never could see my way clear, and I just couldn't stand knowing that my family wanted and needed things I couldn't provide. Love doesn't grow freely in that environment, and the conflict between your mother and me got worse and worse. One day, when I was just about to leave, it finally occurred to me that I'd be miserable without my family. I sat down and told myself that my wife never complained, that she accepted whatever I could do, that I was the problem. I weathered that temptation, and it was the last. After nearly ruining my life, I loved your mother more every day. You can't blame Delia for hating poverty. It's vicious and destructive. If you love each other, make up your minds to work out every problem together, and you'll have a good life. Your life doesn't automatically shape up the way you want it to, Son. You have to do the shaping."

Whatever he'd expected, that hadn't been it. Days after his return to New York, his father's confession haunted him, and he could think of nothing else.

Several days after she got back to New York, Delia sat on a high stool in Kate's kitchen watching her friend make buttermilk biscuits. "You go to all that trouble just for you?" she asked Kate.

"You mean I'm not worth it? I treat myself well, kiddo, and I love biscuits. You could try that. Make yourself happy for a change instead of always doing what you mink's good for you. How's Luke?"

"I don't know, and if you insist on talking about him, I'm leaving."

"Suit yourself," Kate advised. "If it was me, I'd call him up and tell him my TV wasn't working."

"But that wouldn't be true."

"So what? It would be the excuse he needed."

Delia stared at Kate. The woman was serious. "And you wouldn't be ashamed for him to catch you lying?"

"Not one bit, honey. You may turn on logic alone, but take my word for it; Luke does not."

Delia sucked on her bottom lip for a second. "See you later."

She spent half an hour in a bubble bath, dried off and applied *Opium* body lotion on every inch of her skin, combed her hair down and went to her closet in search of her best armor. Red bra and matching bikini panties underpinned a red, wide-legged silk jump suit. She went to the phone. No. That wasn't the right move. She sent an e-mail to him at home, stating that her computer wasn't working, needed urgent repair and could he come over right away.

As Luke walked into Delia's apartment building, it hit him like a hammer that if her computer was out of order, she wouldn't have been able to send him that e-mail. His heart began thumping with such force that he grabbed his chest as though such a move would slow it down. He got off the elevator on her floor and told himself not to run, but he couldn't resist walking faster. He hadn't seen her in nearly three of the longest weeks of his life. He pushed the bell and thought she'd never answer. Finally it opened, and she stood before him. Beautiful. And smiling as though he were the only other person on earth.

"May I come in? I'm in my work clothes, brogans included." He'd worn them intentionally.

"Oh, sure," she said, seemingly oblivious to his attire. "Uh… Sorry. I wasn't thinking."

"Did you send me that e-mail from your computer?" He looked at her hands, always a giveaway, and noticed that she rubbed and pulled at her fingers..

"Of course. Where else?"

"Hmmmm. It's out of order, but you could send an e-mail, huh?"

She shrugged. "I didn't say which computer wasn't working."

He could have devoured her. "You?"

She nodded, and his engine began to rev. "Come here, baby. You didn't want to see me any worse that I needed to see you.

Come here to me."

He opened his arms, and she flew into them. He need-ed to love her, but they had some fences to mend. They'd already bared their souls; each had stood emotionally nude before the other. Yet on those occasions—painful moments that would stay with him for a long time—neither of them had acknowledged what it meant to see a lover's naked soul. His manhood reacted to her warm body as he hugged her to him, and he set her gently away. He needed to look at her, to gauge her feelings.

Her gaze scanned the length of his bare arms and settled on his hands. He stared at her as she swallowed hard and made his midsection the target of her vision. In that moment, he was glad for all the hours he spent agonizing in the gym. Heat began to claw at him as it blazed its dizzy-ing path through his veins, but he refused to give in to it; he had to see what she'd do. But he could barely restrain himself when she began sucking on her bottom lip while her eyes perused him, a gourmand savoring the prospects of a great meal. Her gaze dropped to his groin but, like a shooting star, immediately found another part of him on which to settle.

He wanted to touch her, but he made himself hold off. At last, she looked briefly into his eyes, just long enough for him to see the naked want in them. Her right hand rubbed her left breast. Any minute, he'd explode. He told himself to think about okra, rock music, rap, all of which he hated, but that netted him no relief. He thought of live wire, the deadliness of which was sufficient usually to ensure his rapt attention to his work, but that brought a vision of Della writhing and moaning beneath him. Breath hissed out of his lungs when, zombie-like, she reached for his belt and unhooked it, not even distracted by the sound of his tools and keys as she threw it on the chair.

He prayed for the strength to hold back what he knew was coming when she pulled his T-shirt from his trousers as though to yank it over his head. Didn't she want to talk or, at least, go to her bedroom? His shirt crawled slowly upward until it hid his face from her. At her mercy, not knowing what she'd do next fueled the blood that shot straight to his groin. He grabbed the shirt, jerked it over his head and threw it across the room, then stared into her smiling eyes.

"Della, what—?"

He got his answer when she reached for his zipper. He'd never had a woman undress him, and when she pushed his trousers down over his hips, watched them fall to the floor, and let her gaze travel at a snail's pace from there up to his eyes, he'd swear she'd never done it before. Inquisitive. Experimenting.

Luke waited for her next move. But she licked her lips and smiled as though in a trance, and he lost it. He kicked the trousers from his feet and pulled her to him.

"You've got me practically naked," he said with labored breath. "What do you intend to do with me?"

"I haven't finished yet," she answered in a voice that quivered from shock as she realized what she'd done. "Piece of cake," Bitsy had said.

"Come with me." She extended her hand, but he didn't move, and she wondered if she'd gone too far.

"Finish it," he growled. "Right here. Right now. Finish what you started."

She took a step toward him and wavered. He wasn't in a mood to have her toy with him.

"I luh—"

"Take them off me, sweetheart. I want to feel your hands running down my thighs and your fingers brushing over me. You staked your claim. Collect what's yours."

Nervous and not a little scared, she knelt before him and pulled down the scant bikini underwear that served to do nothing more than cup him. Unsure as to what should come next, she hugged him to her and felt his hand on her shoulders as he lifted her to her feet. She made herself look into his face, and what she saw grabbed at her heart and sent it into a wild gallop. He picked her up, carried her to her bedroom and laid her on her bed. She reached for the zipper on her jump suit, but he stilled her hand.

"It's my turn."

She couldn't take her eyes from his as he peeled her clothes from her body, for she'd never seen such softness in him, and yet his eyes blazed with a fierce desire. He pulled off her shoes and dropped them beside the bed.

"Della, if we do this, you're making a firm commitment to me. Is that clear? I don't want to come crashing back to earth after you take me to Heaven."

She held up both arms to him in an invitation that he could not mistake, but he shook his head and continued to search her face.

"I've gotten rid of my demons. What about you?"

He was going to give her another chance. She raised herself up from the bed, braced her hands behind her .and told him, "I've done the same. Some of what hurt may be a long time leaving me, but that has nothing to do with my love for you. If you have forgiven me, I consider myself blessed."

"What about your sister?"

"She's getting married and we've found a way for her to go on to college."

"With your help?"

"If you knew for certain that I would continue my work at United Nations and you kept your job there, would you nonetheless be willing to marry me?"

She lost her breath and had to gasp for it. After breathing deeply a few times, she managed to say, "If this is a proposal, yes, I'll marry you no matter where you work or what you wear when you get there."

He bent over her, gripped her shoulders and fell with her across the bed. His hard muscles teased her softness, and he rolled over, pinning her beneath him. She gazed up into his mesmeric eyes that glittered with a possessiveness that she'd never seen in him.

"You belong to me?"

"Yes. *Yes!*"

"You're mine?"

"Oh, Luke. My love. I've always been yours." His body heated up with such speed that a sheen of moisture dampened her belly.

"Kiss me. Open your mouth and kiss me. I need you."

The sound of his hunger roared through her, and his need skittered over her nerves and sent the flame of desire arrow-straight to her feminine core. She waited for his tongue while he teased her, playing with her lips, giving her a taste and withdrawing from her. She grasped the back of his head, pressed her lips to his, pulled his tongue into her mouth and sucked it. The tremors that shot through him heightened her pleasure, and she let one of her hands toy with his left pectoral until he bucked above her and stilled her hand. Why didn't he suckle her? He had to remember how she loved it.

"Luke. Please…"

"What you want, baby? Anything. Just tell me."

Frustrated, she led his hand to her breast, and he rolled her nipple between his thumb and forefinger until she cried out and begged him to take her into his mouth. He spread her legs wide, settled himself between them and bent to her breast, twirling his tongue around the nipple until she thought she would scream in frustration. At last he pulled it into his mouth and intensified the torment. With one hand, he rolled the other nipple, all the while creating an unbelievable friction by moving himself erotically over her.

"Luke, honey, I…"

"Hmmm?"

"Please. I… I'm empty. I… I need you to… to fill me."

He bent to the other breast and nourished himself until she flung her arms wide in total capitulation. His lips grazed her belly and her hipbone, and their unbelievably sensuous skimming along the inside of her thighs brought a keening cry from her lips.

Helpless beneath the onslaught of his loving, she gave herself up to him. His lips settled upon the nub of her passion and a scream ripped from her throat, but his rapacious mouth only tortured her more as he kissed and loved her until she surrendered completely.

He moved slowly up her body leaving no spot unloved. "Look at me, baby." She gazed into his eyes.

"May I?"

"Yes. Oh, yes."

He reached down beside the bed and 'got the protection. "Sweetheart. Oh, Della, take me in."

She found him, and the feel of him, hot and throbbing, sent wild fire through her blood as she guided him to her portal of love.

"Look at me, now." She gazed at him while his hot pulsating body found its home within her, and he began their journey to oneness. This time, they knew each other, and he found at once the place where he could drive her to ecstasy. He carried her to the brink and brought her back, giving a deaf ear to her pleas for relief.

"I can't stand it, Luke. I want to burst. Please."

"You will, love. You will."

He drove mercilessly, and the little tremors began, swelling from the bottom of her feet and coursing through her blood stream to her love nest. When he threatened to make her wait, she grabbed his buttocks, wrapped her legs around his hips and undulated beneath him stroke for stroke. She thought she would die when the squeezing and clutching began in earnest and he gripped her closer and unleased his power. Her screams filled the room as he dragged every ounce of passion from her until she erupted all around him, capturing him in her woman's claws until he cried aloud, joining her in an explosion of passion that rocketed them into the stratosphere.

Their recovery took time. He braced himself on his elbows, looked into her beloved face and adored her with his eyes. "I love you, Woman. You're my whole life, you understand that? When are you going to marry me? I need a date."

Her smile, like no other, sent his heart into a gallop. "Six weeks?"

"That long?"

"Five and a half?"

Laughter came out of him in relief such as he'd never before experienced. He couldn't hold it in. He started to get up.

"Where're you going?"

"I was going to get some paper and a pen. We have a lot of plans to make. I have to speak with your father. A whole lot of things to—"

"Luke, would you please get back in this bed. We can go see my father next weekend. Right now, I... er... re—"

He couldn't help grinning. She wanted some more. "You... er... re what?"

She pulled him to her. "Luke don't be difficult. I refuse to marry a man I have to beg."

He planted kisses along the side of her neck while his long fingers began their torrid dance around her nipple. "Baby, that's the least of your worries."

EPILOGUE

Craig Radcliff looked out of the window of his lavishly appointed office in Geneva, Switzerland. In the distance, he could see the Mont Blanc, its peak gleaming majestically in the sunlight. His desk was neat, almost bare, and no scraps of paper littered his waste basket. He had only to buzz and coffee arrived; his Monday luncheon tray—always the same—came sharply at one-fifteen in the afternoon, as did his Tuesday tray on Tuesdays, his Wednesday tray on Wednesdays....

Too large a part of his days was spent with well-heeled third-world diplomats who didn't focus enough on the plight of the world's children, their main concern being to maintain their status, so as to keep their entitlements, fly first class and live abroad. And his evenings? Women clamored for the privilege of occupying them, but he wanted only Delia Murray. For her, he'd gladly exchange his status as a Director-General. But it was too late.

He walked back to his desk of polished walnut and read again the item on the front page of the newspaper, *Delegates World*. His eyes hadn't fooled him:

Della Murray, Director of the Department of Conferences and Services, married Luke McKnight, owner and CEO of RPM Electrical Repair and Engineering, a company that designs electrical equipment arid holds a UN service contract for repairing machines and equipment at UN Headquarters.

And all the time, he'd thought the man a common laborer. He tore out the notice, put it in his wallet, and tossed the newspaper into the waste basket. He wouldn't mind paying for his sins, if the price wasn't so high.

ABOUT THE AUTHOR

Gwynne Forster was born in North Carolina and grew up in Washington, D.C., where she lived before giong to New York to work as a demographer at the United Nations. When she left the United Nations to forma workign partership with her husband. She was chief of the Fertility Studies section of the Population division. As such, she she was responsible for research and analysis of social, economic, cultural and demographic factors and conditions that infulence fertility levels and trends thoughout the world. The studies were published under the United Nations imprimatur and in the name of its Secretary-General. She lives in New York City with her husband (who is also a demograopher) of twenty-five years. She hold bachelors and masters degrees in sociology adn a masters degree in economics/demography as well as graduate credits from Columbia University. As a demograopher, she has been widely published. Her extensive travels for the United Nations and later for the International Planned Parenthood Federation (London Office) have taken her to Brazil, Mexico, most European countries and throughout Asia, Africa and the Carribbean. Her work on thiese trips included representing the Secretary-General of the United Nations, lecturing, conducting workshops and delivering research or policy papers at conferences. She has acted as president of the Board of Directos of the volunteer library that serves the eight thousadn people who live in her community. She is currently a member of the board, and occassionally volunteers at teh library. Since becomming a published author of romance novels, Gwynne has lectured on various phases of the writing business. At teh 1995 Romantic Times (RT) Conference in Dallas, she lectured on techniques of selling a manuscript, including writing query letters adn synopses amd relating the stodry orally and in writing to agents and editors. She also spoke on these topics at Howard University Seminar in June 1995, and also at the March 1996 annual congerence of Romance Writers fo America/New York City Club (which was convened in Melville, Long Island). She held a workshop ont he subject on the subject at teh 1996 Romantic Tiems conference in Baton rouge, Louisianna. She also lectured on fiction writing at the African American Women Writers Conference. This was held at the University of teh District of Columbia in April of 1997. Since February 1998, Gwynen has lectured on all aspects of fictino writing at the branch libraries fo the Queens Borough Library System. She is also a free-lance non-fiction writer. Her lates article is a profile fo Kofi Annan, United Nations Secretary-General, the coverstory of the April/May issue fo Crisis Magazine. Crisis is the media organ of the NAACP. Pinnacle/Arabesque published her second novella, A Perfect Match which is part of the I Do anthology (a Valentines Day anthology in February 1998 and released her fourth full legnth novel, Obsession, in April 1998. Genesis/Indigo published Naked Soul, Gwynnes first hard cover romance, in June 1998. Gwynne's previous books include Sealed with a Kiss (October 1995), Against All Odds (September 1996) and Ecstasy (July 1997). Her first novella, Christopher's Gifts, is included in the Silver Bells anthology. All were published to wide acclaim by Pinnacle/Arabesque. She is represented by the James B. Finn Library Agency, Inc., P.O. Box 28227 A, St. Louios, MO 63132. Readers may right her at P.O. Box 45, New York, NY 10044-0045. Or by the web at http://www.infokart.com/forster/tgwynne.html or by email GwynneF@aol.com.

2006 Publication Schedule

January

A Lover's Legacy
Veronica Parker
1-58571-167-5
$9.95

Love Lasts Forever
Dominiqua Douglas
1-58571-187-X
$9.95

Under the Cherry
   Moon
Christal Jordan-Mims
1-58571-169-1
$12.95

February

Second Chances at
   Love
Cheris Hodges
1-58571-188-8
$9.95

Enchanted Desire
Wanda Thomas
1-58571-176-4
$9.95

Caught Up
Deatri King Bey
1-58571-178-0
$12.95

March

I'm Gonna Make
   You Love Me
Gwyneth Bolton
1-58571-181-0
$9.95

Through The Fire
Seressia Glass
1-58571-173-X
$9.95

Notes When
   Summer Ends
Beverly Lauderdale
1-58571-180-2
$12.95

April

Sin and Surrender
J.M. Jeffries
1-58571-189-6
$9.95

Unearthing Passions
Elaine Sims
1-58571-184-5
$9.95

Between Tears
Pamela Ridley
1-58571-179-0
$12.95

May

Misty Blue
Dyanne Davis
1-58571-186-1
$9.95

Ironic
Pamela Leigh Starr
1-58571-168-3
$9.95

Cricket's Serenade
Carolita Blythe
1-58571-183-7
$12.95

June

Cupid
Barbara Keaton
1-58571-174-8
$9.95

Havana Sunrise
Kymberly Hunt
1-58571-182-9
$9.95

Bound For Mt. Zion
Chris Parker
1-58571-191-8
$12.95

2006 Publication Schedule (continued)

July

Love Me Carefully
A.C. Arthur
1-58571-177-2
$9.95

No Ordinary Love
Angela Weaver
1-58571-198-5
$9.95

Rehoboth Road
Anita Ballard-Jones
1-58571-196-9
$12.95

August

Scent of Rain
Annetta P. Lee
158571-199-3
$9.95

Love in High Gear
Charlotte Roy
158571-185-3
$9.95

Rise of the Phoenix
Kenneth Whetstone
1-58571-197-7
$12.95

September

The Business of Love
Cheris Hodges
1-58571-193-4
$9.95

Rock Star
Rosyln Hardy
Holcomb
1-58571-200-0
$9.95

A Dead Man Speaks
Lisa Jones Johnson
1-58571-203-5
$12.95

October

Who's That Lady
Andrea Jackson
1-58571-190-X
$9.95

A Dangerous Woman
J.M. Jeffries
1-58571-195-0
$9.95

Sinful Intentions
Crystal Rhodes
1-58571-201-9
$12.95

November

Only You
Crystal Hubbard
1-58571-208-6
$9.95

Ebony Eyes
Kei Swanson
1-58571-194-2
$9.95

By and By
Collette Haywood
1-58571-209-4
$12.95

December

Let's Get It On
Dyanne Davis
1-58571-210-8
$9.95

Nights Over Egypt
Barbara Keaton
1-58571-192-6
$9.95

A Pefect Place to Pray
Ikesha Goodwin
1-58571-202-7
$12.95

Other Genesis Press, Inc. Titles

A Dangerous Deception	J.M. Jeffries	$8.95
A Dangerous Love	J.M. Jeffries	$8.95
A Dangerous Obsession	J.M. Jeffries	$8.95
A Drummer's Beat to Mend	Kei Swanson	$9.95
A Happy Life	Charlotte Harris	$9.95
A Heart's Awakening	Veronica Parker	$9.95
A Lark on the Wing	Phyliss Hamilton	$9.95
A Love of Her Own	Cheris F. Hodges	$9.95
A Love to Cherish	Beverly Clark	$8.95
A Risk of Rain	Dar Tomlinson	$8.95
A Twist of Fate	Beverly Clark	$8.95
A Will to Love	Angie Daniels	$9.95
Acquisitions	Kimberley White	$8.95
Across	Carol Payne	$12.95
After the Vows	Leslie Esdaile	$10.95
(Summer Anthology)	T.T. Henderson	
	Jacqueline Thomas	
Again My Love	Kayla Perrin	$10.95
Against the Wind	Gwynne Forster	$8.95
All I Ask	Barbara Keaton	$8.95
Ambrosia	T.T. Henderson	$8.95
An Unfinished Love Affair	Barbara Keaton	$8.95
And Then Came You	Dorothy Elizabeth Love	$8.95
Angel's Paradise	Janice Angelique	$9.95
At Last	Lisa G. Riley	$8.95
Best of Friends	Natalie Dunbar	$8.95
Beyond the Rapture	Beverly Clark	$9.95
Blaze	Barbara Keaton	$9.95
Blood Lust	J. M. Jeffries	$9.95
Bodyguard	Andrea Jackson	$9.95
Boss of Me	Diana Nyad	$8.95
Bound by Love	Beverly Clark	$8.95

Other Genesis Press, Inc. Titles (continued)

Other Genesis Press, Inc. Titles (continued)

Falling	Natalie Dunbar	$9.95
Fate	Pamela Leigh Starr	$8.95
Finding Isabella	A.J. Garrotto	$8.95
Forbidden Quest	Dar Tomlinson	$10.95
Forever Love	Wanda Thomas	$8.95
From the Ashes	Kathleen Suzanne	$8.95
	Jeanne Sumerix	
Gentle Yearning	Rochelle Alers	$10.95
Glory of Love	Sinclair LeBeau	$10.95
Go Gentle into that Good Night	Malcom Boyd	$12.95
Goldengroove	Mary Beth Craft	$16.95
Groove, Bang, and Jive	Steve Cannon	$8.99
Hand in Glove	Andrea Jackson	$9.95
Hard to Love	Kimberley White	$9.95
Hart & Soul	Angie Daniels	$8.95
Heartbeat	Stephanie Bedwell-Grime	$8.95
Hearts Remember	M. Loui Quezada	$8.95
Hidden Memories	Robin Allen	$10.95
Higher Ground	Leah Latimer	$19.95
Hitler, the War, and the Pope	Ronald Rychiak	$26.95
How to Write a Romance	Kathryn Falk	$18.95
I Married a Reclining Chair	Lisa M. Fuhs	$8.95
Indigo After Dark Vol. I	Nia Dixon/Angelique	$10.95
Indigo After Dark Vol. II	Dolores Bundy/	$10.95
	Cole Riley	
Indigo After Dark Vol. III	Montana Blue/	$10.95
	Coco Morena	
Indigo After Dark Vol. IV	Cassandra Colt/	$14.95
	Diana Richeaux	
Indigo After Dark Vol. V	Delilah Dawson	$14.95
Icie	Pamela Leigh Starr	$8.95
I'll Be Your Shelter	Giselle Carmichael	$8.95

Other Genesis Press, Inc. Titles (continued)

I'll Paint a Sun	A.J. Garrotto	$9.95
Illusions	Pamela Leigh Starr	$8.95
Indiscretions	Donna Hill	$8.95
Intentional Mistakes	Michele Sudler	$9.95
Interlude	Donna Hill	$8.95
Intimate Intentions	Angie Daniels	$8.95
Jolie's Surrender	Edwina Martin-Arnold	$8.95
Kiss or Keep	Debra Phillips	$8.95
Lace	Giselle Carmichael	$9.95
Last Train to Memphis	Elsa Cook	$12.95
Lasting Valor	Ken Olsen	$24.95
Let Us Prey	Hunter Lundy	$25.95
Life Is Never As It Seems	J.J. Michael	$12.95
Lighter Shade of Brown	Vicki Andrews	$8.95
Love Always	Mildred E. Riley	$10.95
Love Doesn't Come Easy	Charlyne Dickerson	$8.95
Love Unveiled	Gloria Greene	$10.95
Love's Deception	Charlene Berry	$10.95
Love's Destiny	M. Loui Quezada	$8.95
Mae's Promise	Melody Walcott	$8.95
Magnolia Sunset	Giselle Carmichael	$8.95
Matters of Life and Death	Lesego Malepe, Ph.D.	$15.95
Meant to Be	Jeanne Sumerix	$8.95
Midnight Clear	Leslie Esdaile	$10.95
(Anthology)	Gwynne Forster	
	Carmen Green	
	Monica Jackson	
Midnight Magic	Gwynne Forster	$8.95
Midnight Peril	Vicki Andrews	$10.95
Misconceptions	Pamela Leigh Starr	$9.95
Montgomery's Children	Richard Perry	$14.95
My Buffalo Soldier	Barbara B. K. Reeves	$8.95

Other Genesis Press, Inc. Titles (continued)

Naked Soul	Gwynne Forster	$8.95
Next to Last Chance	Louisa Dixon	$24.95
No Apologies	Seressia Glass	$8.95
No Commitment Required	Seressia Glass	$8.95
No Regrets	Mildred E. Riley	$8.95
Nowhere to Run	Gay G. Gunn	$10.95
O Bed! O Breakfast!	Rob Kuehnle	$14.95
Object of His Desire	A. C. Arthur	$8.95
Office Policy	A. C. Arthur	$9.95
Once in a Blue Moon	Dorianne Cole	$9.95
One Day at a Time	Bella McFarland	$8.95
Outside Chance	Louisa Dixon	$24.95
Passion	T.T. Henderson	$10.95
Passion's Blood	Cherif Fortin	$22.95
Passion's Journey	Wanda Thomas	$8.95
Past Promises	Jahmel West	$8.95
Path of Fire	T.T. Henderson	$8.95
Path of Thorns	Annetta P. Lee	$9.95
Peace Be Still	Colette Haywood	$12.95
Picture Perfect	Reon Carter	$8.95
Playing for Keeps	Stephanie Salinas	$8.95
Pride & Joi	Gay G. Gunn	$15.95
Pride & Joi	Gay G. Gunn	$8.95
Promises to Keep	Alicia Wiggins	$8.95
Quiet Storm	Donna Hill	$10.95
Reckless Surrender	Rochelle Alers	$6.95
Red Polka Dot in a World of Plaid	Varian Johnson	$12.95
Reluctant Captive	Joyce Jackson	$8.95
Rendezvous with Fate	Jeanne Sumerix	$8.95
Revelations	Cheris F. Hodges	$8.95
Rivers of the Soul	Leslie Esdaile	$8.95

Other Genesis Press, Inc. Titles (continued)

Rocky Mountain Romance	Kathleen Suzanne	$8.95
Rooms of the Heart	Donna Hill	$8.95
Rough on Rats and Tough on Cats	Chris Parker	$12.95
Secret Library Vol. 1	Nina Sheridan	$18.95
Secret Library Vol. 2	Cassandra Colt	$8.95
Shades of Brown	Denise Becker	$8.95
Shades of Desire	Monica White	$8.95
Shadows in the Moonlight	Jeanne Sumerix	$8.95
Sin	Crystal Rhodes	$8.95
So Amazing	Sinclair LeBeau	$8.95
Somebody's Someone	Sinclair LeBeau	$8.95
Someone to Love	Alicia Wiggins	$8.95
Song in the Park	Martin Brant	$15.95
Soul Eyes	Wayne L. Wilson	$12.95
Soul to Soul	Donna Hill	$8.95
Southern Comfort	J.M. Jeffries	$8.95
Still the Storm	Sharon Robinson	$8.95
Still Waters Run Deep	Leslie Esdaile	$8.95
Stories to Excite You	Anna Forrest/Divine	$14.95
Subtle Secrets	Wanda Y. Thomas	$8.95
Suddenly You	Crystal Hubbard	$9.95
Sweet Repercussions	Kimberley White	$9.95
Sweet Tomorrows	Kimberly White	$8.95
Taken by You	Dorothy Elizabeth Love	$9.95
Tattooed Tears	T. T. Henderson	$8.95
The Color Line	Lizzette Grayson Carter	$9.95
The Color of Trouble	Dyanne Davis	$8.95
The Disappearance of Allison Jones	Kayla Perrin	$5.95
The Honey Dipper's Legacy	Pannell-Allen	$14.95
The Joker's Love Tune	Sidney Rickman	$15.95

Other Genesis Press, Inc. Titles (continued)

The Little Pretender	Barbara Cartland	$10.95
The Love We Had	Natalie Dunbar	$8.95
The Man Who Could Fly	Bob & Milana Beamon	$18.95
The Missing Link	Charlyne Dickerson	$8.95
The Price of Love	Sinclair LeBeau	$8.95
The Smoking Life	Ilene Barth	$29.95
The Words of the Pitcher	Kei Swanson	$8.95
Three Wishes	Seressia Glass	$8.95
Ties That Bind	Kathleen Suzanne	$8.95
Tiger Woods	Libby Hughes	$5.95
Time is of the Essence	Angie Daniels	$9.95
Timeless Devotion	Bella McFarland	$9.95
Tomorrow's Promise	Leslie Esdaile	$8.95
Truly Inseparable	Wanda Y. Thomas	$8.95
Unbreak My Heart	Dar Tomlinson	$8.95
Uncommon Prayer	Kenneth Swanson	$9.95
Unconditional	A.C. Arthur	$9.95
Unconditional Love	Alicia Wiggins	$8.95
Until Death Do Us Part	Susan Paul	$8.95
Vows of Passion	Bella McFarland	$9.95
Wedding Gown	Dyanne Davis	$8.95
What's Under Benjamin's Bed	Sandra Schaffer	$8.95
When Dreams Float	Dorothy Elizabeth Love	$8.95
Whispers in the Night	Dorothy Elizabeth Love	$8.95
Whispers in the Sand	LaFlorya Gauthier	$10.95
Wild Ravens	Altonya Washington	$9.95
Yesterday Is Gone	Beverly Clark	$10.95
Yesterday's Dreams, Tomorrow's Promises	Reon Laudat	$8.95
Your Precious Love	Sinclair LeBeau	$8.95

Order Form

Mail to: Genesis Press, Inc.
P.O. Box 101
Columbus, MS 39703

Name _____
Address _____
City/State _____ Zip _____
Telephone _____

Ship to (if different from above)
Name _____
Address _____
City/State _____ Zip _____
Telephone _____

Credit Card Information
Credit Card # _____ ☐ Visa ☐ Mastercard
Expiration Date (mm/yy) _____ ☐ AmEx ☐ Discover

Qty.	Author	Title	Price	Total

Use this order form, or call 1-888-INDIGO-1	
Total for books	_____
Shipping and handling: $5 first two books, $1 each additional book	_____
Total S & H	_____
Total amount enclosed	_____

Mississippi residents add 7% sales tax